The Great Texas Dance

THE TALES OF ZEBADIAH CREED, BOOK 2

The Great Texas Dance

Mark C. Jackson

FIVE STAR
A part of Gale, a Cengage Company

Five Star Publishing, a part of Gale, a Cengage Company

This novel is a work of fiction. Names, characters, places, and incidents are either the product of the author's imagination, or, if real, used fictitiously.

LIBRARY OF CONGRESS CATALOGING-IN-PUBLICATION DATA

Names: Jackson, Mark C., author.
Title: The great texas dance / Mark C. Jackson.
Description: First Edition. | Waterville, Maine : Five Star, a part of Gale, a Cengage Company, 2020. | Series: The Tales of Zebadiah Creed; book 2 |
Identifiers: LCCN 2019030905 | ISBN 9781432868505 (hardcover)
Subjects: GSAFD: Historical fiction. | Western stories.
Classification: LCC PS3610.A3543255 G74 2020 | DDC 813/.6—dc23
LC record available at https://lccn.loc.gov/2019030905

First Edition. First Printing: April 2020
Find us on Facebook—https://www.facebook.com/FiveStarCengage
Visit our website—http://www.gale.cengage.com/fivestar
Contact Five Star Publishing at FiveStar@cengage.com

Printed in Mexico
Print Number: 01 Print Year: 2020

Dedicated to Chet Cunningham, my mentor and friend

ACKNOWLEDGMENTS

Thanks to my mother, Judith Ann Jackson, for spending hours on the phone helping me with this book. She knows Zeb better than I do.

As always, thanks to my wife, Judy Walsh-Jackson. Without her patience and love, I would not be the writer I am today.

Thank you to my sister, Linda Fowler, for reading the early chapters and providing her intuitive critiques that spurred me on to continue writing about an era that has been written about so many times before.

Thanks to my sisters, Dawn Varner and Kim Skinner, who allowed me to discuss, in depth, the true nature and consequences of the Texas Revolution, though they live in Michigan and Oklahoma.

Thanks to my children, Denise Liebl, Joshua Jackson, and Sarah Jackson, who have put up with my incessant chatter about where Zeb is at any given time.

Thanks to Kay Walsh, to whom I confided in many years ago while writing the first few chapters, thinking these series of stories would make up one book and that was it.

Thanks to my friends and fellow members of the San Diego Professional Writers Group, Peggy Lang, Tim Kane, Jim Riffel, Lee Polevoi, Jack Innis, Cary Lowe, Bonnie Rea Walker, Heidi Langbein-Allen, Ken Lehnig, and especially Jessica Hayes for their monthly critiques, never tiring of hearing chapter after chapter of Zeb's story.

Thanks again to Heidi Langbein-Allen for making sure my Spanish is indeed the Spanish spoken in nineteenth-century Texas.

Thanks so much to Tiffany Schofield and especially Hazel Rumney of Five Star Publishing for their dedication and patience for this growing writer.

Thanks to Joseph Tyler and Kayli McArthur for being the first to read the full manuscript. Their insight was invaluable.

Thanks so much to my agent, Cherry Weiner, and publicist, Krista Soukup, for keeping me afloat!

Thanks to:

William R. Bradle for his incredibly informative and exciting book, *Goliad: The Other Alamo.*

Stephen L. Moore for his books, *Texas Rising* and *Eighteen Minutes: The Battle of San Jacinto and the Texas Independence Campaign.*

Andrew J. Torget for his book, *Seeds of an Empire: Cotton, Slavery, and the Transformation of the Texas Borderlands, 1800–1850.*

Their stellar research has allowed me to find, buried in history, Zebadiah Creed's story.

And lastly, I thank my friend and fellow writer Robert K. Lewis for his only advice when getting published, "Keep hold of a tight rope . . ."

It is curious that physical courage should be so common in the world, and moral courage so rare.

—Mark Twain

PREFACE

With spring comes storms from the north sending waves crashing into the rocks below my balcony. This morning, the Pacific Ocean is as calm as it has been in a month. I cherish days like today, peaceful. Soon, the dog schooners will make their way up the coast from San Francisco for timber only a big city can demand. Mendocino has grown since I wrote my first book, with the mills working day and night. Some scallywags, but mostly good men come to cut down the redwoods. From my room, I can hear the saws whine across miles of coastline, now barren land. Perhaps one day I shall write a book of this.

Texas, the other side of the world and a thousand years ago it seems, is where I lived for a few brief months. The book I finish, and prepare to send to the publisher, read as history, will join countless other books that tell the tale of a righteous and honorable fight against the brutal Santa Anna and his armies. I hope not, for I have tried reading some of those books and could not complete a one. The tale I tell is not history, but a portrayal of men and the consequences of their decisions, sometimes made during the savagery of battle, most times made in quiet, their desperate acts allowing them no way out other than through loyalty and friendship, or betrayal. The dust of the prairie at Coleto Creek I can still taste in my mouth as well as hear the whispers of the dead in my dreams, for the simple cause: to raise the flag of the Lone Star above the Republic of Texas.

Yet today, the sun shines, the ocean is calm, and my writing is mostly done. In a while, I shall join my good friend Manuel downstairs for lunch. Later, I will go to the bar for drinks and laughs. Tomorrow, it may not be so. Such is life. This book is finished. However, my story carries on.

Zebadiah Creed
The Continental Hotel
Mendocino, California
April 1882

Chapter 1

San Antonio de Béxar, Late Winter 1836

I smelled cooking.

Even with the sun gone down, we could see their camps and while we ate corn tortillas as tough as cows' hides, I imagined Santa Anna and his army feasting on tender roasted beef, boiled potatoes, and wine carried all the way from Mexico City. Overlooking San Antonio de Béxar and the whole of the Mexican army, with their fires a thousand cats' eyes gazing back at me from across the river, all I could think of was how delicious a sizzling beefsteak and biscuit might taste, one last time before my death.

I lay next to Grainger looking west, above the officers' quarters on a flat roof smeared and stained with axle grease, spilt black powder, and tobacco spit. A twelve-pound cannon sat a few feet away from us, manned by a couple of fellow volunteers. Though heavily reinforced, the roof creaked and sagged under the cannon's weight. The old mission, once called San Antonio de Valero and now carrying the Alamo as its name, was never intended to be a fort.

"How many do you figure's out there?" I asked.

"Dunno, maybe a couple thousand er more?" Grainger said.

The sound of boots splashing through the shallow river drifted to us over the barren, no-man's-land that distanced the two armies. Soon, the scrapes of shovels echoed up from the nightly construction of ramparts and trenches. I pictured the soldados, dressed in their red, white, and blue colored uniforms, digging graves, our graves. By sunrise, they would be back across to their side of the river, out of reach of our guns and several yards closer to breaking the siege.

Grainger held his long rifle close and took aim.

I rolled onto my back and stared at the first stars beginning to shine down on another cold and hungry night.

Shhh-boom! Grainger's rifle fired with a cloud of smoke. "Whew there, I got one, Zeb! I got one!" He stood, raised his rifle above his head, and yelled, "One more of ya'll's going to hell, hear me?"

I flipped to my belly and peered into the deepening twilight. "I ain't seen nothin' move out there like somebody's dyin'," I said, under my breath.

"I know I killed one, saw his hat blow right off his head and he fell over." Grainger stood at the edge of the roof, pointing toward the Mexican soldados. Lit from behind by torchlight, he made quite a silhouette. From the trenches, a soldado fired a shot, striking the wall below us, spraying dust and bits of adobe into the air.

"Oh, shit!" Grainger yelped. With a vigorous nod and breathing hard, he thumped down beside me. Scattered laughter floated from outside and inside the walls of the Alamo. The night grew quiet and the constant sound of digging resumed.

We smoked, and we waited.

After a time, I felt Grainger staring at me. "You don't believe I shot a man, do ya?"

I pretended not to hear his question. Several times during our recent friendship, he had asked me to believe one of his tall tales, and right then, I was not of the temperament to argue.

Someone hollered from below. "Creed, Grainger, Colonel wants you."

Using the meager torchlight, Grainger made his way to a ladder. "Let's get a cup and go talk to Bowie 'fore we see Travis."

I stood and winced, the evening chill caused the old wound in my left thigh to pain me some. Pausing for a second to stare into the dark, to listen to the rhythm of the rise and fall of the shovels, I tried to conjure up in my mind the graves they were digging, but saw nothing.

I followed Grainger down the ladder.

Jim Bowie had been bedridden for a week or more. No one was sure what made him ill. Some said he took a terrible fall, others claimed it was consumption catching up with him. I suspected the latter. We took orders from Colonel Travis, but it was Jim Bowie, our friend and leader of the volunteers, we still confided in.

"Come on in boys and have a seat." Bowie took the cup I offered him with shaky hands. Four candles lit a room with a couple of chairs and a large, bare table. He sat on a cot with his back against the wall. "Thank ya for the coffee, but ya got somethin' a bit stronger, do ya?" He covered his mouth and coughed. From the shadows stepped his servant, more his mistress, to comfort him. He waved her off and sat up straighter. She disappeared back into the shadows.

Though the room was cold, I could see beads of sweat on his forehead, and he was shivering. The smell of piss, shit, and burning tallow hung heavy in the air.

"Just so happens I do," Grainger said and pulled a bottle from his coat. He poured Bowie a shot into his coffee, then took a drink himself.

I pushed a chair next to his cot and sat down. "Travis is calling for us. Know anything?"

"Boys . . . Boys, we're in a crux. I been told there's nigh six thousand Mexican soldiers with half as many cannons pointed at this very wall I lean against." He sucked in a shallow breath. "Travis knows we're done for unless he gets us reinforcements.

He means to send another plea for help." He coughed again, this time leaving blood on the blanket he wrapped himself in. "Now, there ain't no men better at sneakin' 'round than you two. An' ain't no men better at killin, 'cept maybe me. I seen that in ya when we took San Antonio from Cos's army." I caught a glimpse of a smile under his beard. "I was the one to recommend ya both."

"Recommend us for what?" Grainger asked.

"Well now, you two'll have to go an' see Travis for that." He pulled his blanket tighter around his shoulders. I saw the edge of a blade exposed to the candlelight.

I looked at him square. "You set if them damn Mexicans come bustin' through this wall?"

Bowie pulled back his blanket and there sat three loaded pistols and two knives in his lap. He grinned at me and said, "If I'm gonna die, more than one'll die before I will."

Grainger waited at the door. Bowie gave him a slight nod, then grabbed my arm and pulled me close. "With the red flag that bastard Santa Anna's a flyin', ain't nobody gettin' outta here alive. I owe you, both of ya. So, go on an' get." He placed the handle of a knife in my hand. "I don't need but one." This time his whole body shuddered when he coughed.

I slid the heavy blade into my belt.

"Good night, sir," I whispered and reached for his hand. Waving me away, he slipped down on his side, the guns and knife rattling as he moved. We left him lying there, facing the table and candles. Three of the flames had burned out.

Colonel Travis stood staring at papers scattered over a door set on sawhorses. He wore spectacles and his uniform well, and though not a particularly tall man, stooped a bit. As we reached the entrance, he did not look up. The room was well lit and smelled of pine resin. A fire burned in a pot stove partially blocked by empty, broken crates. Grey smoke floated up into the rafters and hung like thin clouds. Two huge wooden beams taken from the chapel shored up the roof to accommodate the cannon above our heads. Travis straightened up, peered over his glasses, and said, "Gentlemen, please join me. We have much to discuss and very little time."

There was no door to shut as we walked into the room. Alone in the corner, partially hidden by the pot stove, sat Travis's servant, Joe.

Grainger headed to a small bench where a bottle and clean glasses sat and poured two drinks. I stepped to the makeshift table across from Travis. There were several maps of what appeared to be the town of San Antonio and surrounding countryside. A large drawing of the mission lay under a letter he seemed to be writing. Grainger stepped to my side and handed me a glass.

"Earlier, I heard a shot. You men know anything about that?" Like the rest of us, Travis had not gotten much sleep since Santa Anna and his army's arrival. I saw in his eyes the strain of his commission.

"I killed a man, sir. He was digging on them goddamn trenches and I shot him." Grainger smiled and glanced at me. "I figure one dead Mexican's one less we have to fight later, right Zeb?" He nudged me in the ribs.

Travis nodded to Joe. He pointed at the wall near his head to a small crater blown out of the stucco. "Sir, looks like he shot back."

Grainger glanced at the hole, then to Joe, shrugged, and took a drink, offering no explanation.

With a subtle sneer, Travis said to Grainger, "You came with the Greys," then turned to me. "What about you, Creed, is it? You don't wear the uniform of a New Orleans Grey. What's your story?" Grainger had the remnants of a Greys uniform on under his coat. I did not. I wore buckskins and an old, discarded buffalo cape in place of the clothes I acquired after joining the New Orleans militia five months before.

Travis took off his spectacles and held them in his hand. They shook ever so slightly.

"I come with the Greys. Sailed into Velasco from New Orleans and walked here to San Antonio. I fought 'long side your regulars, takin' this place and here I am, sir." I stared back at him with a stone face, drumming my fingers on the underside of the door.

Travis was silent for a few seconds, then asked no one in particular. "Why did you come here, to Texas? Do you expect to be given land when we win this war, a home to raise a family, a chance to build a new nation? Why did you come here to Texas, gentlemen, answer me that and I will tell you why you stand before me."

He waited for our reply.

"I came to get rich," Grainger whispered.

"And how do you propose to do that?"

"By raising and selling cows, sir. When I smell beef cooking, I smell money. Back in the Ohio Valley, where my dear wife and children are, I own the best livestock in the county. When we take this here country, I will acquire as many leagues of land as a man can handle." He paused, "To raise cows, sir, my answer is to raise and sell cows." He wore a broad grin as he finished his speech.

"A worthy notion, Mr. Grainger. You will build a fine business to help settle this new country, I'm sure of it." Travis then turned at me. "Mr. Creed, do you hold as worthy a notion as your friend here?"

I lowered my gaze to the maps and the half-written letter.

"I'm here for the fight, sir . . ." I finished my drink, set the glass down on the map of San Antonio, and raised my head to look him in the eye. ". . . and a promise to a friend. Don't need no land or cows so I suppose I'll keep killin' Mexicans 'til this fight's done an' move on. Maybe go an' kill Comanche and Kiowa after."

I did not take kindly to preaching or lawyering. Besides, he knew who we were, and why most of us were there.

"Colonel, what do you want?"

Travis nodded toward my belt. "That's one of Bowie's *famous* knives," he said, gritting his teeth.

"Yes, sir, it is," I answered, smiling.

"Did he give it to you?"

"Yes, sir, he did."

"Ah, I see . . ." He surrendered, his shoulders slumped, as if he had lost a fight Grainger and I would never know about.

Recovering his stature, he sighed and placed his spectacles back on. "Gentlemen, I must in some way send out one last plea for reinforcements . . . or all is lost. I fear Santa Anna may attack within four days, as his ramparts get closer and his army swells to well over three thousand or more. Mr. Bonham, one of my early couriers, has returned with word that Colonel Fannin will not be supporting us from Goliad. Though we now have thirty-two more volunteers from Gonzales, my men will not be able to defend this fort. As I said, all will be lost. What I need from you is to deliver this letter directly to General Houston. He must be convinced of our desperate situation. As volunteers, you may refuse my request, though Bowie says that if there are two who can carry word of our plight, it would be you. If caught, you will surely die. However, staying here . . ." He stopped to swallow, as if he were choking. "Doing nothing but waiting for the attack, we will all die. So, what is it, gentlemen? If your answer is yes, then you must leave tomorrow, before dawn."

Travis's hand shook, rustling the papers. He did not lower his eyes from mine. After a few long seconds, Grainger declared, "Well, sir, we both crossed your line same as Aubrey, Crockett,

Bowie, and every other good man here. We aim to fight 'til we die, or win. So, if this will help us, I'm in. Zeb, whatcha say?"

The colonel picked up the unfinished letter and offered it across the table.

I glanced at Grainger, faced Travis, and said, "Bowie's right, there ain't two men better'n me and my friend here. Just one question, sir, you got a way outta this here fort without us first gettin' killed?"

We left Travis and walked back through the old mission's plaza. Five or six fires blazed in the open with a few men each sitting close to stay warm, their eyes dull and distant as they stared into the flickering light. This time of late February, early March, it was cold in Texas. I did not mind, I had lived on the north plains through winters that would freeze most folks. Looking up to the wide roof of the barracks, I saw a couple of regulars sitting with their backs against one of the cannons, smoking and talking. There was not much to do but sleep, stand watch, and tell each other what we were going to do once we got out of this hellhole. Nothing was ever said about dying.

We reached the water well.

"Whatcha really think, Grainger?"

"We can hold 'em for a while but when these walls are broken through, Santa Anna aims to kill us all. The red flag's still flying over yonder in the town square." We leaned against the old stones of the well and looked back down the square. "Hell, the north end of the fort don't even have a solid wall," he muttered to himself.

We smoked. Grainger pulled a bottle from under his coat. He took a drink and handed it to me. The bottle came from Travis's room.

"Helluva spot, ain't it? We could as easy get shot sneakin' outta this place," I said, "but if there ain't no one willing to come back here, well I don't know." I traced a circle in the dirt with my moccasin and spat in the middle of it.

A cold wind picked up. Grainger shivered and pulled his coat tighter around him. "I was too long in New Orleans, I suppose. Ain't used to winter no more."

I heard talk from behind us and turned around. Crockett and a couple of his men stepped through the broken wall in front of the chapel courtyard. His six-pound cannons were set between Bowie's room and the chapel with only a wood palisade protecting them.

"How ya be this evening?" Crockett asked and walked on. He and his entourage pretty well stuck to themselves.

Grainger and I stood for a while in silence.

"I ain't never asked and you ain't never told me, is it true?"

"What are you talking about?" He tapped his pipe against the stone. An ember flicked to the ground. He stomped it out as if it were going to burn the entire fort down.

"That you got a wife, an' children, and cows way up in Ohio . . ."

His laugh echoed across the whole plaza. Wiping tears from his eyes, he said, "My wife and children do live on the Ohio. I ain't been back for a year er more. Thought I'd make my money on the Mississippi and take a steamer home. That just didn't work out now, did it?" He paused. "I'm a river rat . . . I ain't got no cows!"

"Why'd you come here then?"

"I'll just tell ya, there was trouble there and I had to leave New Orleans quick. This was a way to go and here I am standing with you. Understand, I'm better off bein' shot at in Texas than lyin' behind bars, or dead . . . Now, partner, I ain't never asked you the same question. Why'd you come here? Is it to kill Mexicans or Comanche? I can't remember. Either way, friend, that's a whole lotta killin." He snickered, then was straight-faced. "You ain't runnin' from somethin' or runnin' to, yer just runnin' and burnin' . . . And killin' every Mexican and Comanche from here to Santa Fe ain't gonna put that fire out."

"Grainger, you know me better than I know myself," I said, shaking my head. "But that ain't all a' why I'm here."

"What else is there, a man's honor and loyalty?"

"Maybe . . ." I felt my face getting hot.

"Loyalty to Travis? Hell, it seems you despise the man. Bowie maybe? Fightin' an honorable fight alongside him for the sake of a good fight? Or is it really because a poor son of a bitch died savin' your life? Hell, we're a long way from whatever happened six months ago, on that damn plantation."

"I don't stand with anyone lest I trust 'em, or at least trust their intentions." I glanced at Grainger, then looked away and thought, *I don't remember tellin' how Billy Frieze died, or where.* "And I trust a promise I made to a friend."

"That don't answer my question as to why yer standin' with me tonight. We fought a good fight gettin' here and now we're about to run out, leavin' these poor bastards most certainly to their deaths."

"It ain't like we're runnin' out, somebody's got to do somethin'. Besides . . . I ain't ready to die."

Grainger took a drink, then caught my eye.

"I envy you, Mr. Creed, walkin' in yer own footsteps as ya do . . . with such a clear conscience."

We stood silent, our conversation over. I desperately wanted to hold his words in contempt but could not.

Another gust of cold wind blew through the mission plaza stirring dust, sparks, and smoke together. I closed my eyes. When I opened them, Grainger was still staring at me. He looked down and pulled his coat tighter.

I hit him on the shoulder and said, "My friend, we have a letter to deliver."

Chapter 2

Before dawn, four cannons exploded, raining blazing iron-shot down onto the sleeping Mexican army. Ignoring cries of the soldados who lay just across the San Antonio River, the men of the Alamo silently reloaded their cannons and fired once more.

Grainger and I stood naked, covered in black soot from head to toe. In our bags, we carried a bit of food, water, pistols, and knives wrapped in clothes so they would not make noise. The letter to Sam Houston, sealed in wax, lay hidden in a small roll of deer hide. By the first volley fired, we left out the main gate. The second round was shot as we reached the small, shallow lake east of the chapel; the Mexican soldados were up in arms for they began firing back.

Carrying the bags over our heads, we slipped into the water and waded away from the fort. We tried moving fast and quiet with the muck on the bottom slowing us down. The sky was turning purple, the soot began to wash away, and from behind us, more cannons fired, with the Mexicans doing the shooting. We pulled ourselves out the far side of the lake, wiped off as best we could, dressed, and headed south across a brown, barren field toward the only road to Gonzales. A single cannonball screeched past us by a few strides. Grainger and I stopped and by the dawn's light, I could see him grinning. He whispered, "Whew there! That was a close one, Zeb." We paused and took a breath, then lit out running.

With all the commotion, we worked our way into a brush-filled gully beside the road and waited. Not far beyond a grove of oak trees and a little to the west of us lay the Alamo, now quiet except for a few rifles being fired. As the sun tipped the shadowed bluffs to our east, a muster of soldados happened up the road toward us. In the growing light, I counted six along with a sergeant. I put up as many fingers to Grainger. We held two pistols each, cocked and ready. As many as there were against us, we would also have to use the knives at our belts.

The sergeant directed his men to walk slowly along both sides of the road using their bayonets. The first soldado drew close and stabbed through the brush in front of me. *Shhh-boom!* A long rifle was shot from behind me. The man staggered backward and fell onto the road, bleeding from his chest. Before I could think about who was doing the shooting, I jumped up, surprising the next man, and fired, blowing a hole through his clean uniform and gut. The sergeant screamed at the others to take aim. As he pointed his sword at me, there came another shot from afar, cutting him down. Grainger was on the road and firing. He shot one soldado, shattering a leg, and then shot him again, in his face. Dropping both pistols to the ground, he pulled his knife and ran straight at one of the three still standing. Another distant *Shhh-boom* rang out, striking that soldado in his left thigh, spinning him to the ground. Grainger cursed as the last two turned tail, ran down the road between the oaks, and disappeared. Walking back through the dust and smoke to face me, he exclaimed, "Now wasn't that somethin'!" then knelt down and picked up his spent pistols.

I had pulled my knife and was reaching for the hair of the man I killed when one last shot hit the road. Across the field, Crockett and one of his men stood waving their rifles, pointing furiously toward Gonzales. Cannons fired again to our west.

Letting go of the man's hair, I fished both our bags out of the brush and yelled, "We'd better go, *now*!" I threw Grainger his and we ran east, into the early, morning sun.

Grainger hollered from behind me, "Zeb! I can't go no farther!"

I slowed to let him catch up, then stopped and looked back. The sun was still to the east but riding high. Grainger walked to the side of the road and stood catching his breath to relieve himself.

"How far we gone, ya figure?" he asked over his shoulder.

"Don't know. Six miles, maybe seven." We were almost to the top of a shallow bluff, commanding a view of the valley with the Alamo and San Antonio in the distance. "They're not firin' them goddamn cannons at each other. I can't hear nothin' an' don't see no more low smoke," I said. "An' it don't look like we're bein' followed."

"Ain't nobody cares about us two." Grainger stepped up beside me and took a drink of water, then offered some to me. "You're favorin' a limp, you hurt?"

I had told him a little about my time in New Orleans, about the duel. I had not said how deep the cut was in my thigh or how I was stitched up. "I'm well enough."

"Say when at stoppin' for a rest," he said and lit out again.

An abandoned mission sat southeast of where the road crested onto a flat plain. We had seen it on Travis's maps and as the bell tower came into view, we hid in a gully. If the Mexican army had a post there, we needed to figure a way around without being shot at. Out of the late morning silence, we heard a loud, high whistle, then a voice.

"You boys ain't very good at hidin', are ya!"

Up ahead of us, standing in the middle of the road, was the tallest woman I had ever seen. She wore a plain, calico dress and brown bonnet with a pair of dusty, black riding boots. Cradled in her arms was a genuine .50-caliber Hawken rifle, cocked and ready to fire.

"Who are ya?" Grainger hollered.

"Name's Judith Ann Lee and who might you be?"

With our pistols pulled, we stepped onto the road and slowly walked up to meet her.

She raised her rifle. "Lower them guns I tell ya, else one of ya's gettin' shot and it don't mean nothin' to me which one."

Both of us drew down and slipped the pistols back into our belts. We slowly raised our hands.

"Zebadiah Creed, ma'am, this here's Grainger." I nodded back over my shoulder. "We're from the Alamo, down yonder."

"I know where you come from, been watchin' ya since early morning from my perch, up in that tower. Since all them cannons shot off earlier'n usual, I come from the valley to see what the commotion was. Been listenin' fer three shots ever' day, I can hear 'em from my homestead. Says ya'll are still alive. Travis send you boys out?"

"Whew there, we're surely glad to meet you!" Grainger dropped his hands and bowed. "Yes, ma'am, Travis said you might help us with a couple a' horses. We're on our way to Gonzales to find General Houston an' gather more reinforcements."

She did not move to his bow. "Grainger huh . . . what's yer given name?"

"Just Grainger, ma'am." He lowered his head.

"No mama's gonna name her baby just one name, that ain't right. Now what's yer given name?"

Grainger glanced over to me. I could not help him.

"Ma'am, my whole life, Grainger's the only name I ever answered to." He dug a heel into the dirt, then stopped and looked up. "I don't know what else to tell ya."

"Well, it ain't right and that's all I'm gonna say. Now, Mr.

Creed and Mr. . . ." She cleared her throat, "Mr. Grainger, I have cornbread an' beans waitin' and two good horses though I ain't so sure how much you can do for them poor men you just left behind."

She released the hammer on her rifle and walked on up the road. We followed in silence.

East of the old mission by a mile or so, Judith Ann Lee turned south down a narrow trail. We dropped into the shadows of a deep, limestone canyon, widening onto a slope of scrub grass, prickly pear, and a few small boulders scattered about the hillside. We soon found ourselves overlooking a valley full of budding oak, cottonwood, and elm. The sun rode high and though it being the tail end of winter, I welcomed what shade might be offered. By the looks of a few willows to the east, I knew a creek was near. It smelled of cold spring.

We followed Judith south, into the valley. I saw chimney smoke and realized how hungry I was. We had not eaten since leaving the fort hours before. Right then, a two-day-old biscuit would have tasted good.

The trees opened to an empty corral large enough for five or six horses. Past a yard full of chickens sat a two-room cabin built up against a boulder twice its size. A huge, billowing oak towered above both. To the right of the tree were a double-story barn and a smaller corral with two Indian ponies standing at the gate. An outhouse lay under a cottonwood tree past the barn to the west. On the porch of the cabin, there stood a young woman and boy of maybe twelve with rifles pointed at us. Judith whistled and the dog sitting between them came running to meet her.

"Lower them guns I tell ya. Elizabeth, go set the table. These men are our guests and they're hungry!"

As she stepped onto the porch, I said, "Ma'am, we're obliged to you for the horses and food, but I'm afraid our time is short."

"Mr. Creed, if you are to eat my food then you will sit down at my table to do so. 'Sides, I ain't lettin' you ride outta here with two of my good horses lest I know ya better. Now, go clean yerselves up over yonder at the well. The privy's just past the barn. You ain't comin' into my home smellin' like ya do!" She stopped and looked down at both of us. "An' wash yer faces. For some reason, it looks like ya both have walked through a fire."

She handed her rifle to the boy, walked to the door, and ducked into the cabin.

"Mama, I ain't never seen no Injun with straw colored hair an' grey eyes before," whispered the boy.

Judith leaned close to her son and said, "James, he's a white man wearing Injun clothes is all." She passed the cornbread to me. "Ain't that right, Mr. Creed? You ain't no Injun, are you?"

I took a piece. "Thank you, ma'am, no, I ain't."

"He fights and kills like an Injun . . ." Grainger grinned at the boy. "With the devil's own blood runnin' through his veins."

"I'll have no talk of killin' or the devil at my table, Mr. Grainger!"

Still grinning, he said, "Yes, ma'am," and went back to eating.

The one-story cabin was sparse, clean, and made of solid oak. Whoever designed it did well to understand how to defend against attackers. The door and three windows across the porch would open only from the inside by lifting heavy, wood bars that latched to the walls. Slots with removable wedges were cut throughout to allow for shooting, and with the whole cabin built against the side of a boulder, Judith's family only had to defend three walls and the roof. The fireplace ran across the back of the main room with an iron rod run on the inside to hang kettles. A flat iron grate partially covered the fire for cooking. Two empty rocking chairs sat facing the smoldering fire with the dog asleep between them. The oak table we sat at filled half the room and seated six. Judith sat as tall as Grainger and straight as a board, she at one end of the table with the other end empty. The only ornament in the room was a plain, wooden cross hung above the front door.

I reached for another piece of cornbread. "Am I too bold by asking where Mr. Lee might be?"

She stared at her son and daughter for a few seconds, turned to me, and said, "He's gone away," and went back to eating in silence.

"Papa's off fightin' in the war, ain't he, Mama?" Elizabeth answered with a questioning look to her mother.

"Yes, honey, he's gone off to fight." By her tone, I knew she would speak no more of her husband.

Before we sat down to eat, Judith had removed her bonnet to reveal cropped, brown hair and clear, blue eyes. A thin scar ran across her left cheek and over a rather large nose. When she smiled, her straight teeth shined bright. As she spoke to her daughter, she wore a stern frown. Once, she must have been a pretty woman, but there ran a hard streak in her bones that turned her cold.

"How do you know Colonel Travis?" Grainger asked.

"I know Mr. Travis as a lawyer more'n a soldier. We were accused once of stealin' this here land. He helped us. And now I'm helpin' him," was all she said.

Between spoonfuls of beans, I asked, "How'd you know we was comin', ma'am?"

"You two ain't the only ones he's sent out that I helped, just the first two needin' horses."

Everyone went back to eating.

"How is it you two are here, together?" Judith asked, and then added, "If I didn't know it, that's the shirt of some kinda uniform I ain't seen before, Mr. Grainger. And you, with buckskins, Mr. Creed?" I could not tell if she was suspicious or just questioning.

"We're both volunteers with the Greys, ma'am, sailed to Velasco on the schooner *Columbus,* late, last year from New Orleans. We come to fight and that's what we done what with takin' back San Antonio from the Mexicans." I brushed my smock. "I don't cater much to uniforms, ma'am."

"Ya come from New Orleans, a den of thieves, sinners, and whores." She spat the words out. "You both did well to come to a more wholesome place on Earth, here in Texas." Judith paused and looked up at the cross as if she was seeking an answer to a question in her mind.

She closed her eyes and whispered, "It's good you're here."

I took a long drink of buttermilk and noticed the boy staring at me from across the table. I wiped my mouth and winked at him. He looked quickly to his mama, then sneaked a look back at me.

"Ma'am, this here's some mighty fine milk but I didn't see no cows. Grainger here, now he knows all about cows. Did you see any cows, Grainger?" I asked.

"I didn't see no cows," he said without looking up.

"Our milk cow's in the barn. There's a bull and small herd safe in the pasture out back along with our horses." Judith paused, then asked, "Mr. Grainger, you don't strike me as a farmer. Are you?" She sipped her buttermilk and waited for an answer.

He glanced at me and grinned, "Mrs. Lee, my shorthorns are the latest breed and by far the finest in all the Ohio Valley. One day, when we finish this war, I'll go an' fetch my lovely wife, children, and herd. With them cows, we'll build a life right here in the great, new country of Texas."

"How many and what are their names, Mr. Grainger?"

"A baker's dozen or so an' as I said, they're shorthorns is all. My cows ain't got no names, ma'am," he said frowning.

"No, Mr. Grainger, I mean yer children, not yer cows. Do they have given names or do ya call 'em all Grainger?" I glimpsed a smile on Judith's face.

He glanced at me, this time in desperation. Again, I could not help him.

Grainger sighed and said in earnest, "Mrs. Lee, there are my twins, Louise and Jenny, and my boy, Thomas, who's the oldest. They're all good children, ma'am."

"And yer wife?"

"Isabelle, ma'am, Isabelle Grainger." He smiled as he said this.

Judith Lee smiled and finished her buttermilk.

She set her cup down and turned to me. "Mr. Creed, what about you?"

"No wife and children for me, ma'am, though I've thought about settlin' down a time er two." I bit into my third piece of cornbread soaked in beans. I hoped she did not catch the lie I told about not being married before.

She pushed her plate away, crossed her hands on the table, and leaned forward. "Are you also from the Ohio Valley?"

"No, I was born in North Illinois. Chicago, ma'am, Cook County, near the lake."

"And what of yer kin? Any brothers and sisters?" Both her children stared at me.

"My young sister, Cattie, lives with her husband and three children in the Michigan Territory near Dubuque, east of the Upper Mississippi. My brother, Jonathan, is dead."

"And yer folks?"

"Dead, ma'am."

Grainger finished his beans and sat back.

Judith said, "I'm sorry. Our Lord's Heaven is a better place,

I'm sure. May I ask how they were taken?"

I hesitated and then said, "My folks were killed years ago, murdered by the Lakota up near the Minnesota River. My brother was killed just last year by bushwhackin' thieves."

Everyone was still. Grainger's mouth hung open a little. "Whew there, Zeb, you didn't never tell me 'bout this."

"Never asked."

Judith sighed. "Well, that makes all the sense in the world then . . ." She stood and began clearing plates and cups from the table.

"What do you mean, Mama?" Elizabeth asked.

"The Injun dress an' all," she said as if suddenly knowing in an instant my whole life.

The afternoon sun shone through the open door of the cabin. It was getting late. I pushed away from the table. "Ma'am, we're much obliged for . . ."

"Methuselah."

"Yes, sir?" Judith stopped.

"My name, ma'am. My given name's Methuselah. Methuselah P. Grainger, ma'am, from Big Blue Lick, Kentucky!"

"Well, ain't that somethin'. A good Christian name it is," she exclaimed, nodding. Then added, "And what does the P stand for, Methuselah?"

He smiled to everyone and proudly said, "Pippin, ma'am, Methuselah Pippin Grainger's my name."

Judith faced him. She looked genuinely happy. "Why, thank you, sir, fer makin' that mystery clear for us all."

With her daughter, she finished clearing the table.

CHAPTER 3

The boy held reins to three saddled horses, a magnificent sky-grey mare, a buckskin mare with a pure black mane and tail, and a brown and white-spotted Indian pony. Judith opened the corral gate and he walked the horses out to parade them in front of the cabin porch. Grainger and I had slept for an hour or so, and with repacked bags and full bellies, stood at the steps ready to get on with our mission.

After closing the gate, Judith walked up to us. "James'll take ya to the road 'fore dark. With these here horses, you'll be in Gonzales by late afternoon tomorrow."

Grainger went for the grey mare, as the large horse would comfortably carry his weight. He gathered the reins in his right hand and gently separated the horse from the others. He began stroking the side of its head and neck and as the horse rubbed its nose against his chest, he leaned into an ear and whispered something. Grainger stepped back and stared at its black eyes, then swiftly mounted. The mare nodded its head and snorted once. Smiling, he said, "A fine horse, Mrs. Lee, a fine horse she is, ma'am!"

Judith shaded her eyes from the late sun and frowned. "You'd best take good care of her, ya hear?" She laid a hand on the horse's front shoulder, close to Grainger's leg. Still smiling, he tipped his hat and nudged the mare into a prance away from the cabin and corral toward the barn.

The buckskin was beautiful, and feisty. When I went to grab

her, she pulled back, almost getting away from the boy.

"She'll settle once she knows ya," he said, handing me the reins.

This time she did not pull, and I began stroking her neck the same as Grainger did with his horse. I drew the reins up over her head and mounted. The young mare whinnied loudly as she danced circles in front of the cabin, scattering dust, the dog, and three or four chickens under the fence and into the corral. I leaned in close, laying my chest against her silky, black mane. She smelled of wild, winter oats and white sage. Squeezing her ribs tight with my knees, I placed my cheek near the top of her head and began speaking softly, then singing. The swirling slowed until I pulled the reins for her to stand still. I finished my song and sat back up in the saddle. By this time, Grainger had walked his horse back over to us. Everyone was staring at me in silence.

In a quiet voice, Grainger said, "Whew there, partner, you surprise me with somethin' new every day. Where'd you learn that?"

"I been ridin' horses my whole life."

"No, I mean speakin' in Injun."

"From the Lakota . . ."

Grainger dismounted without a word, climbed onto the porch, and scooped up both our bags. He handed mine over, held it for a second staring at me, and let go. I felt the sealed letter safe in the bottom, then pulled two loaded pistols out and placed them in my belt next to Bowie's knife. Grainger climbed back onto the grey mare and waited.

James mounted his pony. Judith watched me as I glanced at his pack, then to her. He seemed to be carrying quite a few supplies for just taking us up to the road and turning back home.

From the porch, Elizabeth threw Grainger and me each a bundle. "Mama said to give you these. There's cornbread, an' biscuits from this mornin', and jerky to chew." She smiled and stood by the cabin door.

"Much obliged." I hung the bundle on my saddle horn.

Judith pulled the reins of the mare to get my attention. "I want my horses back when yer done."

I leaned down and looked her in the eye. "Yes, ma'am, I give you my word. They will be returned to you." I nodded to Grainger. Judith turned to him.

"Yes, ma'am. Much obliged, ma'am," he said and tipped his hat once again. She gave him the slightest of smiles and curtsied.

Judith then said to her son, "You get on back here safe and I'll have supper waitin' for ya." She climbed the steps of the porch and stood at the door next to her daughter. I could see the light from the burning fireplace behind them. I pulled my cap down over my ears. The sun was almost touching the western edge of the small valley. It was going to be a long, cold night.

James headed us in the opposite direction from where we walked earlier in the day. The dog followed close behind his pony, yelping and nipping at its back hooves. As we rounded the far side of the boulder, I thought I heard Judith Lee say, "Take good care of my boy, ya hear?" Then there came a whistle. The dog turned tail and raced back to its home.

For an hour or so James led us east through winter grass and hardscrabble pasture, then up several switchbacks to rest on a narrow trail above the valley. The boulder and oak tree had disappeared below as twilight faded to dark. We sat for a while listening to the silence of the early evening. Except for the echoes of our horses' hooves hitting rock, silence followed us up the black canyon we rode through and out onto the road.

"You ain't goin' back, are ya?" I asked the boy. I could hardly see his face. The half-moon would not rise for another couple of hours to give us a little more light.

"I'm headin' to Gonzales, where my daddy's at."

Grainger's horse danced circles on the road. He seemed anxious to get on. "Your mama's sendin' ya, ain't she?" He sounded angry.

"I'm doin' this on my own," James meekly said.

"Goddamn, boy, that ain't what I asked! Does your mama think you're comin' home tonight?" Grainger's horse stood still.

James did not answer.

"She sent you out," I said, without question. "Trustin' our good nature to take you with us, ain't she?"

"She was figurin' you was headin' that a way and I could ride along."

"She coulda just . . ." I stopped. Then asked, "what's your daddy doin' in Gonzales?"

"He's fightin' in the war."

I pointed west and said, "The fight's back there in San Antonio, not Gonzales."

"All I know's what Mama told me," James stammered.

"Whew there, Zeb, you an' I, we gotta talk." Grainger walked his horse up the road a bit. I followed.

"We can't take this boy along with us, we're already hours later goin' then we shoulda been." Grainger continued with a lower voice. "Besides, what if we run into trouble. What'll we do with him then?"

"Well, we could hog-tie him, set him backward, and send his pony down the trail we just rode up on. But there ain't no guarantee he don't fall off and roll his way home," I said, loud enough for the boy to hear. I was hoping Grainger could not see my grin.

"Zeb, this ain't funny now. What are we gonna do?"

The evening was silent again except for a couple of coyotes yowling in the distance. I rode away from Grainger and back to James. I sensed his newfound distrust of the situation.

"How old are you, boy?"

"I'm thirteen, goin' on fourteen," he proudly said.

He was older than I thought he was. "You ever shot a man, much less killed him?"

"Zeb, ain't he a little too young to be killin'?" Grainger asked.

"Answer the question, boy."

"Yes sir . . ." he calmly said, "I have. At least I think I did. We was attacked by Injuns last summer and I helped shoot. Didn't find no bodies afterward, but they never come back."

"Were you afraid?" I asked.

"Yes, sir, I was."

"Good."

I looked toward Grainger. He and his horse were circling again and I could hear him drinking from a bottle. It was the first time he drank anything but buttermilk and water since the night before, back at the Alamo.

"How fast is that pony? Can he keep up with these horses?" The mare I sat on whinnied, as if she had been listening to the conversation.

"Mr. Creed, this here pony can beat both them horses in a long run. I seen him." I could tell he spoke what he believed to be the truth.

"Well, Grainger, I don't see no reason why he can't go with us. He says he can shoot and his pony's fast. I seen your squirrel gun, you gotta pistol?"

"Yes, sir, I do."

"Is it loaded?"

There was a pause. "No, sir, it ain't."

"Boy, a pistol ain't no good unless it's loaded. Do it now, we'll wait."

James pulled out a shooting bag and loaded the pistol. He was surprisingly quick in the dark.

Grainger and his mare were still walking in circles. Each time around, they went a little farther up the road. I knew he was angry. He would simmer down later. At least, I hoped he would.

"Mr. Creed, my name ain't boy. It's James, sir. James Lee." I heard him cock, then slowly uncock the pistol and place it in his belt, like mine. He seemed ready.

"Well, then, James Lee, let's go."

Grainger was not waiting for us to catch up.

Chapter 4

We lost the moon around midnight. It seemed the clouds came down to meet us. There was no rain, just a damp cold that soaked to the skin. With James behind me, I kept my head down and let the mare find her way. Only once did she guide us off the road. Grainger still rode ahead, how far I did not know. We stopped often to listen for his horse and heard nothing. He began to worry me some.

"Why do ya figure Mr. Grainger got all twisted and run off?" James asked.

I waited to answer. It seemed the fog was heavier up ahead. " 'Cause he don't like surprises," was all I said.

Of all the adventurers, rogues, and idealists that made up the New Orleans Greys, I got on with Grainger the best. We met on board *Columbus,* the schooner that sailed us from New Orleans to Texas. It was the first time on the high seas for me but not Grainger, for he took to the water like an old salt. When I felt I was getting sick, he showed me how to gaze at the horizon and not to look inside the ship. He taught me to walk the decks with more of a swagger than I was used to. He would spend time with the coxswain and captain on the bridge and at least once manned the wheel. In the evening, below decks, there was always a card game to join and Grainger loved playing cards. He insisted on winning.

The second night at sea came a storm. I was in my hammock

early and feeling sick as the ship groaned and rocked to and fro. Grainger had gone up to the foc'sle where the crew slept for a drink and a game. Soon, the young German Ehrenberg was at my hammock stammering something about Grainger ready to kill one of the sailors. As sick as I was, I told him to leave me the hell alone. Minutes later, he came back saying Mr. Morris, the leader of the Greys, claimed that if Grainger killed this man, it might jeopardize our mission. I swung down and made my way forward to see him pinning a man down with a knife to his throat. Cards were strewn about and half-empty bottles clattered with the sway of the ship, spilling rum onto the deck. With little fresh air, it smelled of body stink and old tobacco smoke. Three of the crew stood in half-shadows with knives pulled. Morris knelt next to Grainger attempting to talk him into letting the man go. As I entered the foc'sle, all were quiet except our leader. He nodded to me, stood up, and said, "Maybe you will have more persuasion with your friend. But I must tell you, if he kills this man, he will hang before we reach shore." Morris stepped back.

The faint flicker of an oil lamp caught everyone's eyes, including Grainger. He looked sideways to me, smiled, and said, "Whew there, Zeb, I thought you was sick in yer hammock." A wave hit the bow of the ship throwing Grainger forward, cutting the poor sailor's neck. Blood began dripping into his greasy hair and onto the wet deck. The man closed his eyes and let out a groan.

Holding back the urge to puke, I said, "Grainger, why are you lyin' on him?" I took a step forward.

"Claims I cheated," he said, with a blank look. "Zeb, I ain't no goddamn cheat!" He moved his knee up into the man's groin a little more and smiled down at him. "I ain't no cheat, am I?"

The sailor winced, licked his lips, and cried, "No, no, sir, you ain't no cheat. I'm sorry for sayin' so, sir."

I took another short step, kneeled down to Grainger, and spoke low. "This weather ain't no good for me tonight and it ain't too good fer this here fella you got pinned down. You cut him already and I do believe he has shit his britches. Now, he's taken back his accusation, why don't you let him go and we'll call it a night. 'Sides, if you kill him, the captain of this here ship who's standin' behind me might not be able to stop his men from killin' you."

He hung his head and whispered, "If I drop this here knife, you won't let 'em hurt me, will ya?" I could smell the rum heavy on his breath.

"I can't guarantee that they ain't gonna jump ya. But if you drop that knife and they do, I'll fight with ya."

Grainger thought about what I said for a second, then whispered, "You'd do that for me?"

"Yes, I would."

The knife dropped to the deck and Grainger stood up. He was at least a head taller than any of us and had to stoop in the confined space. The bleeding man lay still. The other men held their knives out and ready.

As I backed up, the captain stepped around me and ordered, "Drop yer knives, boys, we're done here. Mr. Morris, I'm placing this man in irons until we reach Velasco. You can have him back then." He turned to me and nodded. I placed my knife back into my shirt.

Grainger spent the next day and night chained to a bulkhead deep in the bowels of the ship. Either one of the other men or myself brought him water and food. When we reached port, the captain released him to Mr. Morris, and he was again a New Orleans Grey. The next evening, we caught a steamship up the Brazos River to Brazoria, then marched across the low coastal plains to Victoria and Goliad. By the time we were camped outside of San Antonio, Grainger and I were good friends.

I continued to ride slow through the fog with a thirteen-year-old boy behind me, and Grainger somewhere ahead. I reached down and again felt the sealed letter through my bag. We needed to get on down the road.

I wondered where my friend was.

When the New Orleans Greys joined up with the Texas regulars in early winter, we were raring for a fight. What we found was a troop of cold and tired Texans ready to head back to their homes. Colonel Stephen Austin had tried to engage them several times against General Perfecto de Cos and his Mexican garrison, who held San Antonio and the Alamo. When Austin resigned, a man named Burleson became the leader of both the regulars and volunteers. Soon after, we met James Bowie. He was also raring for a fight.

Like everyone else, Grainger and I had heard tales of Jim Bowie's exploits. However, to hear them spoken in his own words, usually told during a night of drinking and cards, only seemed more truth than tale. One evening, after telling us about him running slaves out of Galveston with the pirate Jean Lafitte, I mentioned that I knew a man who lived in St. Louis by the name of Frenchy, and that he was more than likely Lafitte. I told a brief story of how I came to know this. Bowie only raised an eyebrow and said nothing. I could not tell if he thought I was lying or did not want to be upended by the truth. Still, Grainger and I both fell under his spell, especially after he led us through our first battle against the Mexican army.

Soon after hearing rumors about a shipment of silver and gold, the scout Erastus "Deaf" Smith rode into camp one morning hollering about a packtrain headed our way. Before the dust from Smith's horse settled, the men were loading their guns for a fight. Burleson slowed everyone down only by conversing in private with Bowie, then publicly ordering him to take thirty or forty men into the field. This was not to engage the enemy, but to gain information. Bowie in turn picked out the twelve best sharpshooters and riders of the militia and headed off to find the packtrain. Grainger was one of the first chosen and rode alongside Bowie.

The ones left in camp went up in arms, myself included. Those of us who came from New Orleans had not traveled so far to watch a handful of regular militia and one volunteer gain all the glory. Burleson again settled everyone by choosing thirty or so of both regulars and volunteers to back up Bowie's men as infantry. He placed a Colonel William Jack in charge. In a matter of minutes, we were marching after Bowie and his cavalry.

According to Grainger, the battle began about a mile outside of San Antonio. They came upon the packtrain crossing a dry ravine near where the Alazán, Apache, and San Pedro Creeks came together. The mules scattered as the shooting started and the Mexican soldados guarding the animals took cover.

We heard their rifle shots but could not see a thing through the thick bramble brush and trees that grew between the streams. After wading across Apache Creek, we began following the dry bed up the San Pedro. Within a minute, we found ourselves caught under fire. Low hanging willows along the right side of the creek hid the soldados shooting at us. With no sign of Bowie's men, a Colonel Rusk took the lead and with fifteen of us gathered, we began shooting back. The others were able to take cover in the dried cattails and reeds on the far side of the streambed. We got in close enough to push the Mexicans back from shore and up into the woods. This freed up the rest of the men to cross the creek and follow us. We yelled, cussed, and kept shooting until the soldados retreated through a clearing in the trees.

The first shot from the cannon screamed just overhead. Fresh, broken branches and dead leaves showered down upon us covering our hats and shoulders. I thought I would piss my britches for this was my first experience with a six-pound cannonball. I had not heard anything so loud and dangerous. I hit the ground and lay there for a minute smelling the damp earth below and scorched wood above. *Cos must have sent reinforcements,* I thought, for Smith had not mentioned anything of a damn cannon along with the packtrain. A second shot blasted through to my left just missing Rusk and three others coming up from behind. Fine bits of sawdust swirled in the sunlight shining through the trees. I was still on the ground when a horse stepped up beside me and I heard a familiar voice.

"Whew there, Zeb, you'd best get on up lest ya get trampled. The cavalry's a comin'!" Grainger reached a hand down and pulled me to my feet.

"Zeb, them cannons are only as good as who's shootin' 'em and them goddamn Mexicans couldn't shoot a bull in a narrow pasture. Now pick up yer rifle and let's go get that gold hanging off them mules!" He kicked his horse hard and lit out through the trees. Bowie rode past whooping and hollering like a madman. The rest of his men followed.

I picked up my rifle and ran a short distance to the edge of another dry creek bed. The soldados had begun to regroup in bunches along the far side of the creek taking shots at our riders and infantry coming at them. Bowie was the first across the creek bed and climbed the steep embankment straight into battle. Four soldados were furiously repositioning the cannon over a rise for a better aim into the creek. Bowie hit the first one with the butt end of his rifle, breaking the man's jaw. The other soldados stood their ground, one with a bayoneted rifle, the other two held pistols. Bowie's horse suddenly reared up, throwing him to the ground. He lay there stunned. I raised my rifle and from across the creek shot the man about to stab him with the bayonet. Bowie turned his head and for a quick second looked right at me. Another shot rang out from somewhere below dropping the second soldado about to shoot. Before the third one could aim his pistol, Bowie leapt up and sank a knife deep into the man's chest. More soldados rushed in to retake the cannon. More shots were fired from our side of the creek holding them at bay. Bowie quickly climbed onto his horse and retreated down to the creek bed joining Grainger and the rest of his cavalry. Together, they charged back up the embankment and engaged the enemy one last time. I reloaded my rifle, and with my fellow fighters, staved off the Mexicans enough that their cannon did not fire again that day.

Back at camp, Bowie claimed we killed sixty Mexican soldados. I thought it an exaggeration though I never refuted his word. When the soldados retreated to San Antonio de Béxar, they took their cannon but they did not take the packtrain. That day we captured forty mules, not laden with gold and silver, but with saddlebags full of freshly cut grass for Cos's hungry horses. Most of the men did not care. To them, it was a good fight won.

That evening, with the victory celebration well underway, the tales of bravery rang out around the campfires like ancient Greek war songs. Several women came from a hacienda nearby to feed the Texas militia and volunteers with roast goat, pig, and a small calf. General Cos and his retreated troops, who were holed up in town and at the Alamo, must have heard the ruckus. Bottles were passed all around and card games begun. Grainger was drunk by dark.

The poker game began in earnest when Bowie joined. He took my place after I played only a few hands. I was not drunk enough nor had I anything to wager except for a few coins brought from New Orleans. I was not about to accept the credit

Grainger offered me. After losing a couple of dollars, I bowed out as graceful as I could and found another campstool to sit and watch.

Bowie brought the most money to the table as he lived in town. He was a Mexican citizen and had married into a wealthy family. Though his wife and child had died a year or more before from the cholera, he was still close to his in-laws. When the shooting began, he fled their home so as not to be captured and joined the fight. Some said that it was not until after the loss of his family did he commence to drinking, cussing, and gambling. Everything in his life to that point seemed to draw toward the next three months.

"You ain't gonna beat three queens!" Bowie loudly exclaimed to Deaf Smith as if to make sure he heard him. A man of few words, Smith laid down five cards, four kings and a ten. Without even a grin, he swept the coins from the middle of the table to his side. Bowie sat back and did not say a word. He then picked up the cards placed in front of him and began shuffling the deck. "Ya might not be able to hear a damn thing, ya sure can play yer cards right," he shouted.

Deaf leaned toward him, cupped his right ear, and said, "Aye . . . ?"

Bowie gave a slight smile and dealt out the next hand.

Grainger rolled his eyes as he picked up the five cards laid down before him. "Whew there, Jim, you ain't got nothin' better to give me than these?" He stacked them on the table with a jack facing up and threw a dollar in the pot to open. Smith peered at his cards, then looked around the table. He closed them tight against his chest and threw in a dollar. Bowie left his cards facedown without looking at them and threw his dollar in. He took a long drink from a bottle and passed it around. Smith waved it off but Grainger took a drink and slammed it down on the table. Everyone jumped but Bowie. "Damn you boys are slow!" he hollered and took another drink.

The fourth player was a man named Alexandros Robito Obregon, from somewhere south on the coast. He had joined the fight early on, just after the folks of Gonzales kept the Mexican garrison from taking their only cannon. He came to San Antonio with Austin and stayed.

Grainger handed him the bottle and said, "Whatcha gonna do there, mister?"

Obregon laid his cards facedown and turned over a king. "Three dollars to you, sirs . . ." he said near under his breath and threw the coins into the pot. His slight accent was not missed by anyone. With some hesitation, he passed the bottle on to me. I sensed that he might not trust a man sitting out of the game only to watch. I took a drink and set the bottle back on the table in front of him.

Bowie tossed four coins to the pot and turned over an ace. He casually picked up two more dollars and threw them to the center of the table. Smith glanced at his cards, frowned, and laid down two tens. "It's all I have fer now, boys. I call an' bump ye up three dollars," he said and tossed in the coins he just won from Bowie.

"Ever'body's in then, here we go." Grainger turned over another jack. Without a word, he threw what he owed to the pot and five more silver dollars. He then got up and stumbled into the darkness to leave a piss.

Bowie looked right at me. "Yer the man who shot that bastard about ta stab me, ain'tcha?" His eyes were clear but his hand trembled slightly. "I was gonna kill him, ya know." He picked up the bottle. "I expect you saved me from havin' to do so. Fer that, I thank ya." He closed his eyes and took a drink.

I felt his gratitude genuine. A pause came in our talk. Laughter drifted our way from one of the other campfires.

"I shot the son of a bitch who was next in line to kill ya!"

Grainger announced as he sat back down.

Still holding the bottle, Bowie smiled and replied, "And fer that, sir, I will be forever in your debt. Now can we finish up this here hand? My cards are gettin' cold." Grainger frowned a bit, maybe noticing the hint of sarcasm. Nothing more was said about the morning's battle.

Robito turned to Grainger. "What is the pot up to?"

"Ten dollars to stay, mister. Can ya beat two jacks?"

Obregon hesitated. With calm fingers over his coins, he looked around the table. "I believe gentlemen, I shall have to withdraw," he said and turned the king facedown on top of his other cards.

Grainger looked surprised, then angry. "You ain't gonna show yer cards?"

"I do not believe I have to show my cards." Obregon mocked him with a thicker accent.

"Where you from? You ain't no goddamn Mexican, are ya? You don't sound Mexican. Where I come from, you show yer cards, mister." Everyone looked at Grainger, then to Obregon.

"Where I come from, you are being rude and most would not tolerate such indignation. But as you will see, I am a patient man when I choose to be." Obregon paused, straightened up, and laid both his hands palms down on the table. Now, please tell me again your name, *mister.*"

"Grainger . . ." I said.

Obregon turned sharply to me. "Sir, I ask your friend to answer for himself!"

"My name's Grainger an' I don't give a goddamn what yer name is or where ya come from. Either you turn them cards over or I will!" He lifted himself out of his chair.

Bowie quickly stood and leaned over with both hands spread on the table. "Gentlemen, gentlemen, *please*! Mr. Obregon here's from Corpus Christi, just a ways south a' where we're sittin' tonight. I do believe that accent a' yers comes from yer Spanish daddy and yer Greek mama, right, Alexandros? Ain't that what you told me when we was lying in that ditch about ta kill our first Mexicans, oh, two weeks or so ago?" He locked eyes with Grainger. "I've played cards on the biggest steamboats outta New Orleans an' at the best gambling houses in New York City an' Boston. Even played a few hands across the big 'Lantic in Paris an' London an' I ain't never knew a man havin' ta turn his cards if he don't want to." He eased back down into his chair. "Now, I do know a man wantin' to turn some cards so can we get on with this here game?" Bowie threw in eight dollars and turned over another ace. He shrugged and tossed ten more dollars into the pot.

Grainger reached for the bottle and sat back down without another word. I do not think he saw the glint of a palm dagger's blade as Obregon slowly moved his hands off the table. For a time, neither man looked the other's way.

Smith seemed to be sleeping. Bowie threw a cork and hit him in the ear. "Yer turn, Deaf!" he hollered. Smith opened his eyes, calmly stacked up fifteen silver dollars and pushed them toward the pot, then turned over a ten. He pushed another five dollars into the pot and closed his eyes again.

Grainger sat looking at the cards on the table, then casually flipped over another jack. He stared at Smith and Bowie's money for a few seconds, then picked up five coins and juggled them from one hand to the other, letting them fall into a perfect stack next to his three jacks. "Here's fifty dollars' worth a' gold Eagles, gentlemen. I call and I raise!" Grainger picked up the coins and tossed them into the pile one at a time. Each gold piece hit the silver with clear, scattered rings.

Bowie was down to just two small stacks of dollars. Smith did not move. Obregon took the bottle from Grainger and sat back. Feeling a cold breeze, I thought I smelled rain. Talk and laughter from the other campfires were dying down as men drifted off to their tents for the night. A fiddle player finished his last rendition of "Arkansas Traveler" and was silent.

Bowie picked up his remaining coins and threw them carelessly to the center of the table. "I wanna stay in but I don't believe I have the coins to cover." He paused and sat back grasping his coat's lapel. He then reached into a side pocket, retrieved a piece of paper, and said, "If you will accept it, gentlemen, I hold in my hand a deed to property I own just east a' here worth, oh, seven maybe eight hundred dollar 'er more . . . Owned it fer some time now. Should bring a man a handsome profit someday, after this here war's over."

He tossed the partially folded deed onto the heap of gold and silver coins. Grainger picked up the paper and examined it the best he could in the light. He looked at me. I shrugged my shoulders. I could not help him. He refolded the deed and placed it at the edge of the pot.

"Ya sure are a confident man, ain't ya, Mr. Bowie," Grainger said.

Smith opened his eyes. "You turnin' a card or we sittin' here all night. I'm gittin' cold!"

Bowie flipped over another ace.

"Well, I'll be damned." Smith picked up his three tens and placed them facedown on top of his other cards. He stared at Grainger, as if daring him to say something.

Obregon smiled and lit a cigar.

Grainger pushed what remained of his money toward the middle of the table, then stopped and lifted the edges of his last two cards. Taking both hands, he quickly pushed the coins into the pot, crumpling the deed a bit. He turned over a queen.

Bowie's eyes lit up for a quick second. "What ta do, what ta do?" he said to himself, drumming his fingers next to his last two cards. Suddenly he stopped, looked up, and smiled for the first time all night. "Fellas, I ain't seen these here cards same as you. Let's see what's hiding, shall we?" Bowie turned over two queens. "Looks like I got yer queens there, Mr. Grainger . . ."

"Now you show your card, mister," said Obregon with a slight laugh and blew smoke into the cold, evening air. Smith was awake and staring at Grainger, same as the rest of us.

"We ain't got all night!" Bowie said impatiently.

Grainger flipped over a jack, and then whispered, "Looks like these here cards win."

Something in the air changed. Maybe it was the lingering smoke of Obregon's cigar mixing with the smell of coming rain. Maybe, everyone knew the long day was ending.

"Ya got me." Bowie sighed and threw his cards into the pile of gold and silver. The land deed lay half-covered by coins at Grainger's end of the table. By the fading light of our oil lamp, I noticed it was written in Spanish.

Bowie stood and bowed. "Gentlemen, I shall now retire. Tomorrow's another day," he stated and walked away toward his tent.

"I'll be damned . . ." Smith muttered and gathered up his money. Obregon crushed his cigar out with the sole of one of his Spanish, suede boots and said nothing. When they both had gone, I pulled my stool to the table.

"Whew there, Zeb, he didn't look at his cards, not once," Grainger said, shaking his head, and began filling a canvas bag. He picked up the deed and traced the writing lightly with a finger.

"This ain't English, is it?"

I said no, it ain't.

Grainger neatly refolded the piece of paper and placed it in the bag with the rest of his winnings.

We did not see Bowie the morning after or for about a week. The next we met was right before fighting Cos's army again, this time running him and his garrison out of the Alamo, San

Antonio, and all the way down across the Rio Grande to Matamoros.

There were rumors of the card game, that Bowie had cheated. This made no sense because he lost. Grainger never talked about the land he won.

I thought the paper must be worthless.

Chapter 5

Gonzales, Early March 1836

James and I were halfway across the bridge before I noticed the echo of our horses' hooves hitting wood.

"Mr. Creed, I sure gotta piss."

I stopped and looked around. The fog was lifting. The tops of the trees lining the creek below us looked like black boulders peeking out of some lake or ocean.

"We'll reach the end of this here bridge and take a breather, mornin's comin'. I expect we have another day 'fore we get there with this fog slowin' us down."

I dropped to the wood planks and walked a ways to stretch my legs. I had not been off my horse since we left Judith Lee's cabin. My left thigh was stiff and aching. I looked forward to the sun's warmth.

James went on ahead to do his duty. I pissed into a gully at the side of the road and walked my horse up to meet him.

"You ever been to Gonzales?" I asked.

"Been there once with my daddy, last year sometime. Don't like the ferry much."

As the half-moon shown through the clouds, I could clearly see his face. He looked older than he did the afternoon before, sitting at his mama's supper table. He climbed onto his Indian pony, checked the pistol stuffed into his belt, and rode on. I followed.

We reached the banks of the Guadalupe sometime after

nightfall and made camp near the ferryman's empty shack. Across the river lay the town of Gonzales. I slept for the first time since before leaving the Alamo. What little dreaming I did, I could not remember.

We repacked at dawn, ate our last bit of cornbread and biscuits, and waited at the large, rusting, rope pulley next to the landing. We were the first passengers of the morning. The sun was just up when the pulley began to slowly creak, turning faster with an almost silent, steady rhythm. The rope strung to the same rig on the opposite shore sang as the ferry slowly glided toward us. The ferryman glanced up only once or twice as he guided the wide, flat-bottomed barge into the U-shaped pier. We walked our horses on board and rested just forward of the pilothouse.

The ferryman threw all his weight into pulling us across the river. He knew exactly where the knots in the thick rope were to grab hold of, hand over hand, with no gloves.

"What day is it?" I asked.

"Sunday mornin', I expect."

"What's the date?"

He paused, letting the current drift the ferry downstream a ways until what little slack in the rope was gone. The wind had picked up some since dawn and with the sun passing in and out of clouds, I still felt cold from the night before. James stood quiet holding the reins to his pony, staring at the water, then ahead to the shoreline. He looked like he might be getting sick.

"Don't pay much mind to dates. I know the day fer the bell ringin' earlier, sound like Sunday. Any mo' question?" The ferryman began to pull again, slowly, on toward the shore.

"A man rode before us, on a pale grey horse. He may have crossed yesterday, late."

"Big fella, he catch the last trip 'fo night set in. Say he's on the trail a' Sam Houston. Tell him he's wastin' his precious time, the man ain't nowhere 'round Gonzales. Then he ask, where's the tavern?"

"We're lookin' for the same."

"Man er tavern?"

"Both."

"If ya want a bed, Turner Hotel's on St. John. But if ya want a drink and maybe a l'il somethin', well, you know, Luna's where to be, farther up the street."

We were most of the way across when James got sick.

"The water, boy, in the water, not my barge!" the ferryman hollered.

He pulled us up to shore without saying much more than, "Two bits."

James mounted his pony, jumped to the pier, then onto dry land, as if he was riding away from a fire. I told the man thanks for taking us across the river and for the word on Grainger. He took my money and turned away to assist his newest passengers. I felt I would not be crossing back that way any time soon.

James and I headed north on Water Street, ending up at the fort. From across the road, down to the banks of the river were three or four camps of what looked to be Texans with only a few volunteers. I did not recognize anyone nor did I see anything of Grainger. If General Houston was indeed not in Gonzales, then I needed to discuss our plight with the officer in charge. I smelled breakfast cooking from the fires. Damn, I was hungry.

We were tying up our horses outside the fort's gates when I turned and saw Colonel J. C. Neill walking up from the river. "Zebadiah Creed! I'll be, Zebadiah Creed!" It felt good to hear someone call my name and see a familiar, smiling face.

"You come from the Alamo?" Neill asked, shaking my hand. "What word would you bring?" Other men began walking up from the camps to gather around us.

"Sir, it's mighty good to see ya!" I said, "It ain't been more than a month since ya left but you're a sight for sore eyes right now." I waved my hand around to the growing crowd. "All of ya."

"The Alamo and the brave men defending her are in dire straits now, facing thousands of Mexican soldados and cannons. We must gather as many able fighters as there are here and abroad and leave immediately! Hell, it may be too late now but we must try." Not being one for saying speeches, I stopped to reach into my bag and retrieved the sealed letter. "Here's a letter from Colonel Travis written to General Sam Houston requesting the Texas army respond, or else, as I said, all is lost . . ."

"You rode outta there alone?" asked an older man carrying a squirrel gun and wearing a patch over his left eye.

"Me and Grainger left at dawn, day 'fore yesterday. Run out naked, covered in soot. We borrowed horses from this boy's mama a few miles east of San Antonio." I pointed to James, then said proudly to Neill, "Colonel, we left outta there with yer cannons a blastin' that goddamn Santa Anna an' his army!"

"Grainger? And where might he be?" Neill looked around, then down the street as if Grainger might come walking up to meet us. He turned back to me in surprise.

"You ain't seen him? He crossed the Guadalupe last evenin' at sundown. The ferryman sent him on to the hotel and more likely the tavern. I woulda thought he'd go find you first, 'course if he knew you were here . . ."

"I arrived last night, late with my men, setting camp by moonlight. General Houston's over in Washington on the Brazos and will be here any day with more Texans ready to fight. As far as outfitting for goods to take with us to San Antonio, I have begun with my first order for medical supplies and food. I will continue until I feel we are prepared to go and defeat these Mexicans." There was a spattering of applause from the men surrounding us.

"And what of Colonel Fannin?" I asked.

"He and his men are south, near Goliad. Last word sent by the general was for him to retreat to Victoria and hold."

I frowned, then turned away, placing the letter back into my bag. "Must be why he and his men never came. We ain't the only couriers sent out," I said, mostly to myself.

After a pause, Neill said, "So, now you must introduce your new riding partner."

James stepped right up. "Lee, sir. Name's James Lee, son of Jacob Lee."

Neill smiled and shook his hand. "Can you fight, son?"

"Yes, sir, I can!" he said, drumming two fingers on the butt end of the pistol in his belt.

"You ever seen a cannon? Whether you have or haven't, I'll show you the cannon that started this whole fight."

Neill turned back to me. "Zeb, the consult finished our Declaration of Independence on March second, voting it in unanimously." He stepped back to join his men.

I stared into their eyes, one after the other, seeing the pride in what they were doing. Though sorely ill fitted to fight, these men seemed raring to go and face Santa Anna's army.

If only there were two thousand more of them, I thought, suddenly realizing the futility of their efforts. I pushed that thought deep within myself.

"Sir, I know it's Sunday an' all, the ferryman told us as much. What's the date?"

"Why, it's March sixth all the day long."

"I believe it's my birthday," I said, under my breath.

James leaned into me. "Happy birthday, sir."

I nodded thanks.

"Where might the Turner Hotel be?" I asked no one in particular.

"Just up 'round the corner on St. John," said the one-eyed man.

I turned to him. He stood closer than I liked and smelled of rotting chewing tobacco and whiskey. He then winked at me with his good eye. I faced him until he slowly backed into the crowd and walked away carrying his squirrel gun over his shoulder.

Colonel Neill said, "Mr. Creed, I must leave you now and continue my ordering of supplies. James, if you will accompany me, I'm sure there is time this morning to see Gonzales's famous cannon."

The crowd of men broke up with most everyone heading back to their camps. I went to find Grainger.

The hotel clerk peered over his glasses. "He left, early this morning, he did. Stayed the night and was up 'fore dawn. Don't know how, as to him bein' drunk as he was. Had to put him to bed, I did."

The desk he stood behind had not one speck of dust on it with the register and pen laid out perfect. The lobby was decorated with a plant in a pot between two small lounge chairs. A large, ornate mirror, almost too large for the room, hung at the foot of the stairs. A door opened to a restaurant serving two or three customers. Though perfectly clean, it smelled a bit musty.

"Man got throwed outta Luna's. A big fella he was; took five of 'em to carry him out. Found him lyin' in the street mumblin' somethin' 'bout stolen land. Don't know what all it means, I just helped the man to his bed. Paid for the room in gold coin, I do know that . . ."

"Any idea which way he lit out?" I asked.

"Can't say as I do."

The clerk looked me up and down. I must have been a sight

coming through the door as I did in buckskins, with Bowie's knife and two pistols in my belt. I am sure, after being holed up at the Alamo all that time with little water to wash with, I smelled quite ripe.

"You must be Mr. Zebadiah Creed?"

"Yes, sir?"

He slid an envelope across the hotel desk with my name on it. "My wife dictated this here letter for Mr. Grainger last night 'fore he went to drinkin' at Luna's. He also put money down on a room for you an' a boy travelin' with you, said it was somethin' owed in advance."

I opened the letter and read,

March 5th, 1836

Zeb,

Sorry for running off, something hung me back at Mrs. Lee's spread. And, traveling with the boy I just could not stand. I am off in the morning to find General Houston and warn him you are coming. Rest easy, for I will explain things when next we meet.

Your friend,

Methuselah P. Grainger

I placed the letter back into the envelope and tucked it away in my belt next to Bowie's knife. I thanked the good gentleman and asked to see the room.

After having some breakfast and doing my personal duties, I walked back down to the fort. Our horses were still tied up at the gates but with oat bags strapped to their snouts. James was nowhere in sight. Throughout the morning, more men had gathered at the camps and it looked as if Colonel Neill had ordered them to begin marching and fighting drills. I watched for a while. The weapons most of the men carried were nothing more than small-bore hunting rifles at best, guns good for shooting squirrels or rabbits but not fit for killing a man. These men lacked discipline. When a couple of them got tired of marching, they sat down to smoke and then wandered off. One by one, the others did the same. By early afternoon Neill returned to an empty field and the man he left in charge lay asleep under a tree down by the river. He went to fetch him.

James strolled up after Neill. I asked about his father. He said there was a chance he went south to fight with Colonel Fannin's men. He looked sad and undecided as to what to do. It was then I remembered him being only thirteen years old. I also remembered the last thing Judith Lee hollered to Grainger and me as we followed her son up the trail. I could not help but feel some responsibility and, I did not quite know what to do.

"Sad bunch . . ."

"Sir?" I turned from James to Neill, coming back up from the river alone.

He waved his hand, "These men here are a sad bunch. To think of who stands at the Alamo this day and who sits in these camps, well, there is no comparison."

"They need training and arms is all. We was just as green starting out. Why, I remember the first time I felt a cannonball damn near crease the top a' my head, about pissed my pants." I laughed.

Neill smiled. "Speaking of cannons, I showed James the very cannon that lit this whole revolution. Nice and shiny it is, cleaned up and ready for service."

"James, this man here," I placed my hand on Neill's shoulder, "and a handful of volunteers built up all the Alamo's breastworks, palisades, and battlements. We set 'em with twelve or so cannons of all sizes captured from Cos's garrison. Oh, and the Greys brought a six-pounder all the way from New Orleans. He showed us how and we built it all with no help from none of the damn regulars, they all run off. Ain't that somethin'?"

Neill nodded. "I would like to be there now," he said softly and looked at James. "This man is the best fighter I've ever known, bar none." His face showed dead serious as he turned to me. "That is why I must ask you, Zeb, to stay and help me prepare these men for battle."

Standing at the edge of an empty field overlooking the Guadalupe, with the sun finally warming my bones, I fell silent and stared out at the water. South of us, the ferryman had left the Gonzales landing for the fourth or fifth time that day, working hand over hand, one knot at a time to cross the river. With each knot he pulled, ran a wake behind the ferry, washed away by the river's current. *His whole life,* I wondered. *How many folks he'll pull across this river?* I shook my head. *A job like that makes a young man old damn quick.*

"Colonel, I am bound to deliver this letter to General Houston, wherever he may be."

"General Houston will be here any day now, I'm sure of it."

"I feel I can't wait. If he's bringin' more men, I may be able to encourage them to hasten along to San Antonio. Each day goes by, I feel sicker thinkin' our friends and fellows defendin' the Alamo have no chance to survive." I stepped away from Colonel Neill and turned again to James. "Up yonder on St. John Street's the Turner Hotel, you have a room for the night if you'd like. Clean and dry it is and paid for."

I then said to Neill, "If General Houston is indeed on his way here from Washington then I'll be back within a day to ride on . . . Or, if need be, to help in the preparation of these here men to fight."

A cloud passed over the sun and again I felt a late winter chill. The ferryman finished assisting his passengers onto the far landing with no one waiting to cross back to Gonzales. Though the day was still early, I could see him weary as he sat alone.

Three riders approached the landing. The ferryman slowly stood to welcome them on board.

Chapter 6

I rested a spell, then left James at the hotel and rode northeast. The damp air wrapped the early evening in a quiet blanket, muffling any sound my horse may have made. Washington on the Brazos was some hundred miles or more away from Gonzales, a good two days' hard ride at least. I was glad to be alone.

The seventy or eighty odd men and boys camped along the Guadalupe were not ready to fight a minor skirmish, much less battle against an army of three thousand or so trained soldados. I told Colonel Neill as much though I believed in his heart he knew, else he would not have been so determined for me to stay and help train his men. With what little supplies and weapons at hand, a complete rout would be certain. I only hoped there were men with more fighting experience than mere passion riding with General Houston.

The buckskin mare and I got on well. Affectionately named White Socks by the Lees, her three white ankles matched perfect with her light, tan-colored coat and silky, black mane and tail. Guided by my voice and steady hand, the feistiness was replaced with a quiet presence and a fearless will to travel anywhere we needed to go. I secretly named her *Owajila-Tate,* Lakota for Still Wind.

I rode her at a gallop for an hour or so, let her walk for half that to cool down, and then rode hard for another hour. I made good time riding that way without tiring her out. The farther east, the more winding the road became as the prairie and patchy groves of oak and elm gave way to pine forest. When the trees covered the moon, the stars became my guide. Around midnight, I dismounted and walked to stretch my legs.

She seemed to smell the smoke before I did and began nudging me toward the side of the road and into the forest. Seeing faint flickers of light and shadow through the trees ahead, I patted her and whispered I also sensed something amiss, that if there was danger, the forest would not be the safest place to be.

We rounded the next bend and in the middle of the road, a man knelt, tending a small fire. As I approached, he looked up and smiled.

"Whew there, Zeb, am I glad to see you!" Grainger stood and walked toward me with his hand extended. I stayed just outside the ring of firelight. The mare whinnied and backed away, skittish as Grainger stepped forward. I reluctantly shook his hand.

"Where in hell have you been, Grainger?"

He let go and walked toward the fire. "Been on the same road as you, just different places at different times, I reckon. Did ya get my letter?" he asked over his shoulder, then stopped and turned to face me. "You want coffee?"

I did not see a coffee pot.

"Grainger, why'd you build a fire in the middle of the road?" I took one side step toward him.

I heard the brush of a tree limb.

"Grainger, he don't look so goddamn tough ta me, with his pretty hair an' all . . ."

I pulled both pistols, cocked and pointed one at Grainger, the other to my left from where the voice came from. As soon as I dropped the reins, Still Wind quickly walked backward out of the light, turned, and raced down the road a ways.

"Zeb, I'm sorry. But after tellin' me what they wanted, I had to. There's three more of 'em out there with their rifles aimed at ya. You'd best hand me them guns, now." Grainger stood blocking the fire not two feet from the point end of my pistol, leaving me in his shadow. I could not see his face.

The man to my left was the first to show himself. I recognized him from earlier that day in Gonzales, from the patch over his left eye. The squirrel gun was replaced with a .45-caliber trade rifle pointed at my head.

"So, this here's the bastard who murdered Benjamin Brody," he said.

I glared at Grainger. I had told him about my experiences with Brody, how I left him bleeding but alive.

"You, sir, are mistaken. I scalped the son of a bitch but I did not kill him," I said, now staring at the one-eyed man, squaring off more with him than Grainger. I did not relinquish my pistols. "If I die here, sir, so will you."

"Nobody has to die tonight, son. Ain't here ta kill ya. I mean ta take yer young ass back to New Orleans an' stand trial. If yer innocent as ya say, well, sir . . ." I heard the other three men's boots behind me. "You won't hang an' you get yer freedom back. Don't matter ta me much, I get my money all the same." He shrugged and let out something resembling a laugh. The men behind me laughed. Grainger stood stone-cold silent.

"Grainger, I'm much obliged you showin' up like ya did. Yer timin' was 'impeccable' as Mr. Brody would say. Ya see, Mr. Creed, Grainger here, an' I, we used to be partners. 'Til he run off . . ." The one-eyed man gave Grainger a look of disdain and spat on the ground near his feet. He inched closer. I could see his trigger finger tremble in the faint light. The fire crackled and with a loud *pop*, sparks flew into the air. Everyone jumped.

Grainger slightly opened his coat. "You scalped Brody? Why, I'll be goddamned! I was told ya killed him, cut him through the gullet."

"That was Baumgartner I killed, with a knife through the neck in a whorehouse. A few days later, I scalped Brody clean, and like I said, left him lyin' under the oaks, still breathin', his wife cryin' for him. Hell, she got stabbed by this gal named Sophie le Roux, the one who owned the whorehouse." I backed away a bit, still pointing my pistols at Grainger and the bounty hunter. The men behind me moved back.

" 'Nough a' this chatter! Don't mean a thing. Brody's dead an' Creed's accused a' the deed an' I aim to take him back to New Orleans."

"Zeb, you swear ya didn't kill him?"

"Grainger, I swear."

There was another *pop* from the fire. Everyone jumped, but me.

Pulling off Grainger, I twisted all the way to my left and with the pistol in my right hand, shot the one-eyed bounty hunter. At the same time, I shot the man who stood directly behind me. I heard two other pistols fire, then a groan and a rifle shot. Two of the men crumpled to the ground. I glanced at Grainger as he jumped toward the third man left standing. The bounty hunter must have shot his rifle or maybe it jammed for he then used it to take a swing at my head, hitting me hard on my right shoulder. I fell to my knees and he tried to hit me again, this time with the butt end. I pulled the Bowie knife and stabbed him in his right thigh, slicing clean through artery and bone. Blood gushed down his leg onto the road. He dropped the rifle and stood over me for a few seconds, then fell to his knees. We both sat facing each other as his blood pooled around us. A hole was in his left shoulder where I shot him. The patch pulled away from his bad eye revealed nothing but a sunken scar. His good eye stared wildly down to the ground, then rolled back to me. He slumped into my arms and whispered, "Ain't supposed to die like this, I got grandkids." His last rattling words were,

"Fuckin' Grainger . . ." I laid him down, and using clean dust from the road, wiped most of his blood off my buckskins. Grainger was behind me with the last bastard still alive. I heard a scream and turned to see him standing over the man with a boot pressed down on his bleeding belly.

"You ain't hurt so bad as ya can't go back to New Orleans and tell Broussard that both Grainger an' Creed's dead, ya hear? If you don't an' anybody, *anybody* comes a lookin' for me or Zeb, I'll kill 'em! Then I'll come find you and Broussard and kill ya both!!" Grainger stomped on the man's belly one more time, then helped him to his feet. He staggered into the forest. Grainger and I both reloaded our pistols. A few minutes later the man rode east on his horse, passing us as we stood by the waning fire.

"Where's the coffee?" I asked.

Grainger laughed and walked away into the forest. My horse had trotted back up the road to me and nuzzled my right ear. I touched the top of it and felt blood. *I'll be damned,* I said to myself, *piece a' my ear's shot off.* I cleaned it up the best I could.

Grainger rode out of the forest on his horse. Except, it was not his horse. Rather than the pale, grey mare Judith Lee had loaned him, he rode a pure, black stallion.

I followed him east, leaving three dead men in a ditch, the stench of black powder smoke in the air and a fire smoldering in the middle of the road.

"Houston and his men are 'bout three hours' hard ride back up this a way at Burnham's Crossing, should be there by mornin'," was all Grainger said for a long while. I kept him a little in front of me as we rode through the night in silence.

"So, how long did ya work for Brody?" I asked during a walking spell.

"Didn't, worked fer a man named Broussard. I met Brody only once, the evenin' of yer famous challenge at the opry house.

You set him up good, cuttin' his face an' breakin' his nose an' all. Then scalpin' him like ya did and leavin' him alive . . . Whew!" Grainger stopped his horse to let me step up beside him. The half-moon shone down to light us and the road.

"You knew back there I didn't kill Brody."

Grainger raised an eyebrow and nodded.

"Why didn't you tell me about this before?"

"Ya never asked." His eyes narrowed. "Zeb, you're a loyal friend. Maybe too loyal . . ."

He kicked his horse into a gallop. From over his shoulder he hollered, "Come on, Houston's waitin' to meet ya!"

Chapter 7

We rode into camp before sunup. I found a patch of ground to lay my blanket down on and went to sleep. After a couple of hours, I woke smelling coffee. The air was clean and it seemed the ground was not nearly as cold as the morning before at the ferry landing. I lay there a few more minutes not moving, staring up through the pines at a clear blue sky. Spring had arrived.

I closed my eyes and stretched, then looked up to a man leaning over me. This was not the way I intended on meeting General Sam Houston.

"Mr. Zebadiah Creed, I presume?"

I stood, dusted myself off as best I could, and extended my hand. The general was as tall as Grainger but not as large with his uniform clean and pressed. He held himself with experienced dignity.

"Yes, sir, Zebadiah Creed. I have something for you from Colonel Travis, sir." I reached into my bag, pulled out the sealed roll, and handed it to him.

"Mr. Creed, before I sit and read this, you will walk with me over to my secretary. Your ear needs cleaning else it will turn rank. Later, you might need that ear, eh, Mr. Creed?" He gave me a wink, then a good look, and said, "I have spent time in buckskins and moccasins myself. Yours, my young friend, have seen considerable wear." He glanced down at the dried blood left on my britches. "We'll get you cleaned up and fed and then we will talk awhile."

I walked with General Houston toward an open tent with an empty folding table and two camp chairs. The pale grey mare stood nearby, with its reins staked to the ground. We walked on past to a smaller tent. He introduced me to a Mr. Andrew Horton, bowed, and said he would return shortly. With only three other tents scattered about, there were no fighting men at his camp.

My ear was better than I thought, with the ball just grazing the tip, leaving more blood than damage. After smearing a salve over my wound, Horton wrapped a clean, white bandage around my head. He suggested I find a way to bathe the rest of my body and either wash or replace my buckskins. I had not removed them since long before leaving the Alamo.

Grainger poked his head inside the tent and laughed, "Whew there, Zeb, yer lookin' just like a sheik from all the way over in Arabie!" As there was no mirror, I could or would not disagree. He handed me a white shirt and britches with suspenders. "General Houston gave me these to pass on to you. He knows of our plight," he said and left me to clean up and change. Horton brought a pan of fresh water and I began to wash.

"Where's General Houston's army?" I asked.

"I expect they're gathering in Gonzales," he said, and left the tent.

I was dog-tired, a mess, and after almost being killed twice and killing as many men in the last few days, I did not care much about an army or a fight. The letter Colonel Travis entrusted to me was in the possession of General Houston. No matter the outcome at the Alamo, my mission was accomplished. I walked out to find food and a cup of that coffee I smelled earlier.

I sat opposite General Houston in the open tent. I had eaten an entire batch of biscuits and gravy with a couple of pieces of fatback. The coffee was what set me right.

"First, tell of the blood on your britches."

"A bushwhackin'. Last evening, 'fore midnight."

"Bandits on the road?" he asked casually, as if he knew the answer.

"No, sir, they were not. They were lookin' for someone in particular."

"Grainger, then? He left out of here yesterday about sundown, heading back to Gonzales to find you and deliver a message to Neill."

"They wanted me, sir."

He seemed to feign surprise. "Why?"

I told him what happened the night before and the reasons why I thought they were after me.

"So, Brody was alive when you left him at the oaks, missing a head full of hair, mind you, but still alive. And, you killed Baumgartner with the help from a freed black man who you then helped steal back his brother's wife and boys, slaves stolen by a man named Broussard?" He took a breath, and then chuckled. "Hmm, the three B's of Bourbon Street. And what of Madame le Roux?"

"There was somethin' between her an' Brody an' Baumgartner though I never knew what, and never asked. I was in New Orleans only to avenge my brother's death. She allowed me to do that."

"And where does Grainger fit into this puzzle?"

"He said he worked for Broussard for a time, only meetin' Brody once."

"Do you trust him?"

"Yes . . ."

"I sense some doubt."

"Trust depends on the circumstances, I reckon."

Houston looked away to Judith Lee's horse grazing a short

distance away.

"We traded horses."

I nodded.

"I need to be seen in a certain light." He stood and walked to the horse. Taking a small knife from his belt, he reached down and pulled up a hoof. "Been well cared for," he said, more to himself and began cleaning dirt off the one shoe. "I lived with the Cherokee for a time, we didn't shoe our horses. Which tribe took you in?"

"Lakota, sir."

"North plains, as I thought. The cut of your buckskins told me as much." He finished cleaning the hoof, put away his knife, and rubbed the horse's neck.

"I shall rename you Saracen," General Houston whispered under his breath. The pale grey mare responded by nuzzling his chest.

"Won't you walk with me, Mr. Creed?"

The Colorado River was east of the grass meadow where Houston's small party camped. We walked over a rise and down to the water's edge.

Houston picked up a smooth, flat stone and threw it out across the calm water. Three skips and it sank with a splash toward the middle of the river. He handed me a stone. I tried throwing with my right arm but was too sore from being hit with the butt end of a rifle. I tossed the stone to my left hand and side-armed it straight and true across the water, skipping three times before sinking past the middle of the river.

"Ah, a southpaw." Houston sighed.

I nodded.

"And who turned you to the right hand, Indians or Whites?"

"I can't remember, sir."

"I would say the whites. We are a superstitious lot you know. When did you go and live with the Lakota?"

"I was eleven."

"You were old enough to know your white family yet young enough to grow into a man with your tribe." He squared with me. "Pull up your shirt?"

"Why, sir?"

His look was one of mild impatience. "Because, I asked you to."

I reluctantly did what he asked. The old scars on both sides of my chest were fading but clearly visible.

"The Sun Dance."

"Yes, sir."

"You are a Lakota warrior."

"I am not . . ."

"But you show the markings of a warrior," he exclaimed, surprised at my statement.

I broke his gaze and looked away, back across the calm river.

"I stood and fought with my family and tribe as a warrior for years until . . ." I grew silent. Then whispered, "I dishonored my father."

He picked up another stone and held it gently in his hand. "Well, then, you need not tell the details."

Houston stood quite still. "Mr. Creed, we all have secrets along with our regrets. And to dishonor one's father is, well, I certainly understand. You are, however, not the only one to leave his family and tribe, no matter the circumstances." He turned to face me. "Despite the past, you are a warrior else you would not be standing with me along this river, in this fight." He paused, and then said, "Whether you become a great warrior, your deeds and time will tell."

He skipped the stone out over the water five times. "Shall we go? I must sit in counsel and decide, as a general, what my next move will be."

We walked back up to camp, for him to meet with his war

party and for me to have that talk with my friend.

"Mr. Creed, won't you and Mr. Grainger join us?" General Houston asked over his shoulder. "Both you and he have fought the enemy and I welcome your experience."

My talk with Grainger would have to wait.

Chapter 8

I had forgotten about the bandage and must have seemed a horrible sight. I pulled it off and felt my ear. A tiny piece was missing though the salve was working for there was little pain. I tore a bit of bandage and covered just the wound. Every time I touched my ear, I would remember the one-eyed bounty hunter and his words.

General Houston's party consisted of himself and Secretary Horton, a General Hockley, and a recruit named Richardson Scurry. Houston and Hockley sat at the front of the table in the open tent with Horton seated behind, prepared to take notes. After checking my horse, I joined them, squatting in front next to Grainger. The recruit was nowhere around.

Nothing was said for a couple of minutes. The sun burned through the flimsy shirt I wore.

"The Alamo is lost, I'm sure of it," Houston exclaimed to no one in particular.

Grainger and I gave a shocked glance at each other. Neither of us expected such a final statement from the general.

"Sir, we bring the latest news from San Antonio. Unless, of course you have other details we don't know about," I said, questioning him with a direct stare. I stood up. Grainger stayed squatted on the ground.

"You left four days ago, with the general's army of several thousand well-armed men plus artillery surrounding the mission. According to Colonel Travis's letter, he and his men had maybe a week's worth of rations and ammunition left, or less. Am I right?"

Grainger stood beside me. All I could do was nod yes.

"If I was Santa Anna, I'd use those brave men as an example to the rest of us who might fight against him. Yet . . ." He glanced to Hockley. "Because General Cos is his brother-in-law, the man you, Colonel Bowie, Colonel Burleson, and a host of others helped to defeat, he leads his army with a personal vengeance. And gentlemen, no one wins a war by vendetta."

I stepped closer. "And how shall *we* win this war, sir? We expected an army here and you have none. The men at Gonzales are nothin' more than farmers and rogues! With due respect, sir, I feel I don't have to tell you how dismal the future is with those men and their lack of discipline, trainin', and experience. The guns needed to fight three hundred aren't available, much less the food and guns it would take to defeat an army of three or four thousand." My face was burning. I felt a hand on my shoulder.

"Sir," Houston said, slumped in his seat. "I'm afraid I am well aware of my situation, more so than anyone here or in Gonzales."

"Then, sir, I ask again, how will you win this war?"

"Mr. Creed, martyrdom will win our war."

I shook Grainger's hand off. He stepped away from me and continued his silence.

"What would you have me do?" Houston calmly asked.

I stood alone with my arms down by my side and head hung low. There was nothing anyone could do, not I, not Grainger, nor all the men in Gonzales, and especially not Houston. Our mission was doomed as we left out the front gates headed east four mornings before. The men of the Alamo were doomed the day Santa Anna raised his red flag showing no quarter.

"In every war, there is sacrifice. You and Mr. Grainger now

know this more than anyone here today," Houston said staring me in the eye.

General Hockley sat in silence until, "We need only one Alamo's why I'm suggestin' the general send one of ya on ta Goliad an' persuade Fannin he must retreat to Gonzales, er else."

Grainger stepped up beside me. The late morning breeze blew through the tops of pines behind us, moaning like ghosts.

General Houston leaned forward and said one thing more. "You both will rest this afternoon and evening to be gone by dawn tomorrow. Mr. Creed, you will ride straight back to Gonzales and let Colonel Neill know we shall arrive within two days and to continue gathering men and supplies. You, Mr. Grainger, must ride due south to find Fannin."

We were handed yet another letter each to deliver.

Grainger shrugged. "Whew there, Zeb, must be our time in the saddle," he offered and walked off.

With my pistols laid out in pieces on the empty shooting bag, I sat cross-legged on a new patch of grass, my head down cleaning them. My hands shook.

Grainger towered over me. "I ain't never seen you shake like this . . ." For a few long seconds, he fidgeted with a button on his sleeve. ". . . If I hadn't done what I done, you'd be halfway to New Orleans by now, or dead."

I looked up. I could tell he had not drunk since Gonzales. His eyes were clear.

"It ain't the fact that you knew about me and Brody, it's that you concealed it for so long."

"What was the use of tellin' ya? I come from New Orleans. You did. We knew some a' the same folks is all . . ."

"Oh, I don't know, Grainger, because you knew Brody was dead, murdered, and most likely a goddamn shit, one-eyed bounty hunter would come a lookin' for me."

I reassembled one of the pistols, raised, cocked, and pulled the trigger with a click. I laid it back down and reassembled the second one. I loaded both of them. Grainger stood towering above me. My hands still shook.

"And what would you've done if you'd a known, kill him? Hell, you done that, only with my help." He kneeled down in front of me. "And what if I was with ya just ridin' along and them shits bushwhacked us proper? Hell, I'd be dead for certain and you'd be in a New Orleans jail with that letter you delivered this mornin' thrown into the Big Muddy . . ."

Grainger picked at the grass, acting as if he wanted to say more.

"What of Broussard?" I asked.

"What of him?"

"He ain't leavin' me alone, is he?"

Grainger turned away. He may have been good at keeping secrets, but he was no good at keeping his feelings hid.

"What will ya tell Judith Lee about her horse?" I asked.

He looked back sheepishly. "Her horse is bein' ridden by a general, she should be proud."

"Anything else?"

"Nope . . ."

I stood, cinched the bag with my teeth, and held both pistols in my left hand. I reached down and pulled Grainger up.

"Next time I find you tendin' a fire in the middle of a road, I'll just shoot you and ride on."

"Fair enough," he said, smiling.

I smelled rabbit stew cooking.

While the two generals, me, and Grainger and the secretary had our powwow, the recruit Scurry had been out snaring a couple of healthy white tails. I walked to the cook camp and lifted the lid to the Dutch oven. With some winter onions and pine nuts simmering over the rabbits, I did not think I had smelled anything as good. At least I would eat a great supper before riding off again to God knows where.

"Must be hungry," the young man said, walking out of the forest carrying firewood.

"Yes, sir, I am mighty hungry!"

"Oh, please don't call me sir, sir. We'll eat in an hour or so. You like river oysters?" He dumped the wood next to the fire, lifted the lid himself, and stirred the stew.

"Can't say, never ate 'em."

"We're far enough south, I found a dozen or so 'long the shore. I've got 'em buried next to the fire." He paused and extended a hand. "Name's Richardson. Most call me Dick."

We shook. A firm grip he had, strong for as thin as he was. He looked all of fifteen or sixteen years old, with black hair and wire glasses. His uniform was clean and dignified, a cut above most men fighting this war. He reminded me of a young Travis, but without putting on airs.

"Sir, may I speak frankly?"

"Yes, of course."

"The general feels you and Mr. Grainger are the only men to reach Colonel Fannin in time, before . . ." he hesitated, "before the Mexican army gets to him and his men. Sir, my brother's there with them."

"But I'm going back to Gonzales."

"Yes, sir, and on to Goliad." Scurry stopped. Then he said, ". . . once you get word to Colonel Neill of our arrival."

Masking my surprise, I did not know what to say. I was to deliver a letter, nothing more. I could only think of what Houston said, that *martyrdom would win this war.* I did not care to become a martyr.

"General Houston knows he must build an army an' needs

Fannin and his men in Gonzales, includin' you and your brother." I paused, not wanting to disappoint the young man. "I'll do what I can to get 'em there."

Scurry pulled the lid off again and held up the spoon. "Would you like a taste, sir?"

"Why, I'd be honored," I said. "I'd like to try one a them oysters too, if they're ready."

"Yes, sir!" the young recruit proudly exclaimed.

I tasted the stew, the best rabbit stew ever.

Chapter 9

Grainger and I left the next morning, before dawn. General Houston bid us a quiet farewell, and with another sealed letter tucked into my bag, I rode back to Gonzales. Grainger went south toward Goliad.

The only stop I made was three hours west, at the fire. I buried the dead men in shallow graves just off the road. I meant to scalp the two I killed, though the critters had already gotten to them and the smell was withering. It seemed I did not have the sense or urge to save such useless prize. The evening before, I asked Grainger their names. He said he knew only Frank, the one-eyed son of a bitch, and that he was glad I killed him. I sang a Lakota death song for all three men.

I entered Gonzales at twilight with eight new volunteers I met along the way. Campfires littered the shore of the Guadalupe River up to Water Street and from the ferry landing north to the fort. The town was teeming with men of all ages and status, some riffraff, some fighters, most were just farmers and tradesmen. There seemed to be no more organization than there was two days before.

Three blocks east on St. Mathews Street, Colonel Neill had set up his headquarters at the military plaza. I was greeted with a firm handshake. We sat and talked for nearly an hour, about supplies he had sent for and had begun receiving, how the calls for able fighters were heeded, and how starting the next morning, drills would begin again.

When I told him Houston was not bringing any men other than another general, a recruit, and his personal secretary, Neill slumped forward, nearly touching his elbows to his knees. *How are we to win this war,* he whispered under his breath.

I asked if there was word from the Alamo. He said no, but rumors abounded, about how on the morning of the sixth came quite a battle, then all was quiet. The three cannon shots fired daily had not been heard since the afternoon before. The folks living throughout the surrounding countryside were fearful of what most likely had happened and what was to come. Some families had already made their way east to Gonzales, abandoning their farms and homesteads.

Neill fell silent, shaking his head. I had not seen a man more conflicted. To continue preparing for a war with what little there was to fight with, yet feeling most hopeless.

As he opened the letter, I asked about James. He looked up, smiled, and said what a pleasure the young man had been the last few days. He helped Neill with correspondence and as a courier to the contractors with supplies. He said James would grow into a fine, young man, if he survived the next few months.

Neill finished reading General Houston's letter. He asked again about more men. I shook my head no. He then said that Houston ordered me to ride swift, direct as possible to Goliad, and with all my effort convince Colonel Fannin to fall back to Victoria, then make his way to Gonzales. "A split army is a conquered army," he quoted the general. Neill folded the letter, laid it in his lap, and gazed out over the plaza lit by evening cooking fires. With no room left along the shore, new volunteers had begun setting camps in town. Again, he shook his head.

I would leave immediately, I said, as soon as I ate some supper.

★ ★ ★ ★ ★

I sat on a log stirring jerky stew. Two pans, one with cornbread and the other with sourdough biscuits, lay directly on hot coals. Thin strips of venison hung sizzling from green poplar spears that bowed over the burning oak. Deaf Smith sat quiet with his eyes closed, smoking his pipe. I was pleased to be sharing his fire and supper.

"And how is the arcane devil?" he asked, his eyes still closed.

For some time, I thought he might be blind along with being half-deaf had I not seen him shoot a man dead from near a hundred yards.

"Who might you be speakin' of?" I continued to stir the stew.

"Why, Grainger, of course."

"He was part of a bushwhackin' that almost got me killed."

"I ain't surprised at'all. The man's got a shadow followin' him, ain't never catchin' up, where's he at?"

"General Houston sent him to find Fannin an' try an' bring him and his men here," I said.

"Ain't that stew stirred 'nough?" Deaf stood and stretched.

He was a bit shorter than I was and older, but I would not tangle with him, unless I had to. We fought side by side, house to house, in San Antonio, taking first the town, then the Alamo from General Cos and his garrison. He would have died had I not carried him back to camp after being wounded on top of Bowie's in-laws' house. Later, he was the first courier Travis sent out from the Alamo. Deaf Smith was a kind, patient man until you crossed him. He was then your enemy forever. He was not completely deaf, just hard of hearing, when he wanted to be.

I dished us up helpings poured over cornbread. The steam from the stew drifted up, loosening faint memories of home on the cold, north prairie, the prayer Mother sang to us as she ladled buffalo bone soup over cornbread. I closed my eyes and thought how far I was from those evenings long ago.

"I'm sure grateful for supper," I said with my mouth full and shook the memories away.

Deaf nodded and was quiet while he ate. Then, "He ain't gonna come."

"Who ain't comin'?"

"Fannin, he ain't comin' to Gonzales."

"That's what Houston thinks too. Is why I'm lightin' out 'fore dawn to find him myself." I waved my hand back up toward the fort. "Guess the general thinks it'll take both me and Grainger to talk him into joinin' this here ragtag army."

Supper was over in most camps along the river and the fires were dying down. Deaf's camp was the farthest south, near the ferry landing. The only sounds I could hear must have come from Luna's tavern a few blocks away, a distant drum of fiddle tunes, singing, and laughter snaking its way through the streets of Gonzales.

"Yer ear's been shot."

"Yep, a one-eyed bounty hunter shot me with a .45-caliber trade rifle."

"Piss poor shot, an' him?"

"Who?"

"The damn one-eyed man who shot yer ear, what happened to him?"

"He's buried with two others a half a day's ride from here, up in the pines."

Deaf lit his pipe again and sat back. I cleaned up the two plates and stored the biscuits for my ride. I left the venison to smoke awhile longer.

"Grainger's bushwhackin', what'd they want from him, his land?"

"Wasn't him, it was me."

Deaf Smith actually looked surprised. "Bushwhacked you, what for?"

"Claimed I killed a man in New Orleans."

"Did ya?"

"Yes, but not the man they wanted me for, I only scalped him."

"Ya scalped him and he lived?"

"Yes."

Deaf closed his eyes, leaned his head back, and blew smoke into the dark sky. I pulled a piece of the venison off one of the spears, burning my fingers.

"Grainger's land in Kentucky, with all the cows on it, right?" I asked.

"No, sir. The piece a' land he owns ain't but seventy miles west a' here, Jim Bowie's land."

I stopped blowing on the meat and stared at Deaf. "What land?"

He opened his eyes and flashed a rare smile. "Why, thc land he won in that rigged poker game you sat out on. Damnedest thing I ever seen, that poker game. I know Bowie cheated but why would ya cheat to lose?"

With my life more often than not hanging on a limb since that evening some six months before, I had nearly forgotten about the crumpled piece of paper. I never read it, and as far as I knew, neither had Grainger.

"I thought the paper meant nothin', was worthless."

"Zebadiah, ain't no deeds to land worth nothin' 'round here. Depends on where it is, is how much you can resell for, an' ya better believe Grainger's land is prime land."

We both paused, for Deaf to take in the night and for me to take in the conversation. I wondered where this land was located and how fortunate or ill-fated Grainger might be. I thought of Judith Lee and our conversation at her supper table less than a week before. About her family being accused of stealing the land they lived on.

"You know a boy named James Lee? He rode with me on my first day to Gonzales, lookin' for his daddy?"

"I know the boy and he left this mornin', downriver on a barge, headin' to where you're goin'. Brave he is. Ya know Mexican soldiers are headin' there now, to Goliad, I mean. My sources tell me things most folks don't want to know."

"Hmm, like what?"

He cleared his throat. "That the Alamo was more'n likely sacked and burned two days ago with all them men shot an' killed." Deaf lowered his head and spat on the ground. "Wasn't much we could do for 'em, I'm afraid . . ." He stared into the fire, poking at it with a long stick. "More'n likely that son of a bitch Santa Anna's headin' this a way right this very minute."

"No, not him. He don't do nothin' at night but eat, drink, and sleep. An' by the looks of some of them painted ladies we watched from the rooftops of the Alamo, at least a little more than that, I reckon!"

For the first time that night, I heard Deaf Smith laugh hard and long. I started laughing and when I looked over to him, he was wiping tears from his eyes.

I turned away for I did not want to believe him or our talk.

We were quiet for a long while, Deaf smoking his pipe and me watching the stars. I imagined them to be a swirl of pinholes poked through a coal-black riding cape and lit from behind by an oil lamp. Who swung the lamp or wore the cape, and why I thought of this, I did not know.

"Why are you here, Zebadiah?"

I looked over, startled by Deaf's piercing eyes staring at me from the other side of the fire, and from his simple question.

"You ain't got a dog in this fight," he said.

I suppose I could have answered him the same as I answered

Travis only a few days before, or Grainger. Instead I stared back and shrugged my shoulders.

"Who are ya servin'?" he asked.

"What do you mean, who am I serving?" I was getting irritated by the questions.

"Well, sir, are ya servin' General Houston? Some say he ain't nothin' but a drunken fool and Indian lover. Or is it the new counsel and their independence paper, a handful of plantation owners from Louisiana an' Mississippi who want to grow cotton usin' their damn slaves. Are ya servin' all these here landowners, showin' up with nothin' but trade rifles an' no idea of what fightin' an' dyin' for a country is? Hell, the Mexican government give 'em all their land in the first place . . ." He paused to blow smoke into the darkness. "Are ya here 'cause God wants you to be here? Son, in a fight like this, ya gotta serve somebody or some higher purpose, else your just killin' for no good reason at all."

"Well, damn, I've kept myself alive by my own hand so far, by goin' my own way, hadn't I? Sure as hell ain't the God of my missionary folks, he gave up on them, leavin' me and my brother out on the north plains. For years we were slaves to the Lakota." I hung my head. "An' now my brother's dead."

Deaf did not seem surprised that I would mention something so personal, so painful.

After a long silence, he sighed and said, "Don't need to know 'bout all you been through to know you're a better man for it, my friend. Though you'd best find some solace from somewhere, else you'll end your life empty an' all alone."

He bid me good night and good riding in the morrow.

I lay next to the dying fire a long time before sleeping. *Why the hell was I here, diggin' myself deeper into this mess, this cause I ain't really a part of.* For the first time in a long while I thought of Anna, and Missouri. My hands still shook. I did not dream.

CHAPTER 10

There were only two roads to Goliad. One road Grainger traveled on from Burnham's Crossing, the other went south from San Antonio, placing me heading west or east and out of my way. I would have welcomed taking a barge or flatboat down the Guadalupe as James did and when I asked Deaf about this, he said there were no more going south for a day or two. He then told me about an old Indian trail that followed the eastern shoreline. I was glad not to cross the river west on the ferry.

Still Wind seemed to know the way, as if she had traveled this trail before. Following the riverbank close, we were in the open most of the time though the water to our right offered protection from a surprise ambush. It would take a skilled marksman to shoot me at forty yards from the opposite shore. Again, I rode alone with only my horse, and my wits.

By midmorning, it was raining, gentle at first, just a steady spring shower that felt good on my face and the back of my hands. Still Wind smelled of horse sweat, dust, and rain. She reminded me of an earlier time spent on the north plains riding with my brother. A black storm caught us in a draw hunting antelope, until the sky was too dark to see clear to the top of the next rise. We knew not to stay on low ground for the floods always came. I raced up to face the rain, wind, and power of the thunder, laughing like a crazy coyote at the lightning with my brother following close. We stood, our arms raised to the sky singing praise to *Wakatanka,* the Great Spirit. We rode back to camp laughing and joking, trying to knock each other to the ground with our bows, both horses smelling of sweat, dust, and rain.

I missed my brother.

The rain fell harder as I rode. By the looks of the clouds upstream, back toward Gonzales, I knew that very soon there would come a deluge. As the river ran faster, I began searching for higher ground to wait out the coming flood. *Damn,* I thought, *I need to get on to Goliad!*

I came upon deep sets of fresh wheel ruts. They ran out of the river at a wide, shallow bend, a natural ford for crossing. The wagons that made them were heavy, as if they carried much supplies or people. The trail split off east and only wide enough for wagons to travel single file. Yet, scattered about the thinning forest were several wagons and riders pushing their way, struggling post haste, through sagebrush and open patches of waist-high savannah grass. They were not the only travelers that morning for I saw many more wagons approaching the western shore.

I rode down the trail a ways and up onto a slight bluff. While sitting under a willow tree, I watched two wagons and a rider on horseback enter the water. It was raining a miserable downpour and the wind had picked up. In only a few minutes, the river had risen more than a foot, not too deep to cross, but hazardous. Everything from clumps of grass and branches to whole trees raced along through a swift current.

One of the wagons, heavy with household belongings and no cover, reached the middle of the river, then stopped. A woman furiously snapped reins at her two mules to get them moving forward again. The second, smaller wagon stopped with its mule's head almost smacking the first wagon's backboard. The rider had nearly reached the shore and was hollering at the woman to get rolling again, then rode back toward her, sloshing through the water. The woman began to panic. The more she whipped the animals, the more they worked themselves sideways and downstream. The young driver of the smaller wagon pulled around and went ahead, grabbing part of her harness to help steer the mules forward. With help from the rider, both wagons again rolled toward the shore, one in front of the other with the young man leading the woman.

I turned away, then heard a muffled crack and a splash. In seconds, two mules rushed past me tangled in harnesses trailed by a broken tongue, their brays choked off by the water they swallowed. I looked back through the rain to the woman's wagon lying on its side. Water swirled over the bottom ribs and down through the shallow side-slats, creating a small rapid. All their belongings swept away. The woman clung to the buckboard rail as the rider reached for the back of her dress, then hair, and tried pulling her up onto his horse. Perhaps they were both too soaked to hold on to each other, or maybe she let go of the buckboard to reach for the horse's saddle and slipped from his grasp. In an instant, she was underwater, then popped her head up halfway between the rider and myself. Before I could doubt my reaction, I leapt from Still Wind down to the riverbank, dropping two pistols and my knife to the ground. As she swept past me, I dove into the choked rapids. She was a few feet ahead, her arms thrashing about, grasping the spindly branches of a young sycamore tree floating past. She pulled herself into the tree and it rolled her under. I fought the churning water, keeping my head up and an eye on the tree. My left foot touched the sandy bottom and I thrust myself forward, nearly out of the water onto its muddy roots. With both of us clinging to the branches, it seemed the force of the flood grew less. As I worked my way to the center, I tried rolling her to the surface but could not. Through the branches, her hand shot up out of the water in front of my face. I grabbed her wrist and rolled myself under, pulling her to the surface to lie on the floating tree. With my feet firm on the river's bottom and hands on the trunk, I walked us to the shore.

The rider dropped from his horse, entered the river to pry her from the branches, and lifted her onto the bank. I let go of the tree and pulled myself out of the water to lie on the shore, out of breath, staring up at black clouds and rain.

Without a word, she and the rider mounted the horse and rode the trail back upriver a ways to the deep, muddy ruts, joining the young man sitting in the one-mule wagon. After a minute or two of desperate discussion I could not hear, the woman slid from the horse down next to the young driver and all three headed east through the savannah grass. The man on horseback tipped his hat my way as they rode on. She looked back to me only once.

On the western shore, through the rain, more wagons entered the river, past the broken frame that lay nearly submerged in the rushing water. Though soaked to the bone, I gathered my weapons, mounted Still Wind, and rode hard, south toward Goliad.

In the afternoon, farther downriver, I found one of the mules still alive. I cut away most of the harness and led it up the bank to safety. I cut off the rest of the harness and left the mule to graze on new spring grass, in the sun next to the serene Guadalupe River.

Chapter 11

Goliad, Mid-March 1836

I arrived in Goliad with the letter from General Houston, ordering Colonel Fannin to remove all his charges as quick as possible from the Presidio La Bahía. Most were to go to Victoria and more than a third of his men on to Gonzales.

The fort was much larger than the Alamo, with actual walls on all four sides and more cannons by maybe three. Most of his men, some Grainger and I knew from the San Antonio fight, wore ragged coats, partial uniforms, and trousers with no decent shoes or boots. Good that spring was upon us for these men would only have to contend with the rain and not the cold.

I spotted Grainger as he had arrived first. He seemed glad to see me. There was nothing mentioned of our time and conversations with General Houston or the incident at the fire on the road. He had already presented his identical letter to the colonel and said Fannin did not take kindly to the orders. I told him about my supper conversation with Deaf Smith and the crowds of wagons at the river crossing, full of desperate folks.

Grainger accompanied me to deliver the letter. I presented it to Fannin and he shoved it into his breast pocket without a glance.

"Has Houston raised his army?" he asked, turning away from me to stare out over the parade grounds of Fort Defiance. He had insisted on renaming the old presidio. We stood on the roof of the corner blockhouse, next to a six pounder with only four cannonballs stacked up and no one manning it. Some of his militia milled about below us in groups of nine or ten with the sole purpose of digging in to hold the fort. Yet, their efforts seemed listless, lacking guidance or discipline. Not at all like the men of the Alamo.

I had yet to sit down and eat a meal, to know the food, of whether all they had to eat were cowhide tough, corn tortillas.

I'll be damned if I'm part of another siege, listening to our graves being dug outside the gate. Night after night, smellin' their suppers cooking, waiting to be killed.

I'll be damned . . .

"I'm sure he's in Gonzales now, along with Colonels Neill and Burleson . . . I left three days ago, Texans an' volunteers and the like were streamin' in, takin' their place among the ranks." I stood a step behind him, Grainger stood beside me.

"The general figures the Alamo's fallen. It's that he don't want another rout . . ." He glanced at me and hung his head.

"Santa Anna's armies are headin' this way," I said in a tone as matter-of-factly as I could muster. "Any day now . . ."

Fannin whirled around to face us. "I will not be dictated to by a couple of subordinate . . ." He paused, wiping spit from the corners of his lips with his fingers ". . . indigent volunteers. I've had my fill of you Greys, and Rovers, grubbing for a place here among righteous Texans, with little regard for the sacrifice it takes to lead such men."

I clamped my jaw shut to quell my rising anger. By this time, it was clear to me that Fannin was, as suggested by Houston himself, a raving ass.

Grainger raised his head, daring Fannin to look him in the eye. From a step back, he still towered over the colonel. "Sir, we come from the Alamo an' in my mind, I'm reasonably certain I hear the ghosts a' them poor souls callin' my name. To do somethin', to kill as many Mexicans as I can . . . Well, sir." He glanced out over the parade grounds and canvas tents lined along the walls of the fort. "I'll hide in a forest behind a tree with my pistol an' long rifle an' take my chances. Sir . . ."

Fannin waved us away. "You both shall stand midnight watch beginning this evening and every evening until . . . as you say, the Mexican army arrives. For now, you're dismissed."

I did not move. "Sir, an' I call you sir outta habit more than respect . . ." My face burned. I gripped the handle of Bowie's knife and slid it to an inch of leaving my belt. "If you'd read that there letter, we, meanin' Grainger an' me, ain't obliged to take our orders from you." I spat on the roof of the blockhouse, then rubbed the spit away with my moccasin. "We are only to escort you an' your men to Victoria an' back to Gonzales . . . sir."

The colonel stared at my waist. Most all of the knife's wide blade shimmered in the early morning sun. His face turned ashen. Yet, he would not look me in the eye. It was only then did I realize what I had done.

Grainger gently placed his hand over mine and eased the knife back down. "My friend here says the damn Mexicans are comin', *soon.* You can bet them tassels you're wearin' . . ." He pulled his hand away and stood beside me with his arms folded. "Both me an' Zeb have seen the army that's marchin' here. An' from the rooftops of the Alamo, we seen the red flag a-flying no quarter over the town of San Antonio, as if it flew over the whole a' Texas."

A few of our fellow New Orleans Greys had gathered below us at the bottom of the dirt ramp. Fannin glanced at the men, then back at Grainger and me. The smirk on his face showed only contempt. Again, he nervously wiped the spit from his lips and stalked off down the ramp, the volunteers parting way. Grainger shrugged and followed him, leaving me alone. He joined the men and stood with them in silence.

In that moment, for the first time since sailing to Texas, I felt afraid that I might soon be killed.

That afternoon, Grainger and I watched as a Colonel Ward and his Georgia riders stormed out of the fort. We were told they rode south to Refugio, near the coast, to search for Amon King and his men, who had left several days earlier to rescue colonials from a band of Mexican loyalists. By then, the whole camp knew why we were there. I accepted a few smiles and handshakes from the regulars, but most ignored me. Near sunset, the Greys gathered around their fire, first to welcome us, and then to argue whether it was time to leave Fannin behind and go their own way. Ole Dan Padgett was the most vocal.

"I'll be damned if we stay and wait 'til King's men show back up. Hell, there's not a one who can shoot straight anyhow," he said, "I'll take my chances aiming from behind a tree, like my daddy, shooting at those damn Brits way back yonder in Virginia."

Whoops and hollers went up from most of the men. I sat silent, eating a warm tortilla swiped in beans and peppers. Ehrenberg, the young German, who six months earlier helped me save Grainger from knifing a sailor over a card game gone bad, stood next to Padgett with his arms crossed. A frown creased his face as he glanced around at the other volunteers. "I do not know if this is a wise thing we do," he said. "We are only thirty or less, and to fight the whole of the approaching army . . ."

Padgett broke him off. "We can scurry through those woods all around and pick off a dozen at a time." He glanced to me, then Grainger, as if we would help in his argument.

"My place here's to get Colonel Fannin's army to Victoria and on to Gonzales, to join General Houston an' win this war, Now, I've seen this here Mexican army, close enough to smell their cookin', and to see Santa Anna's young señoritas a sashayin' 'round San Antonio's town square, pretty in pink." I paused to allow the few chuckles I garnered pass through the men and to bite into my tortilla. The peppers burned my lips and tongue, sending me to the jug Grainger offered. I instantly spat his whiskey, the tortilla, and peppers into the fire, causing a bright whoosh. "Shoulda known it wasn't water, goddamnit . . ." I turned away from Grainger's grinning face toward the watering hole by the chapel across the square. Through the shadows of the sunset, two men approached us, one tall and lanky, the other short and thin. They both carried themselves with the same proud manner I had seen before.

"I'll be damned, it's young James Lee!" I said, handing the jug back to Grainger. I jumped up and hurried toward the middle of the parade grounds to meet the boy and his walking partner.

"Mr. Creed, I presume?" Standing head and shoulders taller than his son, James's father offered a hand. "Jacob Lee, sir."

"Pleased to make your acquaintance," I said and stepped back. "Don't it beat all; you're the spittin' image of the other." Though, in the fading light, as James glanced at his father and back to me, I caught a flash of the cold, hard streak of suspicion hidden behind his mother's eyes.

I motioned toward the crowd. "Grainger, James found his papa!" There came no answer.

"James has told me the tales of yours and his exploits, from the time leaving his mama, riding the ferry . . ." He glanced to his son and smiled. ". . . until walking into this fort on his own three days ago." Standing in the waning twilight, I saw how proud this father was of his son.

As Jacob talked, I noticed for the first time, the evening fires surrounding us, close to the walls of the fort. There was a separate fire for each company of volunteers and regulars, bands of tribes from across the United States and Texas, many more men then the Alamo held, some men I knew and fought with, strong of will with hard ways about them. I stopped listening to Jacob and James. Panic seeped into my thoughts. I felt my hands begin to tremble and stuck them into my belt.

We strolled back to the Greys' fire, all the while James excitedly narrating his exploits down the Guadalupe, to find his father, but I could not pay attention.

"Mr. Creed, you seem distracted. I believe we shall bid you good evening?"

As best I could, I shook away my thoughts and fears, giving Jacob a most genuine smile.

"Yes, yes, of course, I apologize."

We stood in silence just outside the fire's light as Padgett and Ehrenberg continued arguing whether or not to leave, abandon the fort, in defiance of their commanding officer. Some agreed with Ehrenberg that what Padgett suggested was sedition; another called it outright treason.

"Mr. Creed, do you intend on leaving us?" James asked.

Taken off guard, I was not sure how to answer him. I took a few seconds, then, "My intentions are drawn by my orders from General Houston . . ." I said, loud enough for all the Greys to notice us and to hear my speech again. ". . . and that is to convince Colonel Fannin *and all his men* to abandon this here mission and join the gatherin' forces in Gonzales."

"Well, sir, you have a mighty fight coming your way . . . with the colonel," Jacob said.

James looked at me square. "We aim to hold this here fort, no matter what." His words sounded as resolute as his father's did.

No one spoke for a few long seconds.

Padgett took a step forward to face Jacob Lee. "You go and tell your friend the colonel the New Orleans Greys won't be stayin' 'round much longer because we ain't dying for a . . . lazy coward."

Jacob slid his right boot forward and laid a hand on his pistol. James followed his father's suit.

"Sir," Jacob said. "I will remind you that Fannin is your commanding officer."

Padgett laughed along with most of the men. "He's no commander . . ." He tilted his head toward James and back to Jacob. "Yes, sir, I got it right, a lazy, incompetent coward."

Jacob pulled his pistol.

From around the fire came the double clicks of hammers cocked, the leathery rustle of pistols and long rifles drawn and pointed in Jacob's direction.

I raised both hands up and stepped between the two. "Now, now, friends, I just met ya both an' I don't know you from one hill a' beans to another." I faced Jacob. "An' I don't know the particulars as to why these here brave volunteers don't trust Colonel Fannin." I turned around, with Jacob's pistol at my back. "I do know we're fightin' against the very same bastard who's marchin' his army this way, and like I keep sayin', *he aims to kill us all!*"

I eased away, leaving both men facing the other. Jacob gingerly placed his pistol back into his belt. Padgett took three steps back, joining his fellow Greys. James gave me a quick glimpse with both panic and pride in his eyes. No one from around the fire lowered their guns.

"There's more to this." Jacob Lee nodded to me of his departure and began walking back across the parade grounds toward the chapel and officers' quarters. His son did not move, looking as if he might have seen my point.

"James!" his father called, and they both disappeared into the night.

Later, over an honest plate of beans and a biscuit, Padgett and I sat together.

"That son of a bitch Lee is loyal only to Fannin. He's proven himself."

I thought for a second. "Fannin is your commander, an' I suppose he will be until he's either relieved of his duties by General Houston or . . . killed." I bit into the biscuit and with a mouthful, said, "an' I ain't come to do either one."

Padgett gave me a surprised look. "Houston knows?"

"The general knows Fannin can only be trusted so far. And that's why me and Grainger are here."

"We were supposed to go and help you men holed up at the Alamo, was out the gate and down the hill. The bastard changed his mind."

He spoke as if pleading, "We could've done something."

"I know, we heard." I lowered my gaze to the fire. "Wouldn't have done no good but maybe get yourselves killed."

Padgett gave a slight nod, as if he might agree.

I ate the final bite of the most delicious biscuit I had ever eaten.

I bedded near the stables, away from the Greys, who were still drinking and arguing over their latest plans, and fell right to sleep.

The instant I felt the kick to my foot, I reached for Bowie's knife. A man knelt beside me, a pistol wavering close to my nose.

"Mr. Creed, we're to escort you to the stockade, sir." A Texan by the name of Jones took a step back and held up a lantern in one hand, his pistol in the other still square to my head. In the shadows behind him, three men crouched with their long rifles aimed at me.

I lay back and raised my hands. "I suppose I should ask what for?"

Jones hesitated, with a nervous glance to the other men. "The attempted murder of Colonel Fannin, sir."

I closed my eyes and sighed, not at all surprised. "Because a' my reaction to him bein' a willful ignoramus?"

Jones took my weapons, allowed room to stand, and they escorted me off, leaving all my possessions behind, lying on the ground.

"I should've killed him, the son of a bitch," I said, under my breath.

Chapter 12

Jones placed rusted shackles around my wrists.

"Is this necessary?" I asked, rattling the chains that bound me to the adobe wall. Padgett sat on the floor next to me, his wrists also in shackles.

Jones nodded and shut the wood-slatted door, leaving us in near darkness but for the frayed light from an oil lantern set on a table in the outer room, shining through the open, barred window. I wrapped the chains around my hands and tugged with all my strength, wiggling and yanking on the ring attaching them to the wall. The adobe did not give except for dust stirred into the air. With my palms and fingers scraped raw, I let go.

"They said they were going after you," Padgett whispered. "Said they needed me first, thinkin' I might run, come back later an' start up more trouble is what they said I'd do. They said you wouldn't run . . ." He took a breath. "That you ain't like that."

I did not know how to reply. *They think they know me, do they?* I rattled the chains again, slamming them against the wall several more times. I gave up and leaned back in a sweat.

As I grew accustomed to the dim light, I saw a man lying on the only bunk of the cell. He appeared to be sleeping, with knees propped up and hat over his face. I recognized the Spanish, suede boots, the same boots worn in San Antonio a few months earlier, now caked in dried, black mud.

With all the racket I made, he had to have been awake. I

shook the bunk frame. "Long time . . ."

Alexandros Robito Obregon slowly raised his hat and turned to face me.

Surprised to see him locked up with us, I said, "Last I saw you, we was leavin' that card game Bowie lost in. Before takin' the Alamo for the first time."

"*Sí,* long before the fall." He laid his hat back over his face.

"Before the fall?"

Still thinking Deaf Smith's rumors were only presumed to be true, this was the first I heard anyone recognize the likelihood of my friends' and companions' deaths with such assuredness, such certainty.

Padgett was silent, until, "Were you a witness?"

Obregon sat up, the hat falling into cupped hands, and swung his boots to the floor, stomping off flakes of mud. "I am the only, the one witness, except of course for the Mexicans and the murderer Santa Anna himself."

"We were on our way to help. Fannin turned us back," Padgett said, repeating what he confessed to me earlier in the evening.

"Would not have mattered."

"I don't remember you bein' there. Inside the Alamo, I mean." From the time we met, this man rubbed me wrong, something about him, an air of entitlement, an arrogance . . . He acknowledged my statement only with a slight nod.

"Why are you here?" Padgett asked.

Obregon smiled. Through the thin light, I could see him missing half a front left tooth. "Ah, señor, I ask you both the same question." His gaze was razor sharp. "Especially when the Mexican soldados come this way so soon. Any day now, as I have warned, and the both of you locked up tight." He pointed to the chains that bound us.

Padgett lowered his voice to a near whisper. "Fannin's gone

mad and going to get us all killed. I've said as much to the Greys, pushing us toward leaving on our own."

Obregon did not respond to him but stared at me.

"You know why I'm here," I said.

"*Sí,* a man of no lies you are, my friend. In the open, the light of day, you make bold threats against the colonel. I, on the other hand, am not so fortunate to live as, how shall I say, as conspicuous as you."

I shook my head. "Sir, I have no idea what you are sayin'."

Obregon's smile shifted to a slight, mischievous grin. He glanced around the cell, as if the walls themselves might be listening, and whispered, "I am a spy."

"For who, them or us?"

"Ah, life can never be so simple, now can it, Mr. Creed?"

He toyed with me, as he did with Grainger, back at that damn card game.

"I'm not sure I follow. Life is as simple as ya make it, sir."

"How do you think I witnessed the fall of the Alamo, in hiding? No, señor, in plain sight I was, so near General Santa Anna I could cut his throat and no one would stop me."

Padgett understood before I did. "You stood and watched all our friends and compadres die . . . ?"

Obregon sucked in a breath. "I did not stand for long. The next day I was caught on the road to Gonzales and thrown into chains. I must admit, this room is nothing compared to the room Santa Anna ordered me into. I was tortured for three days . . . until I escaped." He slid a sleeve up, held his arm out, and slowly raised it. A healing wound, a purple, scabbed bracelet, circled his wrist. "Is what I have to show for my suffering."

"Why didn't they just kill ya?"

He looked surprised by my question. "Señor, the red flag flies against patrioteers from America and white, colonial rebels, and pirates. I am but a mere foreigner from Spain . . . on an adventure."

"How did they die?" Padgett asked.

I turned away and closed my eyes. Those brave men were my friends. I shook the chains again, clanging them together three or four times, opening my fists and yanking on the shackles. *Maybe I can slide 'em off my wrists, like our spy here did. Then wrap 'em 'round his neck an' strangle him so he would shut the hell up.*

Ignoring me, Obregon began in a calm voice. "The sky is black, before the dawn. Someway, my eyes clear and I can see. A swarm it is, like white and red beetles with rifles and swords. Scurrying up ladders and over the walls they go with hardly a fight against them. The north wall falls first. As the sky begins to lighten, a door to the inside is broken open." He stopped to clear his throat. "It is then that I hear screams."

I sat still, dried up, watching him speak but hardly listening to his words. I did not care how they all died. Knowing they were gone was enough.

"The last shots sound as if they come from behind the fort. Cries of the escaping, they do not run far before the shooting and cries stop."

Padgett hung his head, as if he were weeping.

"By noon, all the bodies are burning." Obregon gently waved a hand below his nose. "It smells of . . . of . . ."

The three of us sat in silence for a long while, Padgett and I on the filthy floor chained to a wall, Obregon on the bunk, leaning over, and with his palm knife, scraping bits of mud off the soles of his boots. I thought of the man I watched burn to death no more than a year before, lit on fire by my own hand.

I glanced at Obregon once. As he wiped his eyes with a sleeve, the wound circling his wrist shone in the early, morning light.

"The worst is his laugh," he said.

"Whose?"

"The general . . . Santa Anna."

Chapter 13

Rings of smoke blow from behind the grassy rise; the boom of cannon shakes my entire body, the ground I kneel on. A click, the cap of Judith Lee's Hawken hits the striker with only a pop rather than a flash. The rifle misfires, then explodes back into my face and I am blinded. The cries of the battle surround me. I cry out for help. Large hands grip my shoulders and turn me toward the booming cannons. Even through the dark of blindness, I can see grey smoke, black-horsed caballeros rush headlong, lances extended, pointed at my heart.

Again, I woke by someone kicking my foot. I reached for my knife. Coming up empty handed, I struck the man who stood above me, hard, with a fist full of chain. The dream disappeared.

"Goddamn, Zeb, why'd ya do that?" Grainger hollered and plopped down on the bunk, holding his right shin.

"You surprised me," I said, rubbing my eyes.

Though the sun was up, I did not know how long I had slept, leaning against the tan, adobe wall. Padgett was still shackled. Grainger sat on the bunk alone.

"Where's Obregon?"

"Walked out 'bout an hour ago," Padgett said. "Jones wouldn't say a word for what."

The door to the cell was left open along with the door to the parade grounds. I caught a glimpse of someone running past lugging four or five long rifles cradled in his arms. Shooting bags hung against his chest with powder horns slung over a shoulder. In the distance, near the middle of the grounds, Fannin, wearing a peacock of a hat, seemed to be directing several men who, in a frenzy, were digging large holes in the ground. Farther still, along the opposite walls of the fort, the New Orleans Greys were deflating their canvas tents, breaking camp.

I shook the bunk. "Why are you here an' what's goin' on?"

Grainger still pressed a hand on his shin where I hit him. In his other hand, he held up the key to the shackles. "I come to get ya out."

Padgett and I helped each other to stand. I stretched my back, stepped toward the door, and rattled the chains together. "Well, sir, let's get on with it." With my head and heart still ringing from the prior evening's revelations, I was not in good spirits and certainly was not willing to wait on Grainger as he nursed a growing bruise.

He slowly stood, limped a step to me, and with a couple of clicks, I was free. He unlocked Padgett's shackles allowing them to fall to the floor.

"Thank you, sir," Padgett offered and walked swiftly across the grounds toward what was left of the Greys' camp.

I simply nodded and headed for the outside door. Granger stepped sideways, blocking my path.

"Hold on there, partner. Ya need to know where Fannin stands with you."

I tried to move past Grainger but he held up his hand.

"He thinks you've come here on General Houston's accord . . . to assassinate him."

"I come here to save him and his men," I said, shaking my head. ". . . and he accuses me of assassination. He ain't just damn crazy, he's insane."

"The only reason you're not still in chains is because I talked sense into him and . . ." He slowly dropped his hand. "Amon King and his men have been executed and the Mexican army's gatherin' just south of Refugio, no more'n thirty miles from here."

My heart dropped to my gut. I stood still, gathering my thoughts about what I would do.

I will not again be helpless, overlooking an army waiting to kill me.

Grainger stood, blocking my view of the parade grounds and Fannin. I tried moving around him.

"What are you goin' to do now?"

"I'm gettin' the hell outta here," I said, as calm as I could.

Grainger stepped aside and I walked slowly toward the middle of the grounds; Fannin's men began wheeling a couple of cannons down into one of the holes. Three others sat ready for their burial. Only two cannons remained in place as defense. The one we stood by the day before, during the argument, and another sat alone, unattended on the opposite corner blockhouse. Fannin did not notice me step up behind him as he ordered the fourth cannon into its hole. Six men shoveled dirt onto the first two, clods and rocks clanked against cast iron barrels. I found it odd that he thought it necessary to direct this execution himself.

One of the men stopped and rested against his shovel. "Colonel Fannin, don't you think they'd know what was buried here and seeing how they ain't breached, they'd just dig 'em back . . . ?"

"Shut up, mister, and keep piling dirt! We'll be long gone 'fore they get their bloody hands on them."

"So, you are heeding Houston's orders and abandoning the fort."

Fannin whirled around, nearly tripping into me. His face contorted into a blood-red devil's mask.

"You . . ." He shoved a boot between my moccasins and leaned in close, nose to nose. He opened his mouth, gaping, as if to say something, his gaze fearful, then his eyes shaded with pride, ". . . you are to leave, now."

"All of us must leave, now," I said in a clear, confident voice.

He reached into his coat pocket. I stepped back, hands raised and crouched into a fighting stance. Instead of a weapon, he pulled out two letters. One was clearly the orders I handed him only a day before, the other he wadded up, shoved in my face, then let slip from his hand to fall to the ground.

"You will leave, now."

"I'm obliged, but before I do . . ." I eased up straight and brought my hands down to my side. ". . . you will hear me out." I continued before he could react. "You've heard the tale of the Alamo from Obregon. You know what kind of man Santa Anna is. Yet you stand your ground as if you, with these brave men, will defeat his army." The militiamen leaned on their shovels, listening to my every word. "Sir, I'm afraid you will have these men murdered. And with their blood on your hands, you too will be shot dead and left to burn."

He turned his back on me, jerked a shovel from the hands of the nearest man, and began slinging dirt viciously into the closest hole filled with cannons.

I snatched the paper up before it blew away.

Return to General Houston and tell him I will abide by his orders.

Colonel James Fannin
Commander, Texan Army

I could not help but smile.

Grainger watched us from the door of the stockade. I walked back to him, folding the paper, and placed it in my belt.

"Obregon has gone to scout the enemy. Fannin and this here army are to retreat to Victoria as soon as he gets back to the fort," he said.

"Grainger, as long as we've known each other, you cozy up to whoever's the leader. Ya did it with the captain of *Columbus,* ya did it with Bowie. Hell, ya did it with General Houston, and now you're doin' it with Fannin. Can you tell me if this just happens natural, or is it some desperate need to be standin' close in to the man leadin' the charge?"

He grinned. "I have a need for knowin' what's goin' on is all. And standin' next to the man with the plans is comfortin'."

I glanced over my shoulder to Fannin, then scanned the rest of the parade grounds. Most of the tents were down, a handful of wagons and carts were being loaded with others empty and idle.

"Ain't much of a planner, nor does he have much of a plan, if you ask me."

Grainger nodded. "It's all we can hope for now. Go find Jacob Lee, he has your weapons. Meet me at the stable to get the rest of your possibles. I'll be ridin' along by your side."

I found James with his back to the stable's wide, double doors, bent over examining Still Wind's front left hoof. Some of the other horses huddled outside at a feed trough. With only two bushels of hay for maybe twenty of them, they were already underfed, their ribs showing, and most unbrushed.

Someone stepped up beside me.

"I heard he let you out." Jacob handed me my two pistols. He hesitated with Bowie's knife, balancing it gently with one finger under the handle side of the guard. "First I've held one of these." He whistled. "Must have been something of a man."

"He was indeed."

Jacob handed me the knife. As I took hold, he hesitated letting go. "No hard feelings 'bout last night."

I was not sure how to answer so I shook my head and slipped the blade back into my belt where it belonged, next to both pistols. All my possibles lay in a pile a few feet from Still Wind.

"You've taken good care of her," James said, patting the horse's rump.

"She is a fine horse."

I began gathering my things, preparing for a long walk back to Gonzales.

"You can keep on ridin' her, if you'd like," Jacob offered.

I stopped. Still Wind's black eyes stared at me. James and his father would never know the bond we shared.

"Might obliged . . ." I said.

James stepped away and I stroked the horse's neck as she nuzzled the inside of my arm and shoulder. Within a minute or two, we were ready to ride.

I met Grainger outside the stable. He still rode the black mare. I did not hear if the Lees knew the famous General Houston was riding their horse.

On the way to the main gate, we passed Fannin's hole diggers. They seemed to have run out of dirt and given up. From one of the cannon's graves rose part of a dull, black barrel pointed awkwardly toward the sky.

On top of the wall to our left, one of the Texan regulars standing watch hollered down, "Open the damn gate!"

Grainger glanced at me and smiled. We were ready to ride.

The heavy, timber gates creaked open just enough for Obregon to come rushing through on his horse with Mexican caballeros no more than two strides behind, their lances pointed straight at him.

The gates closed with a shudder. Spanish cursing echoed outside the walls of the fort as the enemy riders headed back into the cover of the forest from where they rode. The Spanish curses inside the walls came from Obregon.

Grainger glanced at me again, this time with fearful surprise. "Whew there, Zeb, we ain't goin' nowhere."

I sank deep in my saddle and simply lowered my head.

Chapter 14

Within minutes of the Mexican cavalry's arrival, the same men who buried the cannons dug them back up, leaving four large holes in the middle of the parade grounds. It did not take long before an axle broke in half by rolling a wagon into one of the holes. Fannin was nowhere to be found. After putting up the horses, Grainger and I retreated to just inside the stockade door where I knew we would not be noticed or bothered.

"What now?" Grainger asked.

"I don't know. Let's wait 'til we see some organizin'." I glanced at him with a frown. "Ain't nothin's changed the fact that we need to get outta here."

He shrugged. "Again, we abandon the fight?"

I did not let show how this question burned, as the chains and Obregon's words from the night before still rattled through my head.

"Oh, no, not this time, we take these men with us," I said, wondering if I really meant it.

I felt Grainger wanted to ask me how, but did not.

With the cannons placed square, six across, thirty or so strides inside the front gates, no one stood by them prepared to fire on an enemy should they bust their way into the fort. The fact that there would more than likely be three thousand or more soldados and caballeros did not matter.

Eight or nine riders gathered near the gates, surrounding one of the colonels whose name was Horton. After a brief discussion, he signaled to the guard and the gates swung open. With his men whooping and hollering, Horton led the charge, his sword raised high. The gates quickly shut as all but a few of the men left inside the fort scattered along the tops of the walls and blockhouses, yelling and egging on the riders. Grainger followed me onto the parade grounds. All preparations for either departure or resisting a siege had again stopped. I turned and began walking toward the bell tower.

"What the hell, Zeb."

I shrugged. "If we're to witness this charade, might as well be as high up as we can be."

At the steps, we met the good Dr. Bernard. I thought I had met him once, as he looked familiar and I was not at all sure what kind of doctoring he did. He seemed to know me. But for a nod, we climbed to the top. The tarnished, brass bell hung silent, listing slightly to one side, tied to a rope that fell a hundred feet to the darkness of the tower's inner sanctum. From the small, covered platform that encompassed the bell and its yoke, we could see the entire fort, the squat buildings of the town outside the walls, and surrounding countryside, including the tree line where the Mexican caballeros fled and into which Horton and his men rode.

I felt a tap on my shoulder. I whirled around to face the doctor.

"Please, sir, won't you hold out your hands?" he asked.

I did so, slowly, palms down. He gently turned my hands over, exposing the cuts circling my wrists, the red scrapes and chafed skin caused by the rusted shackles and chains.

"Sir, I attempted talking him out of it, to no avail." He glanced away, down toward the officers' quarters. "That your confused and angry response, pulling the knife as you did, was natural, considering his . . ." He paused again. ". . . his *un*-natural demeanor."

Without a thought, I said, "You mean every bastard he comes in contact with wants to kill him."

Dr. Bernard attempted a smile, yet his grave glance gave him away. "I would not say that, though your own reaction was certainly true."

"What are we to do, sir?" I asked, lowering my hands.

He leaned in, close, as if Fannin himself might hear. "We must prepare to leave tonight, or at the latest, by the morrow. I will continue in my attempt to persuade him to do the same." He was almost touching my nose. "With or without him," he whispered. "You have stock with the Greys, pull them together and be ready." He paused again, then looking resolute, he said, "You must appear to follow his orders, no matter. Else . . ." The doctor again took hold of my right hand to show my wrist. "This will be much worse."

A hollow shot echoed through the forest below us. Seconds later, a volley of shots rang out. Horton's riders burst through the tree line, across the shallow river and back toward the fort, a band of caballeros twice their size right behind. By the cover of brush and trees, soldados fired at the men strung along the tops of the walls. They had ceased their battle cries and began shooting randomly into the oncoming Mexican cavalry. As the doctor and I peered out through a narrow window of the bell tower, there came a shot and instant explosion above our heads with shattered pieces of red-tiled roof showering down upon us. The next shot struck the bell sending a single, clear ring through the air, along with a ricocheting ball into the inside brick, an inch from Grainger's left shoulder.

"Whew there!" he called out and slid down onto his haunches, holding his chest.

The doctor quickly pulled me back from the window and again came nose to nose. I smelled a whiff of whiskey.

"You must gather your militia together and make ready for

retreat, post haste!"

"Doctor, I'm not their leader, Padgett . . ."

"Sir, we have no time to dally. You are their leader, go, *now*!"

I lowered my head. There was no arguing with him, no matter where I thought my place was amongst these men. Nor did it seem to matter how deeply I felt about my incapacity to lead them.

With a hand still over his heart, Grainger straightened up. "Partner, you just told me no more'n twenty minutes ago how we take these men with us when we go, each an' every one of 'em."

I stood still for a few seconds. Dr. Bernard and Grainger waited. If the lot of us were to make a good run for it, we would need help. At the steps leading down through the bell tower, I turned to Grainger. "Find Padgett and bring him to the stockade, along with Ehrenberg. Tell 'em we're leaving no later than first light, no matter."

"Where are you goin'?"

"I'm going to find Jacob Lee," I said, "and Obregon."

As I reached the bottom steps, another group of riders charged out the gate, riding the last of the horses. I did not see Grainger's nor mine among them. Again, from the top of the walls where most of the men still lingered, came laughing and cursing. I passed below them spying Jacob Lee standing next to Fannin on the same blockhouse where we stood the morning before. I hesitated going up there, as I did not want to cause another ruckus. I walked back to the stockade to ask Grainger to go and retrieve him but he was not there. Although I had seen most of the Greys watching the chase, I still went to their old camp. It was empty but for the four or five tents that lay half-folded, scattered about the ground where they stood the night before. The coals of the fire were still hot and strips of deer meat hung from sticks, turning black in the smoke. This was the only food I saw. A few provisions and ammunition cases lay open, their contents left on the ground as if they might stay there another month. I took a long look at the other camps along the back wall of the fort and they fared no better.

I felt someone's presence behind me, then smelled his cigar.

"Your beloved Greys. It seems they are as ill-prepared as the rest, aye, Mr. Creed?"

I did not turn around and continued to stare at what little was done to prepare for retreat. "Ah, Señor Obregon, just the man I need to see."

He stepped up beside me. "I, sir, am at your service."

"We need to coerce these men into leaving, now and not after there's three thousand more cavalry chasin' those damn fools back into the fort."

"Again, I ask what I can do." He glanced to his own boots, as if he wanted me to see how clean they now were.

I turned toward the blockhouse and pointed. "Up yonder, there stands next to Fannin a man name of Jacob Lee. Bring him to the stockade, without rousing the colonel's suspicions. We will conclude our plans of escape."

I faced Obregon. With an eyebrow raised, he took a long drag from his cigar and smiled, the broken tooth showing slightly. The light brown skin of his face was smooth leather. His blue eyes sparkled in the sun. I realized I had only spent time with him in darkness.

"I will do as you ask," he said, hesitated for a second, then walked briskly toward the blockhouse.

I trotted in the other direction toward the stables. The double doors stood open and all the stalls seemed empty. Still Wind and Grainger's horse were not where we tied them up. In a panic, I turned to hasten around back where Grainger might have taken the horses. From the shadows at the rear of the building, I heard a faint snort. I pulled my pistol. Creeping in silence toward the sound, I almost shot James Lee as he stepped into a beam of light shining through the rafters. He held in his hand the reins of Still Wind, Grainger's large, black mare and the Indian pony.

"Mr. Creed, can you tell me what happened to mama's horse?"

I slowly let out a breath and eased the pistol back into my belt. At that moment, I did not have an answer for him.

"Someday, you'll have to ask Grainger to tell that story," I said, nodding.

"They were going to ride 'em off to chase the Mexicans. I wouldn't let 'em." He was shook up bad.

"Thanks, son, you're mighty brave."

"Mr. Creed, are we goin' to die?"

"Not if I can help it. Neither me nor your daddy will allow that to happen." In my mind, I could hear Judith Lee hollering from her cabin to make sure and bring her son home. "Hell, it's like I promised your mama."

He stared at me, trying not to wipe tears away. Behind him, Still Wind, the mare, and the pony waited patiently.

"Hide the horses where you had 'em in the dark, tie them up good, an' let's go meet your daddy."

He smiled, rubbed his eyes only once, and did what I asked.

As soon as we stepped onto the parade ground, I smelled smoke. James and I ran to the stockade. Obregon and Jacob Lee were there.

"He's burning the town down around us," Obregon said.

"Who is?"

"The Colonel Fannin, of course."

"Why would he do that?"

Shots were again fired beyond the walls with return fire coming from the few men still left watching. The gates flew open and into the fort rode Horton's riders.

The late afternoon sun showed the raggedness of his men, their faces greased with a mix of sweat, dust, and fear. Fannin followed them as they dismounted and walked their worn-out horses to the stable.

"There ain't no hay left," James said, to no one in particular.

The parade ground was filling with slow, drifting smoke and still there was not a soul preparing for a fight or retreat.

I glanced down to my left hand resting on the butt end of Bowie's knife, as if it were not my own. If I anchored it against something, it did not tremble. I took a deep breath and closed my eyes. The smoke made me cough. I kept my eyes closed tight. Along with burning wood, I smelled raccoon stew cooking. I tasted it and for the first time in what seemed a hundred years, I saw Anna's face, her sweet smile, as if I stood in her cabin back in the woods in Missouri. I shuddered at her touch and opened my eyes.

Through the haze strode Grainger with Padgett and Ehrenberg, apparitions carrying long rifles and grim faces.

Grainger stepped up beside me. "Zeb, looks like we're all here."

I collected my emotions and took another deep breath. "All right then, gentlemen, go and gather up all the Greys and whoever else wants to go with us you can trust. Ready or not, we're gettin' the hell outta here!"

Chapter 15

By sunset, the tiny town of La Bahía, a scattering of abandoned dwellings that lay just outside the walls of the mission, had burnt to the ground. Fannin had ordered its destruction in an attempt to offer the enemy no cover. The command passed down to the Texans and volunteers was to stand and fight. Through the thinning haze, campfires were lit for the night, tents were again raised. The New Orleans Greys, with the help of a few renegades, quietly packed two carts with food and ammunition. No one could remember if the oxen were fed that day. Our tents remained flattened on the ground, not moved from where they lay earlier in the afternoon. Gathered 'round the fire, the discussion was when, not if, we would be leaving.

"First light," said Padgett. "And by the back gate, I say."

Erhenberg nodded. "Out the front, we may get shot."

"Shot by our own," someone said.

"I'd like to think not." Jacob sighed. "Colonel Fannin gets . . . confused at times."

"This is no time for confusion. We went over it last night and all that happened was me an' Creed rung up in chains." Padgett stared at Jacob Lee with a look of contempt. "What changed your mind?"

"He wanted to hold a trial and hang the both of you by a rope. I talked him out of it. That's not the thinking of a sound-minded man."

Jacob held Padgett's gaze as most men nodded in agreement.

I moved closer to the fire. "Gentlemen, I stood between the two of you last night, I want us to stand together this night." Both men looked away from the other. "As far as I can see, we've got one choice here. Out the back, quiet as mice and on to Victoria. Take only your weapons for we must be quick as lightning. Now, raise them tents an' get some shut-eye; we'll leave 'em where they lie in the morning. We're out the gate before dawn."

There was no good cheer, only a quiet solitude shared among us all.

James held the reins to four horses, Still Wind, Grainger's black mare, the Indian pony, and Jacob Lee's paint. Fog had settled the early morning into a wet darkness. He led the horses toward the rear gate, riderless ghosts drifting in silvery quiet. The rest of the Greys lined the back wall of the fort, deeper shadows providing more cover. Only one guard, we were told, stood between us and freedom.

"Offer him a chance to go with us," Padgett whispered. "If he refuses, knock him in the head."

I sensed surprise from Jacob at the suggestion of such strong action, however dire our circumstances were.

A Kentuckian named Bratts, who had joined our rebellion earlier that evening, claimed to know the guard. He would persuade him to allow us to pass and disappeared toward the gate before Padgett or I could protest. Within seconds, he returned, motioning for us to move quickly. I reached the gate to allow the men through. It was shut and boarded. There was no guard standing watch.

From toward the middle of the parade grounds came a high whistle. Out of the fog stepped Colonel Fannin with Dr. Bernard beside him. Behind, a band of Texas militia stood shrouded in silence. We pulled our pistols. I pointed mine straight at the colonel. With no more than a stride between us, I could shoot him and not miss his heart. The militia, with Jones in the lead, along with the Kentuckian, lined up beside Fannin and the doctor and raised their long rifles. With the twenty or so of us against the wall, if one fired, the rest of us would follow with our executions certain.

Fannin stepped forward, unarmed, holding his hands behind his back. "I have walked these walls nearly all night, wondering what we must do and have arrived at the same conclusion as you gentlemen have, and as much as I hate to say, it is to abandon this fort." He took a step closer. "If you attempt to leave now, I consider you deserters and will order you shot. However, if you decide to leave with the rest of us, once dawn breaks, under orderly procession, well . . ." He turned slightly to face Jacob, standing next to me. "This treasonous behavior will be forgotten . . . for now."

I held my pistol true and glanced at Jacob. He nodded, staring straight at Fannin.

"We keep our weapons," Jacob said.

"Of course."

The fog seemed a shade lighter as dawn approached, yet there came a chill in the air. The men against the wall began lowering their guns, as did the men alongside Fannin.

"We leave within the hour."

"Of course."

I knew he said a lie, but nodded anyway and lowered my pistol.

Chapter 16

There was no rush to leave the comfortable confines of the fort. Most men took their leisurely time, eating breakfast before packing carts and wagons, milling about nearly as listless as I had seen them two days prior, after entering the mission for the first time.

The New Orleans Greys were ready at dawn.

The few guards that were left defending the walls would holler down reports of seeing flashes of red, white, and blue uniforms among the trees surrounding the old mission, then shooting at them. With each shot, I clutched the handle of my pistol and waited for a barrage of return fire. It was not until nine o'clock and after burning the many provisions left behind, that we pressed out the back gate in silence, abandoning Fort Defiance.

The damn cannons were the worst, taking five men each to get them through the fast-moving water and up the steep banks of the San Antonio River. It being late morning with the fog burned off, the oppressive sun helped to slow our retreat to a crawl. Once all two hundred and fifty of us were through the woods, onto the six-mile length of prairie and headed east toward Coleto Creek, then on to Victoria, though exhausted, wet, and covered in mud, we made good time until the order came to stop. Some of us protested, to no avail. Others chose to snooze under trees, out of the midday sun. Our oxen had their chance to graze. It seemed our colonel was unencumbered by reports back from Horton that there was a large contingency of Mexican soldados and cavalry close enough to attack within an hour.

As Horton and his riders scouted ahead, Ehrenberg, Grainger, Obregon, and a man named Cobbs rode behind us by a quarter mile or so. We began moving again. I could see them on a rise, pointing toward the trees we had come through earlier. All four of them kicked in and rode hard, back to us. The closer they got, I saw Ehrenberg take the lead as the other three lagged behind. He entered the line of men and wagons at full gallop yelling in German. He found Colonel Fannin, pulled up, and leaped off his horse. Our whole troop once again dragged to a stop. The other riders slowed down to a fast trot but did not enter the fray. Instead, they rode past, with the intent, it seemed, to rile up every one of us who were walking. A great noise of booing and cursing arose to mix with the choking prairie dust. Grainger and his fellows were halfway to the forest when he turned and lifted the brim of his hat to me, then pulled it off and slapped the black stallion into a gallop. They disappeared through the tree line to our north.

From the center of our troop came loud talk between Ehrenberg, Fannin, and other leaders of the militia. Padgett and I joined them.

"We have no time . . ." Ehrenberg shouted to Fannin. "A thunder of horses rides this way, straight at us. We must move, *now.*"

Fannin stared at the young German with a look of contempt. Near the same as the day I handed him the letter from General Houston. "We will stand and shoot them down."

"The time is not now, sir," said Shackelford, one of Fannin's colonels. "We make it to Coleto Creek and covered by forest, we can defend ourselves more . . ."

"Defend ourselves? I will not merely defend against the

enemy. I will stand and fight to defeat our enemy."

In the bright sunlight, each man's face turned pale.

Dr. Bernard lowered his head, began to speak, then stopped, looked up and said, "We are on low ground and heading toward the goddamn trees. May we at least gain higher ground?"

Fannin stood still for a few long seconds, then, "We shall move closer to the tree line and out of the depression." He cocked his hat and picked up his long rifle. "There, we make our stand." He turned his back to us and walked away, the conversation finished.

Padgett and I rushed back to the Greys.

"Be prepared to retreat . . . and to, to fight," I said, then stopped. *Hell, there's nowhere to go!*

The troop had shaped itself into an oblong rectangle, a human fort, stretching widthwise across the prairie, thin forest to our north and south with the tree line and Coleto Creek to the east by only a mile or so. Fannin ordered us forward and we began moving again, still keeping our shape. The Greys marched in the rear. Jacob and James walked side by side next to me. I kept a keen eye on the rise we topped no more than a half a mile behind. We had only walked a few hundred yards, deeper into the grassy depression and were about to climb out toward the trees, when through the rumble and dust, I heard a couple of men yelling to stop and the whole troop slowed to a halt. I glanced back to the rise behind us. A cloud billowed up beyond the horizon, and as we had stopped, the rumbling from the earth continued.

This is it, boys, we stand and fight, came the call.

The Greys traveled with two carts, one with our provisions, the other filled with ammunition. I grabbed the reins of one of the oxen and guided the ammo cart to sit sideways as defense.

"Padgett, quick now, gather men and unload, then push it over on to its side, bottom of the floorboard facin' out!"

As I soothed the ox, I looked up at Jacob. He nodded, and I slid Bowie's knife from my belt and slit its throat, then eased the animal down to its knees and over on its side, still harnessed to the cart. Two Greys squatted behind the carcass, away from the pooling blood, and began loading rifles.

Over the top of the rise came a hundred or more Mexican caballeros at full gallop.

"Hold steady, boys," came the call, yet, the closer the riders fell upon us, no orders were given to fire.

Down the line and to the right of us, Shackelford raised and shot his pistol. The volley round that came an instant later was deafening.

Kneeling behind the overturned cart, I waited a few seconds for the smoke to clear, taking aim first at the caballeros' horses as they charged us, their lances pointed straight ahead to skewer a man through. The first one I shot at, I aimed high and missed the horse. The ball hit the rider's chest, dropping him just in front of us. The horse continued at full gallop toward the cart, leaping up to clear one of the wheels. Its back hooves caught a spoke and with a tremendous thud, slammed to the ground between young James Lee and me.

I hollered at the boy, "Shoot the horse!"

He finished loading a rifle and was about to hand it to his father hunkered down on his other side. James stared at me as the terrified animal tried rolling on its side, both front legs buckled, twisted, and broken under its heavy body.

"Shoot him, goddamn it!"

A sudden volley of cannon fire thundered across the tiny valley, shaking the ground. The immediate silence drew out the screams of the injured animal. Through the acrid haze of gun smoke, another caballero barreled down upon James and me, his sword drawn. Jacob Lee snatched up his rifle and fired. That horse crumpled, pitching the rider forward to the ground. The man stood, staggered sideways, and pointed his sword at us no more than two strides away. I picked up a freshly loaded rifle and shot him.

The crippled horse still lay between James and I, on its right side, broken, front legs mere bones punctured through torn flesh, its hind hooves scraping and thumping against the upturned bed of the cart, splintering wood, head slamming against the ground, dirt mixing with the froth around its mouth. I smelled smoke, blood, and for a second, saw in the horse's black eyes my reflection.

I could only look away.

Jacob Lee leaned into his son. "Jerk your pistol and shoot!"

James reached for the grip, slid the pistol from his belt, cocked it, and pressed the shaking barrel to the horse's head, just below its ears. The horse grew calm as James squeezed his eyes shut and pulled the trigger.

I motioned to Padgett and Ehrenberg, who lay on the ground to my left. The five of us dragged the horse's body around to their end of the oxen cart, filling a gap between our defenses. The two men propped themselves against the warm body and continued to shoot into the oncoming caballeros and a thousand or more Mexican soldados descending on us.

Chapter 17

Fannin's been shot!

The word that passed through the ranks did not mean much as we continued to shoot at the attacking Mexican soldados and cavalry. From our left, our right, and in front of us they charged, by the hundreds, yet they could not break our defenses. By the time our cannons ceased firing because of the lack of water to cool the barrels, the sun had set to twilight and the battlefield that lay before us was littered with the dead and dying. I could not tell the difference between our death and theirs, it all smelled of gun smoke, blood, and shit. As darkness fell, their snipers stopped shooting at us. A bugler sounded off from deep inside their camp, not a triumphant call, but perhaps a reminder of our inevitable defeat. To our shock, we were told to allow the wounded soldados to be carried off. Our wounded were tended to with hardly any medical supplies, little water, and no fires to see by. I did not care to know how severe Fannin's wound was; I cared only about Padgett and his shattered right knee.

"Don't you try standin' . . ." I said, in an attempt to keep him settled. "James Lee went to fetch Dr. Bernard." As most of the Greys kept watch over the battlefield, Jacob and I comforted Padgett the best we could. He would never again walk without a crutch.

Ehrenberg presented us with a small bottle. "I have saved this all the way from Paris."

I pulled the cork and smelled its content. My mind reeled

back to a night spent in New Orleans with a woman who lit the same liquid on fire. "Whew, the devil's water," I said, handing the bottle back to Ehrenberg. He smiled and gently lifted Padgett's head and poured a small amount into his mouth. Padgett opened his eyes, licked his lips, and nodded thank you.

Jacob stood and walked toward the front line, motioning me to follow. "Quite the damn predicament."

In the dark, I doubt he saw my nod.

"How's James?" I asked.

"Shaken up pretty bad." He took a deep breath and let it out slow and deliberate. "The boy's done things today no boy should have to do."

"Hell, no man should have to do these things we've done this afternoon."

There was silence between us. The moon broke through the trees to our east to provide a brush of light. I wished I had a drink and a smoke. More so, I needed a cup of cool water and a biscuit, as did every other man I stood with on that blood-soaked ground. None was to be found that night. The bugler continued sounding his call from the Mexican camp, echoing through the forest to the north of us. The bugling stopped with only the moans and cries of our wounded to fill the night's silence of the open prairie. The bugler started again, with renewed vigor.

"How shot up is Fannin? I hear Bernard's tending to him personally."

"Shot clean through his left thigh," Jacob said, leaning against the wheel of the same cart from where we took cover earlier in the afternoon. "Leaving without much food and water as we did and no thought to bring any doctoring supplies has left us in a low place."

"I don't think it matters now. 'Course it might make our plight easier if he were, how shall I say, left unattended?"

Again, silence fell between us. Some of the men, who were not wounded, began digging a trench just beyond our meager fortification. The scrapes of shovels reminded me of long, desperate nights at the Alamo. A different bugler sounded, with a subtler pitch, a sad lilt to his notes, perhaps spelling an early mourning call for those of us still alive. The sounds of scraping and the music seemed to sear my bones.

"I came here to fight, for my land and family, for independence. I aligned myself with Fannin because his values seemed to be mine." Jacob paused and took another deep breath. As he exhaled, he shook his head. "I misunderstood his weaknesses." He continued leaning against the wheel for a few seconds, then stood straight, letting it slowly spin, and turned to face me square. "Why are you here, Mr. Creed?"

I watched the shadows of the spokes blend with deeper shadows of the inside of the cart, moonlight illuminating holes shot through and the scrapes of the horse's hooves. A cloud passed before the moon and the shadows were gone to black.

"A testament to friendship."

I sensed that this was not the answer he expected, nor did I expect to say those words. As the cloud slipped away, moonlight fell upon our beleaguered troop; men, who I fought alongside, some who lay dying in the grass and would not see morning. The others certainly would die by the afternoon surrounded by thousands of soldados come to preserve their country of Mexico. This was not what Billy Frieze had in mind when, hiding under empty bags of sugar beets, in a wagon driven by Olgens Pierre, on our way to free slaves from Broussard's plantation, he casually mentioned that he and I might go to Texas. *There's land for the taking, mate,* Billy said. *'Course we might have to kill a few Mexicans for it.*

"Mighty good friend," Jacob said.

I hung my head. The Mexican bugler sounded his mournful

call. "Yes, he was."

James stepped up beside his father. "Dr. Bernard will be here shortly. Meantime, he said to keep Mr. Padgett's leg perfectly still and find a thin plank to use as a splint . . ." James glanced at me, then to Jacob. "And to clean the wound as best as you can."

I turned to the boy and said thanks. Jacob reached out, offered his hand, and we shook. Walking back to where Padgett lay on the damp ground, I heard James say, "Daddy, he's been crying."

"Yes, son, he has. I think he's just realized there's no other place in the world for him to be but here."

Chapter 18

At dawn, not one, but twenty bugles sounded. Yet, there came no charge, their front line of infantry and cavalry held at forty strides or less in front of our lines, surrounding us. The first cannon blasted grapeshot and chain. Whirring above our heads, it sent us scrambling to the ground. If the artillerymen had aimed a few feet lower, the shot would have cut us in two. There came another blast with thunder and smoke drifting up from beyond a rise on the prairie west of us, blowing to splinters a broken, abandoned ammunition cart near the center of our troop. A call went out for the leaders to gather around Fannin.

"We must fight," said Shackelford.

"Yes, we can beat them off," Fannin said, a weak declaration from a man lying in prairie grass tainted with blood, his face pale as the moon.

Jacob and I stood aside from the others, listening. He glanced at me and shook his head.

"We must surrender, now."

I could not see who said this, nor did I recognize his voice. I lay my shaking hand upon the grip of my pistol. "Then we will all die," I said.

"Then we fight, aye, Mr. Creed?" Fannin leaned up on his elbows and smiled at me for the first time ever, more a crooked, limp grin.

"No, sir, they showed us what they could do with just their cannons. Once we're blown to shits, the soldados will come and skewer any one of us left alive, leavin' the vultures to swoop in and clean up. No, sir, we run; drop everything but ourselves and our guns an' in formation, head for the trees. At least in the trees we have cover to fight."

Fannin's smile grew. "Yes, yes, even if some of us die, some of us may break to Victoria and on to Gonzales," he said, as if announcing his obligation to the orders sent from General Houston, and to me.

Dr. Bernard stepped up. "Then we must leave all the wounded behind?" He glanced down at Fannin and his blood-soaked bandage tied around the hole in his thigh. "Everyone?"

Jacob touched my arm. "And what of Padgett?" he whispered.

"We run as hard and fast into them trees and scatter among 'em and keep running and shooting," I said.

"What about the wounded?" Jacob asked again. "What about Padgett?"

They all turned to me in silence, as if the very silence of the cannons awaited an answer. That by some word, I might offer a way out no one had thought of. Or, that I might simply change my mind about seeing the red flag flying so close above our heads.

"They will kill every . . ." A blast cut me off, this time shot from the north; sending chain whizzing just above our heads, as if the commander told his artilleryman to aim at the small group of men circled around an invalid lying in the grass.

Picking himself up off the ground, Dr. Bernard said, "It's too late to fight and too late to run. We must surrender, offering ourselves to their humanity!"

I could say nothing more.

"But for their good grace," Jacob said, pointing beyond our wretched, human fortress. "I speak Spanish, I'll go talk to them."

The rest of the men nodded in agreement.

Fannin laid back and rested a hand over his eyes to shield

them from the sun. He raised it and looked at me, then covered his eyes again. Only this once did we agree completely on the grave decision made.

Fannin ordered a white flag raised. The cannons ceased their fire and within minutes, three emissaries from the Mexican army entered our square. A call came for Ehrenberg to join in their discussion with Fannin and his leaders. Jacob and I were not invited.

"Why Ehrenberg?" Jacob asked.

Through the dust and smoke, I could see one of the soldados speaking to Ehrenberg who would then turn to Fannin or Shackelford.

"The one still wearing the hat is German, or at least speaks German," I said.

"Hmm. I guess no one can speak Spanish but me."

I did not answer. We had left the group only a few minutes before the flag was raised and had no time to inform the New Orleans Greys of our surrender.

"Goddamn sons-of-bitches. We can still make a run for it," said Padgett.

"Ya can't even walk."

"Put me on the line, I can shoot. Better than being butchered I say and left to burn . . ." Padgett sounded aloud with panic, delirious from the pain of his wound and the liquor Ehrenberg gave him. "Like them poor souls at the Alamo, I ain't burning!"

One of the Greys, name of Johnson, slid down behind the upturned cart, cocked his rifle by two clicks, raised it, and was about to fire into the line of soldados. I kneeled down and said, "If you shoot with that white flag flyin' over yonder, well then, we're all dead. If you restrain yourself and wait for word from our commanding officer, there might be a chance a' gettin' outta here alive." As I lay a hand on the man's shoulder and stood, I shook my head, hardly believing my own words.

James Lee faced his father. "Are we surrendering?"

"They're going to kill us all," Padgett screamed. "Obregon watched those bastards murder our friends!" He tried to stand but could not. The entire Greys' militia gathered around him in a circle.

"Yes, but that ain't happening today as you lie in this field with a broke leg. Today, we're the lucky ones still alive and as long as that white flag flies, they ain't going to kill us, we'll die fightin' if that's the case. If there's a way out, it's through their ranks and more than likely on back to Fort Defiance. They ain't goin' to just shoot us . . ." The breeze shifted and the smell of death overtook me. I tried not to gag but could not help myself. The reek of the bloated horse and ox, their limbs cut off to provide better cover, the sweet stench of our dead lying in the sun no more than twenty feet away, and the bodies of Mexican soldados that still littered the battlefield. I regained my composure. ". . . there's too many of us."

Jacob turned to his son. "They're soldiers, not murderers."

Ehrenberg appeared in the circle, out of breath. "Colonel Fannin will be leaving the square to meet their general and to negotiate the terms of our surrender; he would like you to accompany him." He looked at me, then Jacob. "The both of you."

In my mind, there was no good reason why I should go with Fannin and discuss our terms of surrender, though I had just tried persuading my fellow Greys there was nothing to worry about, that we would not be killed. "Tell him I ain't going."

Ehrenberg gave Jacob a frightened glance. "Sirs, may we speak in private?"

Jacob and I followed Ehrenberg away from the circle.

"Gentlemen, they offer only unconditional surrender.

However, the colonel feels there can be a way to capitulate in our favor."

Jacob's face turned ashen. He stared at his son standing alone a few strides away, gazing out toward the front line of the Mexican army, holding a rifle with a pistol at his belt. "There must be a way to convince this commander . . ."

"Is it Santa Anna?" I asked.

"No, a general named Urrea," Ehrenberg said.

"It don't matter, he's under the bastard's orders."

I looked through the haze to Fannin, who with the help of a couple of men, was on his feet. It appeared he was looking back at me.

"Come talk to the colonel."

"What the hell, Zeb. Can't hurt."

"Well . . ." I lifted my left hand off the handle of my knife, the knife Bowie gave to me only three weeks before. My fingers shook. Besides Grainger, Ehrenberg and Jacob were the only ones to see this. Though I thought I found ways to hide my fears, I had begun to suspect many could see through me. "What the hell, right?"

After Jacob spoke briefly with James, we walked to Fannin. It appeared his wound had been wrapped with fresh bandages, yet blood seeped through them. Crutches fashioned out of wood stripped from the side of a cart allowed him to stand. He showed genuine pain and for the first time since I had known the man, I sensed he might understand the enormity of our situation.

"Thank you for joining me. I would offer you a seat but . . ." He glanced at the two emissaries sitting on small barrels, frowned, and opened a hand in their direction. "May I introduce you to Colonel Juan Holzinger, their interpreter, and aide to General Urrea, José Gonzalez. The third fellow has returned to his commander."

Neither Jacob nor I offered anything more than a cold stare.

"These gentlemen have come to us with nothing more to offer than unconditional surrender. I have a feeling . . ." Fannin stopped and swallowed hard. "They offer no quarter as Santa Anna is still overall commander of the Mexican army. However, they have invited me to join General Urrea in his camp as we might persuade him that to murder over two hundred of us will not stand. That we will fight until the last of us are dead, as well as killing most of his men. That there must be some guarantee, some compromise two commanders can come to agree upon."

"Why us?" I asked.

To Jacob, he said, "Because I trust you." He turned to me. "And . . . you have heard the true story of the Alamo, according to one who was there. Together, we look into the eyes of this man and see if he has the will to do such abominable acts. If so, then we must persuade him not to."

Gonzalez and Holzinger stood and brushed down their immaculate uniforms.

"We leave now," said Holzinger.

"Yes, we leave now," Fannin said.

Jacob looked past me to his son. "Yes."

I nodded in agreement.

Chapter 19

No one spoke a word as we left behind our line of defense, no offers of encouragement or good luck from those still manning the barricades, only grim silence. Under the white flag, the Mexican army went about gathering their dead from the battlefield. We killed many more of them than they did of us, yet we were still outnumbered, it seemed, four or five to one. The dead horses, they left lying on the prairie for the vultures to pick clean. As I passed one, crows began to fight over entrails pulled from the body. Their caws made me shiver. We climbed the rise, away from our human fortress. The stench of death receded to the aroma of food cooking, real food, not just corn tortillas and peppers, but broiled beef. I swore I smelled biscuits cooking. As slow as we walked to accommodate Fannin and his injury, I could well have forgotten how dire our situation was as to how hungry I had become. However, the reason we walked toward our possible deaths did not leave my mind for an instant.

The line of Mexican soldados parted, allowing us into their camp, past cannons, full buckets of water to cool and clean the barrels, and piles of grapeshot to continue the assault. There were few tents, mostly packs with bedrolls leaning against the trees of the thin forest. This army was not to be there for long. As I understood some Spanish, the snatches of words spoken among their troops as we passed were not necessarily harsh toward us, though I was sure we had killed many of their friends. The looks of apathy I struggled with. One soldado ran his thumb across his neck, shrugged, and turned away.

The two emissaries guided us to a large tent, the front open, with a bare table similar to the one General Houston used at Burnham's Crossing. We were told to stand and wait. Fannin leaned heavily on his makeshift crutches with blood soaked through the bandages covering his wound. He looked as if he might pass out and fall to the ground. Holzinger placed our confiscated weapons on the table: Bowie's knife, Jacob's pistol, and Fannin's short saber. I felt as if I were naked standing there.

From the back of the tent stepped a young-looking man in full uniform, about my height, clean-shaven with eyes the lightest of brown. As he pulled the chair back to sit, he stared down at our weapons and picked up the knife. Balancing it in his hand, he looked at Fannin, then Jacob. He pointed the blade at me and nodded. I gave him back the slightest of nods. He laid it next to Fannin's saber and unhooked the sword hanging at his side, gently setting it on the table, its handle toward us. I had never seen such beauty scrolled into silver, lines forming leaves and flowers. The butt end held what appeared to be a piece of amber embedded in a crown to match the eagle gold-plated onto the inside of the guard. The black, leather scabbard was just as ornate with silver and gold binding the seams together. Even in the shade of the tent, the weapon seemed to glisten. *The blade ain't ever felt the skin an' blood of a man,* I thought.

General Urrea sat down. "Gentlemen, you understand my predicament," he said, in perfect English.

I glanced to Fannin. He was in a sweat and seemed about to fall over.

"As you can see, our commanding officer is wounded and until he's able to sit and rest, there can be no official discussion," Jacob said.

"Yes, of course, my apologies." With a wave of a hand, his aid offered a short, three-legged stool to sit down on. As Fannin squatted, I steadied him to balance on his own.

After a long silence, with his eyes closed, Fannin said, "I wish to acquire our honorable surrender."

"Hmm, you must know I am under no obligation to give anything of the sort . . ." Urrea held my gaze. "In fact, it is quite the opposite." He seemed fascinated by my appearance and glanced down again at the knife.

"We have come to you for mercy," Jacob offered, with both hands held out, palms up. "We will fight you no more, and . . ." he swallowed, "be on our way back home."

"And where is your home, señor?"

Jacob did not hesitate. "Just east of San Antonio."

"You are a citizen, then."

"No, sir, I'm not. Though I came here and rightfully acquired my land and have built up a fine homestead."

The general shook his head. "Señor, if you are not a citizen, then you are not the rightful landowner. So, I tell you that your home is not east of San Antonio, it is somewhere else. Now you are either a thief or a liar, maybe both. Or naïve to think that the land of Mexico can be so freely given away."

"It was granted to me and I was told that it was mine."

"Do you have proof, señor? And how much will you sell, how you Americans say, to speculate the sale for a profit?"

"I will not sell; it's my family's home!"

Urrea clasped his hands together, laid them on the table, and leaned forward. "I ask you again, señor, are you a Mexican citizen?"

Jacob shook his head no.

"Then you are a thief."

Urrea's aid brought a pitcher of water with four glasses and set them on the table. The general stood, pushing his chair back, poured water into a glass, and took a sip. I could not remember when I had seen such clear water.

"I can offer you one glass each and no more. Unless . . ." He took another drink and placed his glass on the table. "Every one of you down in that field offers an oath, an allegiance to your country of Mexico. You must agree to give up your lands. Later, you may buy it properly." A slight grin creased his face.

With my hands on my hips, I leaned forward. "The man that knife's named after was a Mexican citizen, didn't save him from bein' murdered."

Urrea shrugged. "I have heard of this man." He picked up the knife again. "His name was James Bowie. I know the family he married into. He wanted too much, too soon. If he had only been more patient, as was the maker of this exquisite knife, he would have owned all the land and riches a well-mannered man could want. And still be alive today."

"Bowie's wife and child died of the cholera a year ago, he had nothin'."

"Ah, quite the contrary, señor, in Mexico you are married to the family for life, even as a widower." He ran a finger along the edge of the blade. "You have kept it in good condition, eh señor . . ."

"Creed, my name is Creed."

"Ah, yes, Creed. What an appropriate name for a man such as yourself. He was your friend?"

"Who was my friend?"

"James Bowie. James Bowie was your friend. You would not have his knife had this not been so."

I glanced to Jacob and then to Fannin, who still balanced precariously on the stool and one of the crutches.

"I have no friends, sir."

Urrea again laid the knife on the table. With a slight caress, he let go of the handle and sat back down. "Señor Fannin, you are injured. I can only offer water." He motioned to his aid to pour Fannin a drink. "What do you say for yourself, leading these men into a battle they cannot possibly win?"

Fannin gulped the water down and tried to stand, only to drop the glass. It hit one of the legs of the stool with a clink. He sat back down and after a few seconds, opened his eyes. "If only I had this for my cannons . . ."

"*Sí,* this liquid," Urrea picked up his glass off the table, "is necessary for many things." He poured the remaining water onto the ground beneath the table.

"As my men have fought bravely, I cannot expect anything other than a conditional surrender . . ." Fannin closed his eyes, took a breath, and coughed, his face pale with tiny beads of sweat on his forehead. "A traditional surrender . . ."

"And where will you go, eh? If you claim a home here in Mexico, then you have nowhere to go back to, unless, as I insist," Urrea frowned with impatience, "you become a good Mexican citizen."

"Most of these men come from America and would likely go back there," I said.

"And where is your home, Señor Creed?"

"I came from New Orleans."

"But is that your home?"

I glanced to where the water had barely moistened the dirt at the general's feet, and then locked eyes with him. "My home is where I stand."

We stared at each other for a few seconds. I saw nothing in this man that offered us either compassion or hatred, only, perhaps, insolence.

"You are an adventurer, as was your friend Señor Bowie. His adventure was short-lived, as yours may be."

"Sir, do you have children?" Jacob asked.

"Whether I have children has no bearing on your case."

Jacob's face turned a shade red. "My son is down there, waiting to know whether he will be killed, murdered by your hand."

"Señor, it was your hand that raised him up to be a traitor to his country."

Jacob said nothing.

"I must ask, señor, are you a slave owner, a freemason perhaps?"

Jacob seemed taken aback by the question. "No, sir, I am not. By Mexican law, it's illegal."

"Yet, if it were possible to win this war, you would own a slave, or two?"

"I don't know, I hadn't thought of it."

Urrea waved a hand, as if he disregarded anything more Jacob might say. "Señor, you do not know what you fight for."

He looked back to me. "And you?"

"No."

"Of course not. You do not dress like the others. I sense you are not here to win the right to own another soul. Why are you here then?"

I lowered my head.

"You have no answer?"

I stared at the knife. "Friendship."

"But, señor, you claim to have no friends." Urrea looked as if he was losing his patience with the conversation.

"They're dead."

His eyes widened in surprise. "To kill others for the sake of loyalty to dead men."

I did not answer.

He stared at me, nodded ever so slightly, and started to speak. Instead, he motioned toward Fannin. "Señor, how many men do you have left uninjured and can fight on this . . ." He rolled his eyes. ". . . battlefield."

Fannin sat still and with his head lowered, began mumbling under his breath, nonsensical words, as if he spoke in tongues.

He then pulled a small pistol concealed inside his bandages, stood, and with his other hand pressed against his bleeding wound, pointed it at the general. "I stand before you, a man of honor."

As I reached to disarm him, his legs buckled and he fell to the ground. The pistol slipped from his hand. Jacob kicked it away and knelt by Fannin's side.

Urrea waved away the five guards, their rifles pointed straight at us. "Brave man he is, but stupid. Leave him lying in the dirt."

Jacob straightened up and stepped next to me.

Urrea stood, placed his hands behind his back, and hung his head for a few long seconds, as if in deep thought. "Though I have given no mercy to some in this revolt, I do not wish to execute you and your band of outlaws and pirates . . ." He looked at me, then Jacob. "If I offer no conditions, we go back to fight and I will lose a few more brave soldados. However, with my artillery, I shall decimate you rather quickly, leaving a pile of bodies to burn on the prairie." He waved a hand in front of his nose, just as Obregon did as he described the burning bodies of the Alamo. "There must be some way to resolve this impossible dilemma." He picked up Bowie's knife and balanced it with a finger between the handle and the blade. "*Perfecto . . . Simplemente magnifico!*"

I nodded toward his sword. "A collector?"

"*Sí,* Señor Creed, indeed I am." His eyes brightened as he laid the knife on the table and picked the sword up. "Given to me by the governor of Durango and close friend of my family. I expect, since you have no home, you do not collect anything, eh, Señor Creed?"

I thought of all the knives I had owned or used, including my brother's, and Frenchy's plain, wooden-handled knife. I glanced to Jacob, then to Fannin still lying on the ground. "I offer a proposal to get us out of this here mess."

"Proceed."

"You take that genuine Jim Bowie knife and add it to your collection. In return, you offer a conditional surrender, letting these men go back, to America, abandoning their homes here in Mexico." Again, I glanced to Jacob. I did not catch his reaction.

Urrea began to laugh, then stopped. "Señor, do I hear you right, you wish for me to disobey my strict orders of unconditional surrender, for a knife?"

"Yes, sir, I do."

"I shall simply take it from you now."

"No, you won't because if we leave here with no reasonable means of saving our friends and our own lives, then, sir, you're obligated, as a soldier honoring his battlefield, to hand me that knife and send me on my way back down into that human fort an' fight you 'til I die. I'll tell ya, the first thing I do? I find the nearest barrel of one of those useless cannons and bust that knife apart." I paused, "Besides, I take it you ain't no thief."

It seemed the whole camp grew silent, as if each soldado was listening in on our conversation. Jacob's mouth hung open. Fannin was still unconscious.

"You would break it?"

"Yes, sir, I would indeed."

Urrea eased into his chair and leaned back, shaking his head. He beckoned to Holzinger and whispered into his ear, then motioned for us to follow him, leaving Fannin be.

The general slowly stood, picked up the sword, and hooked it to his side. As we passed the table, he handed me the knife, handle first.

"I may own this yet, Señor Creed," he said, and disappeared into his tent.

Chapter 20

Padgett lay on the floor of the chapel along with forty or so other injured men. His shattered knee had been set on the battlefield and reset the day after arriving back to the fort; his bandages had not been changed since. I kneeled beside him and smelled a whiff of rot, the same I remembered smelling in a cabin near Arrow Rock, along the Missouri many months before, as I lay dying from being shot in the shoulder by a murdering rogue.

"Did you bring it?" Padgett asked.

"Yes, but this is all of what's left." I handed him Ehrenberg's bottle of absinthe.

"Thanks, Zeb, you're a real friend," he said, and drank it all, wiping his mouth with the filthy sleeve of his smock.

I looked at the other wounded scattered about. It seemed they fared no better than Padgett. "Where is the doctor?"

"I hear he's gone to find . . ." He paused to close his eyes and lick his lips, not to miss a single drop of the magic liquid. ". . . a saw."

I felt a twinge of pain in my knee.

With his eyes squeezed tight, Padgett grimaced and asked, "Zeb, my leg ain't that bad, is it?"

I did not answer. I knew it would not get any better with him lying on that filthy floor surrounded by the many other dying men.

Fort Defiance had now become our prison. Most of the

militia and regulars slept outside on the parade grounds as the Mexican infantry and cavalry took all of our tents. The general occupied Colonel Fannin's quarters. The wounded were housed in the chapel, as was the colonel, laid up in an adjacent room. Four days earlier, as we carried him back down to our meager defenses on the prairie to persuade Shackelford, Bernard, and the others to agree to our terms of surrender, I secretly thanked Jim Bowie for giving me his knife. Questions came, most behind my back, as to how I was the only one allowed to keep a weapon. Neither Jacob nor I told a soul how I would lose possession the hour we left the fort free men, per my agreement with General Urrea.

Padgett opened his eyes. "Have you seen her?"

Taken aback by his question, I asked, "Who?"

"She came last night, late, and offered her services to the doctor." He stared up, into the rafters of the chapel. "Ah, Zeb, she is a beauty."

"Who?" I asked again.

"After soothing me with a cool-water cloth, she kissed my forehead and said she'd return this morning." He grabbed my arm. "When you see her, you'll know. And, send her my way."

I thought he might be dreaming, a fever-induced trance that made his thoughts and wishes seem real. I pried his fingers away and stood. "I'll do just that."

I found Dr. Bernard not far from where Padgett lay, ministering to a Texas regular wounded by flying splinters embedded in his face and neck, probably from a cart blown to bits by cannon shot. The doctor removed a piece of wood that had festered to the surface of his skin, dropped it into a bloodstained bowl, and gave the man a small drink of whatever the Mexican doctor was gracious enough to offer to help kill the pain. As he finished, I whispered, "How's Padgett? He says you went looking for a saw, is that true?"

"Yes, and I was unsuccessful in finding one. I will decide by the morrow if the leg must be . . ." He shook his head. "In the meantime, I'll keep looking for any means to cut off any . . . rot."

"How's Fannin?" I asked.

Dr. Bernard laughed. "Hell, he's as strong as an ox but still acts like an ass. If we survive this, he will outlive us all, I'm sure. The fact is he has gone to Copano with Holzinger to investigate the rumors of a ship being available to take us all home. Speaking of rumors, Mr. Creed, there is one . . ." He spoke low, glancing around to make sure no one was within earshot. "That it wasn't Fannin at all. That you made some kind of deal on your own with the general, something of an arrangement, with a knife, and that is why we are not dead." He stepped back and looked down at my belt. "The knife you still carry, the one James Bowie gave you."

It felt good to smile. I shrugged and said, "I told him I needed it to eat with."

Dr. Bernard turned back to his patient. From over his shoulder, he said, "I'm damn glad you did."

I stepped outside. Blinded by sunlight, I shaded my eyes and nearly knocked into her.

"*Disculpe,* señor," she said, and entered the chapel. I had not smelled the scent of a woman in months. Lilacs lingered at the open door. She disappeared into the darkness; the wind swept her fragrance away. I stood thinking I had just seen an apparition, a beautiful, daylight ghost to lift our spirits out of this prison. *Padgett saw her, she must be real,* I thought. *Though, he's got the fever so maybe not.* I walked back into the chapel.

She stood next to Dr. Bernard, over Padgett, now lying back on his elbows. A shaft of broken, prism light shone through a stained-glass window illuminating them. She knelt beside Padgett and smiled, touching his forehead, wiping his hair away from his eyes. She had tied her black hair into braids, yet one wisp brushed her cheek. She wore a flowing, white skirt that gathered at her feet. As she leaned forward, her blue blouse fell open a bit. I waited in the shadow of the pulpit until Bernard noticed me there and motioned for me to join them. As she looked up, I could not help but stare.

"Mr. Creed, come and meet our new friend," Bernard said, motioning to me again.

I made my way through the wounded men lying on the chapel's floor. Padgett grinned and gave me a wink.

"May I introduce to you Señora Francisca Alavez," Bernard said. "Ma'am, this here is Mr. Zebadiah Creed."

Not waiting for her to stand, I bowed and closed my eyes for a second. When I opened them, her hand was outstretched. I gently grasped her slender fingers and raised the back of her hand to my lips. As I straightened, I did not mean to draw her close. She did not resist. I could not help but stare into her brown eyes.

"Please to meet you, ma'am."

She released my hand and stepped away, not seeming embarrassed at all. She looked me up and down, touched her nose, and said, "*Sí,* señor, it is a pleasure. Are you hurt? Though you might be in need of a good bathing, you do not smell like these other poor men."

"No, ma'am, I have scars from other fights but not from this one, yet."

"You are missing a very small piece of your ear, it is healed?"

I touched the ragged edge of the top of my right ear and shrugged. "Seems to have healed just fine, thanks for askin'." She was the first in a while to mention my ear. I had forgotten about it. "Ma'am, I have to say, your English is very good."

"And your Spanish is bad, or do you speak my language at all, Señor Creed?"

"Un poco," I said, smiling.

She turned back to the doctor and said something I did not understand. He nodded and said, "We must go."

I was surprised at how abruptly our conversation would end. The sun continued to shine through the colored window glass, down upon her, more natural now, the back of her skirt frayed, stained with blood, as she had been in the chapel through the night, helping to save these men's lives. She drew her skirt up to wipe her hands and spun around to face me.

"Well, I'm goin' to speak to Urrea," I said, "about gettin' us some decent food, for we may have a long journey back to New Orleans, or wherever we end up."

"He is not here."

I stared at her for a long second. "Excuse me, ma'am, but what do you mean, he's not here, where did he go?"

She shook her head and again offered a hand. "I do not know, señor. My, umm, husband says he rides on to the real fight. We must leave now, Señor Creed, it is a pleasure to meet you."

I grasped her fingers and gave her a slight bow. "As is my pleasure, Señora Alvarez."

Still holding my hand, she leaned in to me. Through the smell of lilac, I breathed in the strong, natural odor of her body, pungent and sweet. "Sir, my name is Alavez, rather than Alvarez." She came close enough for her breasts to brush my arm. "You shake now, more so than when we first touch each other."

Not letting go, I wanted to stand with her, in the shifting, colored light of the chapel, forever. I wanted to draw her into me, wipe the smudges off her face and kiss her, in front of Padgett and all the other injured men who lay on the ground waiting for her cool-water bath and soothing words. She eased her fingers from mine and walked away with Dr. Bernard. She looked back once, to see if I watched her, and smiled.

"I told you," Padgett said and closed his eyes.

I found Jacob and James at the Greys' fire. As Holzinger had gone with Fannin to secure a ship, the only other man I knew who claimed to speak Spanish was Jacob. He and I walked to the officers' quarters. We did not know who Urrea had left in charge. I tried not to think of the consequences of him no longer being at the fort.

"Podríamos ver al comandante, por favor?" Jacob asked. The guard nodded toward two chairs on the porch and disappeared. We sat down and waited.

"Been meanin' to ask you . . ." I said, after a few moments of silence. "What Urrea was talking about?"

"What do you mean, Zeb?"

"About ownin' negros?"

Jacob's face turned a shade red and he looked down, as if he might be embarrassed. "I suppose some folks here are fighting for the right to own slaves, a lot of them. I'm not one of those folks."

I thought back to Bowie and his negro mistress. She certainly seemed to be in his favor, though I had not thought of her as his slave, but more his intimate servant. With Travis however, he clearly owned Joe. In the heat of the day, I paid them no mind as the few negros at the Alamo mixed with the Tejano families, almost as if they were refugees, same as us.

Jacob turned away. He was finished with our conversation.

"Just wonderin'," I said.

The guard stepped out onto the porch and motioned us inside an office. A second guard did not look up from his afternoon dinner of salt pork, roasted peppers, and corn tortillas. The first guard approached a door and tapped lightly. I heard the mumble of a voice and the door opened.

"*Sí, sí,* come in, come in, Mr. Creed," said Holzinger.

"I thought you were gone, with Fannin," I said.

"I was, until now." Holzinger's English was impeccable as was his dress. "Gentlemen, may I introduce to you Colonel José Nicolas Portilla. He is now our commanding officer."

The man who sat at the desk glanced up. As was his namesake, he was rather portly, wearing a thick mustache and a balding head of hair. An empty plate sat on papers scattered across the top of his desk. He did not smile, yet with his kindly eyes, I thought we could insure our survival.

"Quiénes son estos hombres?" he asked Holzinger.

"Señores, Zebadiah Creed and Jacob Lee."

Portilla stared at us for a few seconds then turned back to Holzinger. *"Encontraste tu nave?"*

Holzinger shrugged saying, *"Tal vez, ya veremos."*

Jacob whispered, "Did you find your ship? And the German said maybe."

The colonel looked directly at me. *"Qué es lo que desea?"*

"When do we leave?" Jacob asked.

Portilla waved Jacob away, stood, and wiping crumbs from his ill-fitting uniform, pointed to me. *"Le he preguntado, no él."*

"When do we leave?" I repeated, as Holzinger repeated it in Spanish.

Portilla sat, motioned to Holzinger to lean down, and as he stared at me, whispered something in the German's ear, then said, *"Se lo dire mañana por la mañana."*

Holzinger stood straight next to the colonel. "Tomorrow morning . . ." he said, looking away. He gave me a glance as if to see my reaction.

Jacob nudged me in the shoulder. "Palm Sunday!"

Portilla leaned back in his chair, clasped his hands behind his head, and said, "*Sí,* señor, Palm Sunday it is."

He knew English, the bastard.

Chapter 21

The celebration had already begun. Even the soldados-turned-guards seemed happy to be rid of us. With the help of Shackelford, Fannin made his way around to each group of prisoners personally announcing that he had found a ship and that we were all sailing away, back to America. I waited outside Fannin's room for him to return, to share with him my uneasiness, if he cared. I wished Grainger to be there with me, though I was sure he, Obregon, and Cobbs had, by then, made their way to Houston and his army. Grainger seemed to see through dark clouds better than most.

I decided not to wait on Fannin and walked around to the front doors of the chapel. Jacob, his son, and a young man about James's age broke from a group of rowdy regulars and approached me.

"Why so glum, Zeb? You look like the sky might fall any minute," Jacob said.

I shrugged and kept walking.

"Mr. Creed, we're goin' home, aren't you happy?"

I stopped and stared at Jacob. *Had he not told his son the truth?* I thought. *That they're not going back home to San Antonio, but to New Orleans, or some such other damn place the Mexicans might send us?*

I looked at James and again to Jacob. "I suppose I'm glad to be goin' back to New Orleans, all of us."

James glanced at his father. "What do you mean, we're goin'

home to Mama and Elizabeth, aren't we, Daddy?"

Jacob and I stared at each other for a few more seconds, and then he turned away from me to James. "Yes, son, we're going home."

I left them standing on the crowded parade ground. I wanted to see her again one last time, the woman from the afternoon, Señora Alavez.

The chapel was darker than just two hours before. The sun did not shine directly through the stained glass. There was a muted silence, contrary to the boisterous activity outside, as there seemed to be far less injured lying on the floor with no one tending them. There was a faint stink of death in the air. Padgett had been moved for I could not see him anywhere. From the side room, off the chancel, stepped Dr. Bernard. As I approached him, he quickly shut the door and ushered me back to the floor.

"My son, what a great day it is! We are leaving this God-forsaken place for good, aye?" His words sounded hopeful, however, with his back stooped and long face, his demeanor did not.

"Where's Padgett?"

The doctor would not hold my gaze. "He's been taken to another part of the chapel, to prepare for our long journey home."

I hesitated. "Where is she?"

"Who, Mrs. Alavez? Why, she is assisting in the . . ." He stammered. "Uh, preparation."

He took my arm and quickly walked me back toward the main doors of the chapel. "Mr. Creed, I'm sorry but you must leave now, for we have much to do. Perhaps you can ensure the rest of our fine, able-bodied men are ready to go home?"

"Doctor, you're acting mighty strange to be so happy about leavin'. And, you know most of these men ain't goin' home.

We're sailin' to New Orleans."

Bernard opened both doors and pushed me out. "Yes, yes, of course, they are," he said, then bolted them shut.

I stood staring out across the parade grounds, wondering what the hell just happened. *He put me out with no real explanation why,* I thought, *as if he just lied to me.* I wondered where Padgett might be.

Twilight had begun and fires were lit. The crowds of men were finding their own small bands, their tribes, to spend one last night as prisoners and fellow Texas militia. Nearly four hundred of them laughing and joking with one another, for they were going home.

I found the Greys, not far from their tents the Mexican soldados occupied. Most had packed what belongings they still owned. There was no food to speak of, though four or five bottles of mescal were given to them by the Mexican officers and were being passed around. Some of the men were already drunk. I waved away the bottle that came to me. With Jacob off with his son and Grainger gone, I felt alone and did not care much for celebrating. I pulled a small stone I used for honing and sat sharpening my knife. Ehrenberg stepped around to my side of the fire and sat down next to me.

"You do not drink?" he asked.

I shook my head. "Don't feel the need."

"Neither do I, my friend."

We sat in silence for a minute, watching the fire. The other men were getting louder, poking and pushing each other the drunker they got. I continued sharpening the blade.

"I do not trust these men," Ehrenberg said.

"Our drunken friends here?" I thought he meant someone might be shoved into the fire by accident.

"No."

I then knew whom he spoke of; I felt the same in my bones.

"Do you remember when we sailed here, the night you saved that sailor from Grainger's knife?"

I nodded. "Didn't know at the time whether he would kill the man or not. If it happened today, I probably would stay in my hammock an' go back to sleep. Why do you ask?"

"He would have killed the man, I know this. You talked him out of it. You have a gift."

Again, I nodded.

From another fire, I heard singing accompanied by someone playing a flute. *Where the hell did a flute come from?* I thought. *Maybe he made a deal with the general.* I laughed to myself. *Wouldn't that be somethin'?*

"I have seen into the eyes of this Holzinger," Ehrenberg said. "He is German, not to be trusted."

"The deal was not made with him, it was with Urrea."

Ehrenberg shook his head. "The general is not here."

"Then you don't trust the new man in charge, Portilla?"

"Neither one . . ." He took a breath. "I do not trust any of them."

We sat quiet for a minute, listening to the singing and watching the drunken men of Fannin's militia dance with each other around the fires.

I pointed to the gates. "The only way outta here is through those, I'm afraid. We'll know in the morning if they intend on killin' us or will truly set us free."

Ehrenberg stood and stretched. "Until then, good night, Zebadiah Creed," he said, and slipped away.

I sat awhile longer. No one else approached me, nor offered congratulations from afar. Again, I wished for Grainger's company.

Near the stable, at the place where barely a week before I was awakened and taken off to the stockade for threatening Fannin, I lay my head down.

I should've killed him, the son of a bitch, I thought, as I drifted off to sleep.

There comes a knock at the door.

The early morning sun shines through the only window, laying familiar light and shadow across the bed and the hand-hewn wall of the log cabin. Anna's fingers caress my shoulder, then she gives me a nudge to make sure I am awake. I reach under the blanket and touch her swollen belly. I turn to her and she smiles. Her blond curls cover half her face; I brush them away to see her shining, blue eyes.

There comes a banging at the door, wood to wood now, as if a club or butt end of a rifle is used. Rascal is barking, a scared, vicious bark.

I rise, throw on a smock and britches, and pick up my Hawken rifle. I peer out the window. Billy Frieze stands at the door. He sees me.

"Hello, mate," he says. "Long time, aye?"

"What the hell, Billy!"

Though a dead man stands on my porch, I am not surprised that he has come to my cabin at Arrow Rock. I step back into the center of the room. Rascal snarls and snaps at two shadows that seep through the crack below the door. Though I am glad to see my friend, I do not open it. "Why have you come here, Billy? And who's with you?"

"Open up, Zeb, and we can talk."

From afar, a lone bugle sounds, mournful. A Mexican death tune blows across the lower Missouri hill country.

"Who's there, Zeb?" Anna is out of bed and wrapped in the blanket.

"An old friend," I say.

Anna steps around me. "Well then, we must let him in." She disappears behind the opening door.

I raise my rifle. General Urrea and Holzinger stand before me in full, dress uniform, unarmed, with their hands behind their backs.

Colonel Portilla is at the steps of the porch and beyond him, in formation, the whole of the Mexican army stretches across the land with their rifles pointed at me.

"Señor Creed, I have come to collect what you owe me," Urrea says, and nods toward the knife at my belt.

"Where's Billy?" I ask.

"Señor Frieze has been dead for some time now," Holzinger offers.

I place my hand on the cool handle of Jim Bowie's knife. From behind the door, Anna steps to me, lays her hand gently on top of mine; our fingers entwine.

"Come back to me," she says.

Pressing her belly against our hands and the knife, she leans in and kisses my neck.

I awoke with a tremble, sat up, and stretched. I was not lying next to Anna in a cabin in Missouri, but sitting on a dirt patch next to a stable, held prisoner in an old mission in Mexico. I hung my head and closed my eyes. I desperately wanted my dream back.

The boy who woke me looked familiar, though I had only seen him once, the day before with Jacob and James.

"Who are you?" I asked.

"My name's Will, sir."

"What's your last name?"

"Scurry, sir."

I rubbed my eyes and looked past him to the grounds. The whole of the Texas militia was lining up at the gate. The Mexican soldados were in full-dress uniform with their rifles, the officers with swords at their sides.

"You have a brother? I don't remember his first name."

Will Scurry's eyes grew wide and began to water. "How do you know him?"

"He rides with General Houston."

James Lee stepped out of one of the lines and strode over to us. "Daddy and I want to walk with you and, figuring you'd be with the Greys . . ." He offered a hand to pull me up.

"Any food?" I asked.

James slowly shook his head.

"Well, I guess where we're goin', there'll be plenty soon enough."

As I had no possessions to gather but my knife, the three of us walked together across the parade ground to find Jacob and the Greys.

Chapter 22

We lined up with my fellow New Orleans Greys, two by two, Jacob and his son in front of me, beside me stood Ehrenberg. The gates swung open and the men before us began walking, some singing "Home Sweet Home." Others were deathly quiet. We followed. I said a word to no one.

Beside the gate stood Colonel Portilla, a woman who appeared to be his wife, Holzinger, and standing next to an officer who must have been her husband, was Francisca Alavez. I stared at her as we passed. She glanced to me, quickly looked away, then pointed to James Lee and spoke rapidly in Spanish to Portilla. He waved a hand. A soldado stepped to James, grabbed his arm, and pulled him from the line.

"What are you doing?" Jacob asked and took hold of his son's other arm. We stopped. The men ahead of us kept moving.

Francisca said, "I will save him."

"From what? He's going home with me."

The soldado tried pulling James toward Francisca with Jacob holding him where he stood.

As if in a panic, she pointed to someone behind me. "Then I will save that boy."

I glanced over my shoulder just as another soldado jerked Scurry from our ranks and placed him next to her. She wrapped her arm around a shoulder and whispered in his ear. A look of surprise and fear shaded his face as he watched the rest of us file through the gates without him.

Jacob and James again joined our ranks.

Holzinger stepped before me with his hands behind his back. “I shall take the knife now.”

I took hold of the handle. “The deal was made with Urrea. ’Sides, we ain’t free yet.”

“This morning, I shall represent him.”

He reached for the knife. I slid the blade from my belt. Three soldados aimed their rifles at my head.

“You ain’t takin’ nothin’ from me.”

I glared at him, sensing his fear that I would kill him before being shot. Looking away to Portilla, he backed off and motioned for us to continue through the gates.

Ehrenberg leaned in to me, close. “They intend on shooting us all.”

I ignored him.

I felt no freer outside the mission. Clouds covered the sky, yet with little breeze, the heat was near unbearable for early spring. I sniffed the stink of our bodies, men who had not bathed in months, with blood and shit still on their clothes from battle on the prairie five days before. I did not sense fear as much as exhaustion of minds and souls, and the slight hope walking away from the mission gave. Silence overwhelmed those few who still sang “Home Sweet Home.”

The soldados split us into groups and we were sent walking down three roads with most of the Greys headed toward Victoria. Some of the men wondered aloud why we went east rather than south to Copano Bay, where a ship waited to take us back to America. The soldados marched in line on both our sides, in step, to a cadence only they could feel.

Jacob began to whistle, stopped, smiled at his son, and said, “It will be good to see Mama and sister.” He glanced at the soldados, frowned, and went back to whistling.

Ehrenberg pulled off his satchel and let it drag on the ground between us, then let go. He peeled off his threadbare jacket and dropped it on the road. I looked back as the men behind us trampled the uniform in the dust. He stepped closer to me, pulled his hat down to his eyes, and shook his head.

"When you run, zigzag," he whispered. "You will become less a target."

I nodded. I wanted to say I knew this but could not.

Jacob stopped whistling.

Ahead, the soldados guided the men off the road, to our left, past a chest-high brushy hedge stretching halfway across a field of short prairie grass. Between this and the trees beyond, two caballeros sat on their horses, holding lances, dancing in nervous circles. The line of soldados on our left joined ranks with the other to make a new line no more than three strides away, leaving us with our backs against the hedge.

We still stood two by two. In my ear, Ehrenberg whispered, "Head for the trees . . . and the river."

The officer in charge attempted to talk with a couple of the men, cordially trying to spread us out more.

A volley of rifle shots rang out in the distance, from another road, with men screaming.

"The first click, fall down!" I yelled.

Ehrenberg disappeared through the hedge.

The soldados aimed their rifles. Someone hollered, "Hold steady boys, we'll all die together!" Others cried out no words.

One click, I dropped to the ground.

Jacob glanced over his shoulder and said, "Stay behind me, son!"

Shhh-boom!

A hundred rifles fired at once; a hundred men fell, most dead before they hit the prairie grass.

Jacob toppled backward onto James, knocking him down.

I lay still, with the sweet smell of morning dew, the roiling black rifle smoke, the cries of the dying. I did not want to move. *I must get up and run,* I thought, *the smoke will clear and I will be shot dead.*

Beside me, Jacob clawed at the spurting wound in his throat, making a gurgling sound as he tried to speak. A shadow fell across us. A soldado raised his bayonet and thrust it into Jacob's chest. I reached up, took hold of the soldado's baggy crotch, pulled him near me, and buried my knife in his side. He fell onto the butt end of the rifle, driving the bayonet deeper. I shoved both bodies off James, grasped his shirt collar, and pulled him to his feet. Except for the breath knocked out of him, he was unscathed.

"This way!" I hollered.

Covered in his father's blood, he stumbled, falling into the hedge. A hole seemed to open before our eyes, Ehrenberg's escape route. "There!" I said and pushed him through the brush. I followed and we lit out toward the trees and river with rifle shots whizzing past us.

"Don't run straight!" I yelled, and we each ran in diagonal lines, back and forth toward the tree line. A caballero rode hard for James, his lance lowered. At the edge of the field, he slowed to a trot, about to pin James to a tree. The rider did not see me for I was able to get behind and shadow him, close in to his horse's hindquarters. I reached up and snatched a piece of the tie around his waist, jerking him backward. With my other hand, I slapped the startled horse in the haunches. The horse took off at a run; the caballero slammed to the ground with my foot at his throat. James picked up the lance and held it over the man. He spit on him and raised the weapon.

The caballero cried, *"Niño, por favor, tengo una familia!"*

"To hell with your family, you killed my father!"

James looked at me. Rage filled his eyes, tears and hesitation.

I stepped away. He plunged the lance into the prairie, close enough to the man's head to slice his cheek just below the eye. He raised the bloody lance, tears streaming. Another caballero and his horse thundered toward us. I nodded to the river. James sank the weapon deep into the dirt next to the writhing man and, again, spit on him. Ten strides later, we met the bluffs overlooking the swift-moving San Antonio. Shots echoed through the trees.

James shouted, "I can't swim!"

"Take a breath, hold on, and don't let go!" I said, grabbing him tight in a bear hug.

We jumped, falling thirty feet below the top of a bluff, hit the water, and sank to the bottom. James panicked and climbed his way up my body; I held his legs before he could reach the surface. The current carried us downriver, but not far enough out of range of the shooters trying to kill us. Each ball pierced the water, leaving a trace of air, closer and closer, with a couple missing by only a hand's width. The shooting stopped. I let go of James's legs and he bound to the surface. I came up gasping for air. He floated on his back, as if he was dead, allowing the water to take him away. I followed right behind for three or four miles until we found a shallow inlet, pulled ourselves from the river, and lay in the mud. James rolled over and puked, then sat up and cupped river water into his hands, drank, and spit it out. Breathing hard and without opening his eyes, James asked, "What are we gonna do now, Mr. Creed, and . . . what about Daddy?"

"Maybe head north," I said, facing the young man. "I'm afraid we can't do nothin' for your pa." I could not tell if there were tears or river water running down his cheeks. "From here on, though, suppose you call me Zeb, will ya?"

He wiped his eyes, stood, and offered a hand. "Well, then, Zeb, we'd best be on our way."

Chapter 23

Rancho Cuero, Late March 1836

"Don't look like anyone's home," James said.

The ranch house sat back in the middle of a grove of oaks, off the main road and north of Victoria by a couple of miles, the same road Grainger traveled to get to Goliad. From where James and I stood, in tall grass and cattails on the shore of a shallow pond, we could not see whether the house was truly occupied. Between a low wall of stone and the main entrance, in the shade of an ancient, gnarl-plagued oak, a few chickens pecked at gravel and dirt. After three days of hiding from the small patrols of Mexican soldados and scavenging nothing but roots and berries to eat, we both were too weak to be chasing chickens.

"Must be a henhouse somewhere," I said. "Six or seven eggs would taste mighty good right about now."

All James could do was offer a nod. The young man was strong, but he was not used to going days without food . . . "Zeb, I'd eat a dozen if we could find 'em."

"To hell with the eggs," I said, not caring if anyone was around, and walked straight toward the chickens with my knife pulled. As soon as I hopped the stone wall, the chickens scattered, leaving puffs of dust in their wake. I chased after a black and red-feathered one, closing in enough to take a swipe. The damn bird stopped in its tracks and flew back through my legs, tying me up. I fell, skidding on my hands and knees across the gravel, the knife flying from my hand to hit the hard ground with a clank. James sat on the wall holding his belly, laughing.

"You ain't never caught a chicken before, have you, Zeb?"

I picked the knife and myself up, dusted off, and sat down next to James. "Maybe it's better we find those eggs."

James shrugged, stood up, and in seconds stalked the same chicken into a corner, against the wall, slowly swaying back and forth, as the poor animal tried to get past him, each time driving it back to the corner. He moved to one side of the chicken and motioned me to stand on the other side to keep it from flying away. James continued to sway, creeping forward, extending a hand. The animal did not move. In one fell swoop, James scooped up the chicken and held it gentle in his arms. I sat back down.

"You know how to build a fire without char and a striker?" James asked, then nodded toward the front door of the house. "I bet we can find something in there."

"I might take a chicken or two 'cause I'm starvin', but I ain't no thief." I swiveled around to the outside part of the wall and stood up. "Come on, I'll cut some cattail and we'll go to those woods back a ways an' have us a nice meal."

James cradled the hen as he would a baby, cooing softly, smoothing its ruffled feathers. He carefully placed his thumb on top of its head and with its neck between his index and middle fingers, let go of the body to fall, and jerked up. The chicken landed on its feet running, blood squirting from its neck. James opened his hand and showed me the head he held between his two fingers. "Mama taught me that." The headless hen danced for a few seconds, froze, and fell over dead. James picked up the animal, stepped over the wall, and stood in front of me, holding the swaying, dead chicken by its feet. "Zeb, you never said whether you can make a fire, can you? I'd hate to eat this here bird raw." He raised it to my face. I must have stood there with my mouth hung open, staring at the last of the blood draining out of the chicken's neck. James wore the broadest smile I had seen in days.

"Of course I can, ever' bit as good as you catchin' an' killin' that chicken," I said, embarrassed that a kid had showed me up. Though the look of pride in his eyes was a sight to behold, after all he had been through.

We headed back through the woods a ways, far enough off the road and away from the ranch house not to be seen. A fallen tree with a trunk three or four feet thick, its bare limbs still attached, blackened, as if lightning had struck many years before, offered us some protection from our enemies. With the knife, I set about digging two holes a foot and a half deep and half as wide with a through hole between them. As I gathered leaves, dry twigs, and small, dead branches, James pulled all the feathers from the chicken and scraped its skin with the sharp edge of a rock he had found. He cut a fresh branch from an elm tree, cleaned it straight, and skewered the raw meat, making it ready for cooking. After filling one of the holes with the leaves and twigs, I cut two branches, one from the elm, the other from a white oak, and shaped them into sticks two fingers wide and each a foot long. With the oak being much harder wood, I fashioned a narrow, dull edge to fit into the two slots I cut out of the elm. I scraped bark from the oak tree and crumpled it up, making it ready to help start the fire. Sitting cross-legged with my back against the trunk, I held the two sticks in front of me.

"Gonna need your help. When the shavings spark, add the tiniest pieces," I said to James, pouring the bark tinder into his palm. After greasing the slots with earwax, I rubbed the edged stick back and forth, keeping a steady rhythm, scraping bits of shaving into the front slot. As the wood began to smoke, I rubbed faster, furiously scraping the wood against the other, with James lightly blowing into the shavings. A spark, then a tiny flame appeared. "Quick, add the tinder," I said. The flame grew higher. On my knees now, I placed both sticks of wood into the hole, on top of the kindling. James continued to blow on the growing flame. In another minute, the kindling burst into a fire.

There was no smoke.

Relieved, I sat back with a smile.

"I'll be damned," was all James said as he positioned the meat over the fire. Soon, the entire woods smelled of roasting chicken.

James tended our meal while I looked on, with my knees drawn to my chest. This was to be our first cooked meal since before our escape three days earlier. On the run, we were nearly caught twice by patrols out searching for survivors. Once, we stumbled upon two of our fellow rebels, shot in the back, then stabbed through the chest, same as Jacob, and left lying in a field for the vultures to get at. The crows had begun to pick at their skin. James insisted we bury them. I dragged him away, swearing that we would be caught and killed in the same way if we did not stay concealed and keep moving north.

Not once did he speak of his father's death. I closed my eyes and listened to the cooking chicken sizzle.

"It'll be done soon," James said.

"Smells great!" I had not realized how hungry I was.

As the meat was falling off the bone, he used the knife to cut it in two and handed me half. We sat side by side and devoured the chicken in minutes.

"Best tastin', ever," I said.

Licking his filthy fingers, he gave me back a huge grin. "Not bad."

"Oh, the cattails!" I lay what was left of mostly bones down on a patch of grass and stripped back the roots of a plant to its tender center, then took a bite. The juice burst into my mouth.

I just shook my head. Together with the chicken, it tasted so good! I handed the rest to James and stripped another root. He ate the cattail, then ate the chicken's bones. Between the both of us, not a trace of the food was left to toss.

"We must be on our way," I said, and leaned my head back against the tree trunk. *I'll close my eyes for a quick second.* James was already snoring.

One click and I woke. Three more clicks and I jumped to my feet with my knife pulled, staring at four rifles pointed at us. James continued to snore. I gave him a sharp nudge with my foot. He slowly stood and raised his hands above his head.

"Olía mi cocina de pollo, no fueron difíciles de encontrar," said the lead man, his mustache drooping so low I could hardly see his mouth move. He wore a wide-brimmed straw hat tied around his neck, pushed back off his forehead, and a poncho the same bright colors and design I saw some of the Tejanos wear back at the Alamo.

"He says he smelled the cooked chicken we stole," James said.

I shrugged and rubbed my belly. "We were hungry . . ."

The man laughed, turned to the others, and said something I did not quite hear. All of them burst into laughter.

I glanced at James. He wore a fearful look on his face. "He said, 'that's good because we will carry full bellies to our graves for stealing Don Padilla's favorite chicken . . .' Zeb, I don't want to die for stealing a chicken."

The Tejano motioned toward my knife I still held in my hand, to give it up. The other three men held their rifles pointed at us. I offered it handle first. "Tell him we are not the enemy." James repeated it in Spanish.

He shrugged and took the knife. *"Don Padilla decidirá."*

Our captors chattered and laughed all the way back to the ranch, taking us behind the main house and yard, between two outhouses and a barn. One of the men opened the door to a small henhouse. *"Tened cuidado, estan enfadadas porque habeis matado a su amigo, os pueden picotear a muerte!"*

James and I stepped through the tiny door. The putrid smell of chicken shit was overwhelming. James pointed to a hen sitting on her nest. "It's looking like we got our eggs."

CHAPTER 24

After the stir of feathers and choking dust settled, the chickens nestled themselves back onto their perches and sat quietly clucking. Darkness came quick and soon we could see nothing. James and I found corners to sink into and we both fell asleep. Sometime in the night, I awoke to the chirping of crickets and frogs croaking in the pond. The hens were asleep, the smell of chicken shit only a little less reeking than when we were first locked in. I thought I heard the whinny of a horse and the roll and creak of a wagon. With no voices to go with the noises, I paid no attention. I closed my eyes and opened them. There was no light to make a difference. *I ain't dead . . . but damn, what a place to be, in a stinking chicken coop, in Texas. No, Mexico! I'm in Mexico, damnit.* I leaned my head back against a wood slat. *At least I ain't dead . . .*

"Zeb, you awake?" James asked.

"Yep."

There came a long silence. I could hear James breathing. He stirred, as if he sat up. "I want to say thank you."

"For what?"

"Saving me."

"I didn't save you, your papa did."

His breathing stopped. He let out a slow, deep sigh. "Daddy was already dead . . ."

"James, he stood in front of you so you wouldn't be shot and killed."

He began to sob, softly, hesitating, as if even in the dark with only the two of us, he was embarrassed to cry for the loss of his father.

"I lost my brother, shot through the head. Killed leanin' against me. Both of us tied to a tree in Missouri . . ."

"What did you do?"

"I sang him a death song." *One day,* I thought, *I'll tell ya the whole story.*

We sat in silence for a minute or two. Then, "Zeb, would you sing Daddy a death song?"

I had not shown anyone other than General Houston my true nature. I wondered if James might understand the depth and meaning of the song, or think me a crazy Injun in straw-colored hair and grey eyes. What else would I do but to share in his loss and grief the only way I knew how, while we sat in a dark, smelly henhouse?

"Yes. Get on your knees." I rocked onto mine and took a deep breath. I closed my eyes. Softly, I began . . . *"Jacob, at-eyahe, Wakan Tanka kinya, Maka, Han hepi wi, wi, ista yuganhwo, Inistima hwo?"* I paused and listened for James's breathing. I opened my eyes. The beginning of morning lightened the inside of the coop. The hens began to stir.

"Ista Yuganhwo na kinya."

Three times I sang this, with a lilt to my tongue, sadness for a man I knew so brief, though he was my friend.

"Will you sing it in English?" James asked. I could make out his body's outline but not his face.

"Lakota don't translate too well into English, but I'll try." I took a breath. *"Jacob, your father, the great-spirit flies. Earth, Moon, Sun, open your eyes, are you sleeping?"*

I paused again. His head nodded ever so slight.

"Open your eyes and fly . . ."

"Fly to where, Heaven?"

"Everywhere on the earth and in the sky," I whispered.

We kneeled in silence. James began to hum the melody. I chimed in. We sang Jacob's song, over and over, until we could see each other's face in the morning light.

We stopped singing and waited, for Jacob's spirit to fly, for James to release his father? I did not know. The hens began to cluck. One flew down to land in front of us, leaving a beautiful, brown egg on her nest. She paraded back and forth, as if to gain our attention and then flew up into the rafters of the coop to disappear. I felt comforted that by some means, Jacob was there with us in that stink of a henhouse.

Loud voices sounded near the ranch house, urgent and angry. The men who spoke seemed to be headed this way.

"A Mexican patrol!" James whispered.

We still kneeled, as if in prayer and had nowhere to hide, defenseless. If we were caught . . . I wished I had not given up my knife so easily. *Jacob, we may be followin' right behind,* I thought.

I motioned for James to crouch on one side of the small door while I stooped on the other side. "When they poke their noses in, we take hold of the barrels of their rifles and then . . ."

A woman's voice rang out, saying something to the patrol.

The soldados' harsh words softened, as if they knew with whom they spoke, yet they did not stop their search. Through the cracks between the wood slats of the coop, I saw three of them enter a small barn, their rifles raised.

"We're next," I whispered.

"Se donde se encuentran las cenizas de una hoguera en el bosque," said one of the Tejanos who captured us.

The soldados left the barn and quickly walked away, following the man toward the woods.

"He's taking them to our fire," James said.

"We must get away, now."

A shadow fell across the door, its latch raised and swung open. I stepped back into the center of the henhouse and peered outside. There stood a woman, silhouetted. The morning sun shined through her white dress.

"Señores, it is safe for the moment, but we must hurry. They will surely return," she said.

I followed James out the door. He gasped, as if he might have seen a ghost, for before us stood Señora Francisca Alavez.

"Ah, the boy I tried to save," she said, smiling at me. "Señor Creed, is it? You kept him from his death?"

"We kept each other from dying," James said.

I stood still and could not move, in shock as to how in the hell she happened to stand before us. I asked, "You're here, now?"

"I am friends with Don Padilla, as is Dr. Bernard. This is his home. There will be time for talk later, we must go now, those three soldados are not the only ones near," she paused. "And your friend Padgett is in danger of dying and needs your help."

She led us back to the house, past the stone wall, the gnarled tree, scattering three chickens off the path, and to the front door. Without a knock, she opened it wide and we walked into a mudroom. Ponchos and coats hung on small, mounted antlers. Four or five pairs of riding boots were lined up neatly against the wall, a couple of them caked with black mud. "Please take off your clothes, quickly. I will retrieve new ones and be right back. This will help to disguise you." She held her nose. ". . . though will not help you with your stink."

James and I slowly peeled off our clothes and laid them in a pile. The smell of sweat, blood, and chicken shit filled the room. I could not tell if it was the clothes or our own bodies that stank so much. *Oh, to have a warm bath with soap,* I thought. James stared at the scars on my chest and the dent in my shoulder where I had been shot. He glanced down once to the cut Brody gave to me on my left thigh, still bright pink, and turned away. I was certain he had noticed the scar on the cheek of my face, but never asked about it. On his right arm lay a deep, jagged line, as if he was on the run and caught in heavy thornbush, an early mark of a young man's life.

Francisca came with clothes for us both, handing them through the partially shut door. "José has brought water to wash with, he's waiting outside. You may not enter smelling as bad as you both do." I opened the front door, the same Tejano who held a rifle on us now stood by three pails. We stepped back outside into the sunlight, naked and stinking of chicken shit. He handed me a scrub brush and a bar of soap, then walked away. James and I took turns washing ourselves, and rinsed, all the while looking out for the soldados who might come back to catch us completely unarmed. We wrung the water off our bodies and reentered the mudroom. I could not remember a time when I felt more refreshed.

Once we were dressed, Francisca joined us. We both wore Tejano riding britches, brown boots, and colored smocks, mine bright blue while James wore red. Our hats were made of straw, wide brimmed, with a string to hold them onto our heads or hung down our backs. Francisca bound black sashes the proper way with her slender fingers wrapping the fabric twice around our waists, then tied. She leaned into me, close, as she did in the chapel; her arms around my hips pulling the sash down a bit, then with a gentle tug, let go and stepped back with a smile. She did the same with James. His face turned as red as the color of his shirt. I thought, a woman so beautiful had never touched him in such a way.

"Now you may enter Don Padilla's home proper."

We were in disguise, to be seen in plain sight.

If the antlers in the mudroom were taken off young deer, then in the living room hung the antlers of their mamas and daddies. Over the cold fireplace hung the head of a buck the size of a horse, with its antlers reaching into the rafters. Broad windows stretched along the opposite wall, open to the morning breeze, with a hint of sage wafting through the air. Above the windows hung more heads, of deer and elk, bison and antelope. A large cougar stood at the far corner of the fireplace, ready to pounce on three, stuffed geese. To our left, against a wall, next to an open door, sat a desk cluttered with books and papers. Above it hung half of a brown bear, its claws raised and teeth showing. *If I had killed that bear, the teeth and claws would be hangin' around my neck.* The other animals would certainly have been eaten and their skins tanned to be worn. I shook my head at such a waste.

Two round tables with chairs sat in the middle of the room, as if ready to accommodate nightly games of cards or poker. One armchair faced the fireplace. Don Padilla rested a hand on its back, the other he held in the pocket of his vest. He was not an old man, yet stood with the confidence of age, expressionless, as he watched us enter the room.

"Ah, señor, you are up and about," Francisca said, greeting him with a kiss on both cheeks. "Already, this morning has been busy."

She stepped back and turned to James and me. "May I introduce to you, Don Juan Antonio Padilla."

The gentleman stood frozen as if he were a statue, not blinking an eye. Then, "you have visited my henhouse?"

I nodded. "Yes, sir, we have."

"You ate my *Gallo del Fogoso.*" His eyes flashed anger, then sadness and back to anger. I almost laughed as I realized he had named the bird. Like James, though, I did not want to die from killing and eating a chicken.

"He was the finest rooster and cock fighter in all of South Tejas. I won many pesos because of his fierceness." He spoke with a slight lisp.

I glanced to James. He had not mentioned that we ate a rooster, and I apparently could not tell the difference. Besides, the damn chicken did not seem so fierce when James popped its head off, running around squirting blood all over the gravel and dirt.

"We were very, very hungry, sir," said James.

Padilla's eyes softened. "You come from Goliad?"

"Yes, sir," I said.

"Who are you?"

I had a feeling he already knew who we were.

I reached out my hand. "Zebadiah Creed, sir."

He did not take my offer of a handshake. He nodded to James.

"James Lee, sir." He too offered to shake with Padilla. The older man looked him up and down and slowly reached out and grasped the young man's hand.

"We are deeply sorry for eating your prizefighter . . . sir," James offered, and bowed.

Francisca smiled and said, "Ah, we are all friends now?"

From behind us, I heard the clink of a glass and dishes laid upon a table. Then I thought I smelled biscuits! It had been nearly a day and a night since we ate his rooster and desperately wanted to turn around, but did not wish to appear any more disrespectful.

Don Padilla slowly waved his hand as an invitation and said, "Señores, sit *por favor.*"

It was the first time in weeks that I had sat at a real dining table, even though it was more likely just a fancy card table. A young woman of maybe sixteen, wearing a flowing, yellow dress and white apron stood next to a rolling cart filled with food, ready to serve us.

"Lady's first," I said, and pulled a chair for Francisca. I sat down next to her. She nodded without looking at me and whispered, "*Gracias . . .*"

Don Padilla sat on her other side, shook his napkin out, and tucked a corner of it into his shirt at the neck, spreading it across his chest. James and I did the same thing, although we were not as elegant as he was, with me fumbling to keep the napkin in my shirt. I was so hungry; I did not care if I spilled food on my clothes.

The servant poured hot coffee along with glasses of water for each of us. James and I drank our water in one gulp leaving empty glasses on the table to be filled again. The coffee was the freshest, strongest coffee I had drunk since leaving New Orleans six months earlier. James tasted his, frowned, and then blew over the top of the cup to cool it down. The young woman dished a stew with whole kernels of corn and meat into bowls. I thought this looked familiar, as I had eaten something similar with my Lakota family. Before tasting it, I held a spoonful up to my nose. It smelled similar to the stew of buffalo guts my mother would boil for days and share with our entire tribe.

"It is called *menudo,*" Francisca said. "Here in Mexico, a pig's *intestinos* are a great delicacy."

James did not wait to smell the food, and in less than a minute, ate all the stew in his bowl. He asked if more could be served to him. The young servant smiled and accommodated his hunger with larger chunks of meat and less soup. He was a little slower at eating all the contents of that bowl. The last time I sat at a table with him in someone's home was with his mother, sister, and Grainger. *How far you've come, young man,* I thought, *how far you've come.*

The four of us were silent while eating our breakfast. When Don Padilla finished, he sat back in his chair, pulled the napkin from his shirt without wiping his mouth, and asked, "How did you escape?"

James laid the spoon in his bowl, hung his head, and waited, to gather his thoughts, maybe to try and understand what happened three days before?

"We ran," he said.

"And never looked back," I added, staring straight into the eyes of this man. A simple question about the past could have several different meanings affecting the present and future.

"Many men were killed," he said. "Francisca, you were there, tell them what you told me, *por favor?*" He seemed to carry no feelings of remorse or sympathy in his voice, nor any real interest in a discussion other than mere conversation.

She stared at him for a long second, perhaps wondering how she might share something so horrific and be so casual.

"It took only an hour in the morning to shoot them all. It took all afternoon and evening to burn their bodies." Her voice quivered as she spoke.

I felt as guilty and helpless as I did after Obregon described the fall of the Alamo. I stared at my half-empty bowl and was no longer hungry. James and I glanced at one another. As we escaped by following the San Antonio River back north and east, we had to pass close to the mission. In darkness, we saw the sky lit up by fire, and smelled flesh burning. I had to keep pulling James along, whispering there was nothing to do for them. We were alive and needed to stay that way.

"Fannin?" I asked.

"Executed, shot in the face, and his body dumped into a ditch, along with most of the wounded left in the chapel." Her eyes brightened. "Some, I was able to help escape, including your friends who you call Padgett, and Dr. Bernard." She paused. "Oh, and the boy of course."

Scurry's still alive! I thought.

"Where are they?" I asked.

"Not far from here, on my land and safe," said the Don.

"And Padgett, how is he?"

Francisca said, "Not so good, Señor Creed, he has lost a part of his leg."

It seemed Dr. Bernard found his saw.

"The surgery did not go so well, just as we were preparing him to leave the chapel." She paused. "So he might escape being executed. On the way here, he again extracted the poison and now more of his leg needs taking to keep him alive."

I sank back in my chair. "Where did you say he was?"

"I did not say," Padilla said.

"Can we go there?" James asked.

"*Sí,* I will take you to your friend, and the doctor," he said. "However, you must do something for me." He rose from his chair, walked to the desk, and stood behind it. "You must deliver two letters, one to Stephen Austin, and another to a man you might know?" The bear above his head appeared to be alive, ready to attack. "Alexandros Robito Obregon."

Black mud on the boots, I had seen it before. I was not surprised that this man standing behind his desk knew the bastard.

"May I ask how you know them?"

"Señor Austin and I spent time together, north of here and east. I helped him build his colony, and not long ago, helped write a constitution, to break from Mexico. He was my friend."

"He's not your friend today?"

"No, he is not."

"And Obregon?" I asked.

"My agent, of sorts."

". . . and friend?"

"No, I would say not. Now I ask the questions . . . How well do you know Señor Grainger?"

What the hell does Grainger have to do with any of this? I thought, shocked that Padilla would mention his name. "We both came to Texas on the same ship six months ago, I've known him since. How do you know Grainger?"

"He, Señor Obregon, and one other man were here more than a week ago, on their way to find Señor Houston and his army. They spent one night."

That was indeed the plan, for Grainger to meet with Houston and convince him to send part of his army to Goliad. I was against it, knowing Houston would not agree to split his forces, no matter the cost of losing Fannin and his men. Grainger tried talking me into going with him. I refused to leave and abandoning my fellow fighters as I felt I had done at the Alamo.

I nodded for Padilla to go on, then asked, "Did he get drunk?"

"Ah, well, drunk is not the word, señor. I will say . . . he became very talkative."

"Yes, he can be that."

"He spoke of you. This is how I knew you would come." He frowned. "Though he did not say you were a thief."

I wanted to ask how James and I ended up there, at the same place where Grainger and Obregon stopped on their way north, and how Señora Alavez, Dr. Bernard, and Padgett happened to also arrive days after the massive murder. Perhaps it was a confluence of grace and providence. Others would believe it to be the hand of God that guided us all there. Part of me refused to believe anything other than the random chance from the choices all of us made.

I was bewildered, but I would not show him. "Sir, again, we are very sorry for eatin' your rooster. Had we known he was your prize, we would've eaten one of your other chickens."

Francisca rolled her eyes and smiled. Señor Padilla seemed unamused by my comment.

"You have me curious, what did my friend say?" I asked.

"He claimed he owns many leagues of land north of here, east of San Antonio, land for grazing, land to raise cattle. He has a very good plan. When this fight is finished and Santa

Anna is driven to the sea, we will need strong men like him to hold the land, from the Comanche, from ones who would raise cotton, populate all of Tejas . . . with slaves." He said these last words as if he had poison in his throat.

My mouth must have hung open. "Are we talkin' about the same Grainger?"

"He says that you will provide the cattle for his venture."

For a moment, I was unable to respond. Then, "I have no idea what he meant by that. I ain't no cattleman."

My thoughts swirled back to our conversations, trying to remember any promise I made to Grainger, which would make him think I would accompany him in his ventures after the fighting was done. Not one word came to mind.

I shook my head and looked at James. He shrugged. "Daddy talked about raising cattle, said it was a solid investment come our independence."

"I know nothin' about no damn cows," I said.

"Well, Señor Creed, you would rather have a country filled with slaves?"

"Of course not, I was a slave once myself, held by the Lakota for years until . . . I know what bein' a slave is." I felt as if I had drunk a little of Padilla's poison. "It's just that, I ain't stickin' around when this here war is done."

"Then why are you here, if you do not want something from its outcome?"

Again, that question.

"I'm here to make sure this young man gets home alive. Like I promised his mama I would."

James sat in silence.

"We come all this way, through the blood and killin', to sit here discussing my intentions and plans?"

Don Padilla shook his head. "I must know if you are to be trusted."

"Why? We were just passin' through. If we hadn't stole your rooster and got caught, James and I would be long gone from here."

"Señor, I knew you would come. My *Gallo del Fogoso* saved your lives. Saint Teresa does not lie."

"Who the hell is Saint Teresa?" I asked.

"She is a messenger from Jesus and the blessed mother Mary. She came to him during prayer, in a vision," Francisca said, not allowing herself to be put off by my cursing. "Do you believe in visions, Señor Creed?"

As she asked me the question, I remembered the dream Jonathan shared with me the night before he was killed. Afterward, for several weeks it seemed, while I was healing from my wounds, my brother would come to me in my dreams, consoling me, until he left this world trailed by fireflies.

I nodded.

"Well then, you must know Saint Teresa only gives us her love and compassion, and willingness to help shape our new country in a righteous way. You have come to help, Señor Creed."

Don Juan Antonio Padilla stared at Francisca with the eyes of a man carrying deep sadness. I was wrong in thinking he did not care, about our plight, or the land where he and generations before him had lived.

"One last question. Are you aware of the Order of the Lone Star, Señor Creed?"

I was confused by his inquiry and shook my head.

"Are you a freemason, sir?"

Again, I shook my head. This was a question General Urrea had asked Jacob during the surrender.

He looked me up and down, then frowned. "Of course not," he said.

There came a light tap on the door. Señor Padilla stepped

outside the room for a few seconds, then leaned his head in and said, "It is time for you to go, the army patrol has moved on for now. José will take you to your friends."

I turned to Francisca and asked, "Will you be accompanying us?"

She smiled and said, "*Sí,* Señor Creed, of course. You and Dr. Bernard will need my help with your friend Padgett."

Chapter 25

José gave back to me my knife, along with a pistol, hunting rifle, and shooting bag. He gave James the same. We wore our hats pulled down to our eyes. I no longer felt naked. We rode in the bed of a field wagon with wood planks for seats. Three armed ranch hands sat with us. Señora Alavez sat next to José, our driver. Two *vaqueros* rode behind us on horseback; both held scatterguns in their laps. I carried a leather pouch with food and at the bottom, concealed in wax, sat two letters, one for Stephen Austin, the other for Alexandros Robito Obregon. Again, I was to be the messenger.

James seemed in good spirits as he asked the men about their families and how long they had lived in Tejas. A couple of them said they went back generations, certainly as long as Don Padilla's family had lived there. Like his father, James spoke Spanish very well. However, I did not, so I would ask him what they said. After a few moments, I could tell James grew tired of translating so I sat quiet, enjoying the cool breeze and late morning sun.

Francisca turned around and motioned to me. "Señor Creed . . . Señor Creed."

I carefully stood, held on to James's shoulder to balance myself, and sat down behind her. "Señora Alavez?" As the wagon moved forward, the smell of lilac nearly overwhelmed me. I could not help but smile. She gave back to me a wisp of her smile.

"Are you a good friend of the doctor?" she asked.

"I've only known him since our defense of Goliad, attempted escape, and stay as prisoners. As far as I could see, he saved the lives of many of our wounded . . ." I stopped and swallowed. "He's a man of integrity and courage."

Francisca nodded. Though the noonday sun offered her no shadow, I sensed great sorrow. Staring ahead, she did not speak for nearly a minute. When she turned back to face me, I wanted desperately to brush the tears from her cheeks.

"He is not well."

"He's sick?"

"You must understand, we have seen so much," she said.

I nodded. *Did she not know what we'd been through? No, how could she? And how selfish of me to think like that.*

"I helped them to escape, only after watching many men be killed, most of the wounded . . . taken from the chapel and shot. The doctor and your friend would be dead had it not been for me. Once we got here, he fell into a stupor. I went to get help from Don Padilla, and found you."

As José steered us off the road, the wagon hit a rut, shaking us all out of our conversations. Across a small field, we entered a grove of trees. A house came into view, built of rough-cut squares of stone with a massive wood frame and roof, well hidden from the road by the dense green of fresh, spring leaves.

"Pabellón de caza de Don Padilla," said José.

James leaned into me. "His hunting lodge."

As we pulled to a stop, no one came on to the porch to greet us. José snapped a finger and pointed to the front door standing ajar. The three men riding in back with us stepped off the wagon and approached the porch, their pistols drawn. James and I pulled ours. The *vaqueros* placed themselves between the porch and us, still on horseback, holding their scatterguns and ready to shoot.

One of the men entered the doorway. A shot rang out with wood splinters flying down around his head. He held up his hands and walked on in, speaking loudly, admonishing someone in Spanish.

From inside came, "Hell man, I could have killed you!"

The ranch hand walked back out onto the porch, placed his thumb near his lips, and tilted his head, laughed, and went back into the lodge. Everyone lowered his weapons.

Francisca stepped off the wagon, climbed the porch steps, and disappeared through the door. James and I followed.

Before we entered the front room, I smelled flesh rot and stopped. James stumbled into me.

"Zeb, are you all right?" he asked.

I had no time to answer. Francisca called out for help. In an armchair positioned to face the door sat Dr. Bernard, holding a smoking pistol in one hand and a bottle in the other. Padgett was not in the room. Bernard seemed not to recognize any of us. He looked at the man he nearly shot and began to cry.

"I am so sorry, sir," he said, took a swig from the bottle, and let out a loud snort. "I . . . I thought you were going to kill me."

"Where is Señor Padgett?" Francisca asked.

The doctor drew a strange look, as if he did not recognize the name.

"Where the hell is Padgett?" I asked.

His look turned to shock, then fear, as if he suddenly remembered where our friend was. He tried to get up from the chair, but could not, and again began to cry. "I could not save him . . . I could not save any of them."

I shook him, hard. "Where is *Padgett*?"

He nodded to a closed door and lowered his head. In a second or two, he was passed out. Francisca opened the door and entered a room as dark as if the bright sun outside the lodge did not exist. The smell of rot overwhelmed James and he began to gag. The man Dr. Bernard came close to killing held his nose and walked out the front door. *"El hotel huele a muerte,"* he said to his fellow *hombres.*

From the darkened room, I heard a groan.

"He is alive, Señor Creed, your friend Padgett is still alive!" Francisca said.

Chapter 26

James went to find water and I pried up two windows and opened the shutters. Fresh air and sunshine flooded the room, causing me to blink. Padgett kept his eyes closed. He lay on his back in a four-post bed, covered in a sheet. His left foot stuck out. The sheet lay flat and blood soaked where his knee, lower leg, and right foot used to be.

"Zeb, do you have any more a' that damn good drink?" Padgett asked.

"Don't have any more, my friend."

Francisca leaned over him and cleaned sweat from his face. He opened his eyes and smiled. "Ah, my angel . . . has come to save me."

A breeze rustled the curtains, pushing some of the stink out of the room. James entered carrying a pail of fresh water. Francisca dipped a cloth and wiped Padgett's eyebrows, the same as she did in the chapel the first time I saw her. He smiled and closed his eyes, then winced and reached for his upper leg. Francisca dropped the cloth and slowly pulled the sheet away from his body. He was naked, except for a bandage wrapped around the stump of what was left of his leg, soaked with blood and colored by a rank, greenish-yellow stain. Above the bandage, shooting up into his thigh were red strains, like branches of a tree. Francisca covered his privates with the sheet, glanced to me, and shook her head. She went to soothing his face again and gestured for me to pull the bandage away from the wound. I hesitated.

"We should get him something for the pain," I said. "James, go and fetch a bottle of whatever the doctor's been drinkin'."

James came back with half a bottle of mescal. "I found three empty bottles and this . . ."

"We'll need more. Go and ask your new friends if they might have somethin'," I said, and gave the bottle to Francisca.

James left again. I heard him speak to the fellows on the porch. One of the men answered and walked away. James came back and said, "José has gone to the fields to find something. I've never heard of it, but the other men nodded, as if they knew what he was looking for."

Padgett took a swig, with some of the liquid dripping from his mouth to the bed. Francisca did her best to wipe it away. I began to unwrap the bandage, letting it fall to the side of his leg. The closer to the stump, red and black patches of skin appeared, oozing blood and pus. The flap to cover the bone had been hastily sewn on to the rest of the skin and the stitches had loosened. The stench filled the room again. I had to turn away. Padgett attempted to look and Francisca gently pushed his head back onto the pillow.

She glanced up, and with a look of tearful composure, said, "We were in such a hurry . . . they would have killed them if we were caught."

I covered his amputation up with the bloody bandage, then covered the rest of him with the sheet, and sat down in the one chair in the room. He offered me the bottle and said, "Zeb, ya look like you need a drink worse than I do."

I took the mescal and stared at Francisca. She looked up again, this time with a smile. At that moment, with her doting after Padgett, I truly admired her courage and compassion.

From the front room came a moan, then, "Where's my bottle?

I know I had a drop or two left."

Francisca's smile turned to a frown. "He promised he would not drink for the short while I visited Don Padilla." She shook her head. "We arrived two days ago and since he found the mescal in the cupboard . . . I hid two of the bottles."

Dr. Bernard stood in the doorway to the bedroom, swayed forward, then backward, and leaned against the doorframe. He focused on me sitting in the chair. "Zebadiah Creed?" he asked, and rubbed his eyes. "What the hell? I'm seeing your ghost for surely you are dead, sir."

I approached my friend. "No, sir, I ain't dead, yet," I said, and reached for his hand. He stood up straight and we shook, then he pulled me into him and gave a hug, tight. He slowly released me from his arms, hesitating, as if were we to let go of each other, I might disappear.

James had slipped behind me while I sat, and kneeled, with his back to the wall next to the open window, partially hidden by the chair. Bernard had to look around me to see him.

"Your father . . ." said Bernard. "I saw him. Well, his burning . . . you know, amongst the others." He stopped, lowered his head, and asked again, "Where's my bottle?"

James rose to stand beside Francisca. She grasped his hand. "Enough talk of death and the past." She nodded to Padgett. "What are we to do, Doctor?"

Dr. Bernard kept his head lowered. Without a word, he stumbled to the front room and sank back down in his chair.

There came a knock on the door. "Señor Creed?" José entered the front room and held out a fistful of plants for me to see. "*Toloache,*" he said. I recognized the plant from my childhood. If eaten by a horse it would, for a while, go crazy. A man, sometimes much worse if not careful. In his other hand, he held a bouquet of purple flowers. I also knew this plant as it grew wild across the north plains. My mother used it to soothe a sore throat. We would need much more to stop Padgett's infection from spreading.

I motioned for James to join us. "Will you go to the kitchen and start a fire, find a large pot, and boil some water? We'll need to dry these leaves an' make Padgett here some strong tea. Be quick about it. Oh, and please ask José to gather more flowers, we will need a bunch."

Francisca pulled on Padgett to sit up in the bed. "A few sips," she said, handing him the last of the mescal. He took a long swig. She pulled the bottle away from his mouth. "Not so much, señor, this is all we have for now." He seemed more comfortable, though I knew that if we did not do something very soon, he would die. Francisca's glance told me she knew the same.

She came to my side, leaned into me, and whispered, "We must find a saw."

I shook my head. "I don't know if that will help, or just kill him."

"You must do this," she said and placed her hand on my arm and squeezed. "We will do this together to save your friend."

I laid my hand on hers. "Our friend."

I broke away and joined James in the kitchen. He stood next to a bare table, more a butcher's block, in the middle of the room. On one wall there hung pots and pans along with quite the variety of cutting utensils, against the other wall sat a cooking stove, cold and dusty, as if it had not been used in years. The table was large enough to accommodate the butchering of a full-grown buck. I pulled the latch up, opened the back door, and peered outside. In a clearing, wood lay piled next to a tree with an axe buried in a stump. I turned back to James. He stared at the stove, as if he did not know what to do. He closed his eyes; tears streamed down his cheeks. He wiped his nose with a sleeve. "I know he's dead, but did they have to burn him?"

I took hold of his wrist and led him out the back door to the woodpile. "We need wood chopped small enough to make a fire in the stove. If we don't hurry, Dan Padgett may die; one more of us gone from this old world. Sometimes, that's the best, I suppose. Your daddy died quick, well, quick enough not feel too much pain. Padgett, he's feelin' a lot of pain, and we can do somethin'. Now, I need you to chop this here wood."

James peeled the axe from the stump and stood up a log. He held the axe in his right hand for a couple of seconds staring at the round piece of wood. In one swift, violent move, he stepped a foot back and swung down. With a crack, the log split clean in two, both pieces falling to the ground. He set up an even larger log, and with a groan and more vicious swing, split that one in two. I backed away to the kitchen door.

Francisca joined me and for a moment, we watched James. "He will grow into a fine man," she said.

"He already is."

She left me standing alone at the door.

Chapter 27

I did not like butchering. I was not any good, for I was always making a wrong cut. As often as I had been dripped, sprayed, and had laid in blood, mine or someone else's, I never did get used to it, and here I was expected to cut two inches off a man's leg and not kill him.

Padgett took another drink and gave me the bottle. His ruddy complexion seemed to be returning and he was visibly drunk, though when I checked, his leg looked worse. He closed his eyes as if to sleep.

In the front room, Dr. Bernard still sat in his chair, snoring.

James hollered from the kitchen that the water was boiling. I walked back to see him, Francisca and José separating the coarse leaves from the pods of the jimsonweed, breaking the pods open and scooping out the tiny seeds with spoons. José placed the leaves and stalks in a pot of cold water to soak. He laid the flowers of the snakeroot onto the stove to dry out. The afternoon sun shone through the open back door. We would have to hurry to beat the coming darkness.

"Heat the seeds 'til they're dry, then we'll crush them into as much of a mulch as we can and swirl it into a glass of the boiling water. Not too much though, we don't want to kill him."

Francisca stared at me. "How do you know this?"

"My mother was a medicine woman."

We worked in silence. José crushed the dried snakeroot and with the last of the mescal, mixed up a thick salve. We would use the jimson leaves to wrap the wound.

I found a short saw hanging on the wall and held it up to look for rust. "Francisca, did you not say you had two more bottles of the drink?"

She nodded, left the kitchen, and came back holding two full bottles. I opened one and doused the saw blade. I was about to dry it with my shirt when Francisca motioned that she would use her dress. "You still stink of the henhouse." I held out the saw as she gathered the white cloth in a bunch. After wiping the blade clean, with her left hand she reached for and steadied my shaking hand, let go of the saw, and picked up the other full bottle. "For your nerves, Zebadiah Creed."

I had never tasted mescal. I uncorked the bottle and drank a bit. An instant heat expanded in my chest and belly, as if I had breathed fire into my lungs. I desperately wanted to cough, but did not want to lose face in front of José or James. The second drink went down much smoother.

Francisca smiled and said, "You must take one more drink and you will be in love with our mescal for life."

José nodded and waved a finger to put the bottle back to my lips. "*Sí*, señor, *un poco más*."

I hesitated and then took a long slug. The kitchen seemed to brighten, as if the sun had become stronger, or the very walls shined of their own accord. I offered the bottle to José. My hand did not shake any longer. He took a strong drink, passed it on to James, and said, "*Ahora eres un hombre, no un niño!*"

"What did he say?" I asked.

James smiled, as if he was embarrassed. "He says I'm a man, now I must drink."

"Well, drink up then, Señor Lee," I said with a bit of a slur.

James guzzled enough for the three of us, then slammed the bottle down on the table. "That's how ya do it, Zeb!"

Francisca picked up the bottle and took a sip. "Is enough for me," she said, smiling.

A loud groan came from the bedroom where Padgett lay. We stared at each other, perhaps forgetting for just a moment, how dire our situation was.

The pot of water continued to boil. José removed more of the dried flowers off the stove, then crushed them. In a bowl, he mixed the powder with the mescal to finish making his salve. I took a small handful of the jimson seeds, and in a glass, smashed them into a pulp, then mixed it with the boiling water, the liquid turning a golden brown.

"James, pull those leaves from the water, quick so's they can become like a wrap." I felt my tongue thick.

I guzzled down more mescal. Francisca pried the bottle from me hands. "No more for you."

My belly started churning. I knew I had enough.

Soon, our medicines were ready. Padgett was steadily groaning as he felt more pain. Outside, the sun waned past the trees. Soon, we would have to light a fire in the front room. José went to fetch lanterns for the evening.

"Shall we move him?" I asked. "This table's large enough. This is where all the butcherin's been done."

Francisca and James agreed. I took the jimson concoction to Padgett. His face had again become drawn and pale.

I handed him the glass. "Here, drink."

He did not question me and slurped it down, then coughed. "What the hell is this?"

"It's gonna help ya, my friend. Now, just lay back and let it kick in." From what little experience I had with doctoring, I figured it might take only ten or so minutes. "You're goin' to a whole, new world, my friend, a place where no one else has been."

Padgett closed his eyes and smiled, for the first time since our arrival to the hunting lodge. "You're taking the rest a' my leg, ain't you?"

"Yes," I said.

I called James and José to help move Padgett into the kitchen, his groaning was certainly better than screaming. A thin trail of blood followed us from the bed to the butcher's block. Francisca covered him with a clean sheet, his infected stump of a leg lying bare. He began to mumble unintelligible words. His eyelids moved, as if his eyeballs rolled side to side, up and down, seeing a world in his mind. I had taken jimson weed. The chances of experiencing a world of pleasure or pain were about even.

"Ready?" Francisca asked.

"No," I said, took another drink of the mescal, and handed her the bottle to clean the skin where I was to cut.

James must have seen my hands shaking, contrary to how much I had to drink. "Shall we try waking the doctor again?"

I shook my head.

I touched Padgett's leg with the saw. He screamed, full-throated, filling the kitchen, the lodge, with a fearful noise that surely Don Padilla could hear at his ranch five miles away. I lifted the saw off Padgett's leg. He continued his bloodcurdling cry.

Footsteps sounded behind me. *"What in hell are you doing!"*

Dr. Bernard stood at the door to the kitchen. *"What the hell, you will kill him if you do that!"* He walked to me and eased the saw from my hand. "Less than thirty seconds, he will have bled to death. Besides, you use a knife to make the first cut, the saw's for cutting through the bone. Hell, you didn't even give him a stick to grit his teeth on."

Padgett continued to cry out. Francisca rinsed a cloth with water and began to soothe him. The doctor stared at me, as if in disbelief that I was actually going to cut the rest of Padgett's leg off. He laid the saw down, bent over, and looked at the infected stump, then stepped to the stove and picked a leaf of the jimson weed out of the water. He touched the last of the dried flowers and said, "You were certainly on the right path." He reached for the bottle of mescal sitting on the butcher's block and started to take a drink, then thought better and set it back down. He picked up the bowl of salve José had concocted, sniffed it, then moved me away and began to slather the edges of the wounds, working his way to covering the whole stump.

"He'll die anyway if we do nothing," I said, feeling angry. "You were doin' nothing . . ."

Dr. Bernard interrupted me. "You've done plenty, my young friend," he said. "The jimson and snakeroot your idea?"

I nodded and then pointed to José.

"Muchas gracias, mi amigo."

Padgett, still with his eyes closed, his eyelids moving less now, whimpered like a baby. Francisca looked to the doctor. "Shall we move him to the bedroom?"

After we carried him back to the bed, José and James left the room. Dr. Bernard sat next to Padgett and finished applying the salve, then wrapped the whole area in jimson leaves. "Give him more of the mescal than the tea." I sat slumped in the chair. He turned and looked me dead in the eye. "You would've killed him, you know. With all you've done, by not cutting him, you may have saved his life."

I shrugged. "Maybe, but we couldn't just let him die on his own."

The doctor nodded and finished wrapping Padgett's stump with the leaves. Francisca brought a clean cloth as a bandage and left us alone. "Let him sleep. If he's not dead by the morning, he will live a good, long life." He sat at the edge of the bed, held his head, and moaned. "Ugh . . . I need water." He coughed, then "How long have I been out?"

"Two days or so."

He sniffed, raised his head, and sniffed again. "I smell chicken shit, do you?"

I smiled. My quick bath must not have been as good as the doctor's keen sense of smell. "Shall we go an' sit in the front room? I can tell ya how James and I came to be here, and you tell me how in hell the three of you came to be in the same damn place as us, aye?"

The doctor smiled and said, "Good to see you alive, my friend."

I nodded. "Yes, sir, it is indeed good to still be livin'. Now, how do we get outta here and find our way back to Sam Houston and his army?"

Chapter 28

Through the cracks of the outhouse, I could see the hunting lodge lit up, with at least one lantern burning in every room. Off the front porch by only a few strides, the Tejano ranch hands had set up camp, with a few chickens run onto a spit and hung over a cooking fire. One of the *vaqueros* strummed a guitar and sang a song, a mournful tune, perhaps reflecting the treacherous times they lived in. Yet, if an army patrol happened by, we were well protected within our disguises, of where our loyalties lay, as long as I was not asked to speak any Spanish.

I finished my duties and sat for a while. The last time I stayed in a privy longer than needed was at Anna and Dr. Keynes's cabin in Missouri. I decided then to go after the men who killed my brother and stole our furs. If I had not made that fateful decision and stayed with them . . . Oh well, *regrets don't lead ya forward, they only try an' take you back to where a man can't go, and livin' in the past can surely get ya killed today.* I listened to the end of the song and then there was silence. *If Dr. Bernard had not awakened . . . Indeed, there might be a God after all.* Sitting alone in the dark, I sighed, and shook my head no. *God sure as hell didn't stop my friends from gettin' shot in the first place, now did he?*

I left the outhouse and walked back inside. With the lantern turned down low, Padgett slept peacefully, his bandages dry and expertly wrapped. Francisca sat in the chair, also asleep. In the light, she did indeed look like an angel, black hair barely pulled away from flush cheeks and closed eyes, her head lowered, hands in her lap with legs spread slightly apart. I stood in the corner and held my breath, watching her breathe.

She awoke, looked directly at me, and smiled, as if she knew all along that I was there watching her. A feeling passed between us, a spark of something more than friendship, more than a simple attraction. Before she turned away to check on Padgett, I saw in her eyes a sense of wanting, a need to be nurtured, and touched, yet disappointment, as if only in another time and place might we grow fond of each other.

She looked back to me. "How long have you been here?"

"Not long . . ."

She lowered her head and brushed the wrinkles out of her dress, then glanced out the open window. "I heard a song, I thought I was dreaming." She began to hum, then sing in Spanish.

She finished, I said, "Beautiful, it sounds sad. As I know *sólo un poco español,* what are the words in English?"

"I will try and translate, however, it may not have the same meaning, for you must know my people."

She leaned back in the chair and closed her eyes.

"I leave my love each day, to work the fields, to plow
the earth,
Covered with sweat and blood, I return each evening
to find her arms open
A warm meal and bed
But tonight, she is gone to the town, and I am alone
with my toils
My love,
Lost in the forest
Lost on the road
Lost in the town
Tomorrow, I go to the fields

And hope she returns home
Back to me . . ."

The whole world seemed hushed by her words and melody, her voice, a sadness only she knew.

Francisca opened her eyes and wiped away tears. "I am sorry, Señor Creed. You have once more caught me off my guard." She again pressed the wrinkles from her dress. Without looking up, she said, "I am that woman."

I stepped to her and offered my hand. She touched my fingers, then slid her palm into mine and rose up out of the chair. We stood facing each other; she smiled and turned away, wiping the last of the tears from her cheek, turned back, and tenderly laid her head on my chest.

"I will never go back," she whispered.

I smoothed her hair and smelled a faint scent of lilac. My hand shook. As much as I willed it to stop, it did not. I tightened my grasp around her waist. She raised her face to mine, and we kissed. I brushed her lower back. She quivered, froze, then pulled me tighter and again, we kissed.

A groan and a cough from the bed reminded me that we were not alone. Padgett sat up and stared at us. "Is the rest a' my leg gone, Zeb?" I am sure he wanted to say more as he witnessed Francisca and I embrace and kiss not two feet from his bed. She let go and left the room as if she were embarrassed.

"What the hell, Zeb?" He feigned anger, but he could not help but smile.

"The doctor stopped me," I said.

"Stopped you from what?"

"Cutting off your leg. Said you would bleed out if I kept on. Caught me just in time, else . . ." I did not need to tell him more. "You're alive is all that matters."

"I do feel much better, the roots and leaves you dug up

must've done some good." Again, he smiled. "You act like the danger a' me dyin' has certainly passed."

I was about to say something in response, when Francisca and Dr. Bernard came into the room. Francisca would not look at me and went straight to Padgett to check his temperature.

"Hi, Doctor, thanks for savin' my life," Padgett said, "I mean, for not letting Ole Zeb here cut off what little leg I have left, would've been a big mistake . . ." To himself, he whispered, *"Thank God."*

Bernard tried to smile with some reassurance. "We'll see tomorrow."

Francisca retired to the other bedroom across from Padgett's; the doctor took up his armchair in the front room. James lay on a blanket on the floor next to the fireplace, I sat in the chair while Padgett slept. The night was quiet with the *Tejanos* settled in. I wanted to smoke but had no tobacco or pipe. I could take a swig from the bottle of mescal that sat on the table next to Padgett's bed. My head still hurt from the drink I had earlier in the day. All I thought about was her kiss. *Damnit, Zeb,* I shook my head. *She ain't that kind a' woman.*

The door to her room opened a crack, then was pulled back. She stood just inside the doorway wearing only her underclothes, and whispered, "Tonight, I will share my bed with you, Zebadiah Creed."

I slowly rose, blew out the lantern, stepped across the hallway into her arms, and shut the door.

Chapter 29

I woke to a scuffle of boots in the hallway, then a knock.

"Zeb?" James asked, with a harder, more urgent bang on the door. "Zeb, if you're in there, you must come out now."

Francisca lay asleep in my arms, naked but for a sheet covering us. She stirred, placed her hand on my chest, and whispered, "What is it?"

"Zeb, I know you're in there, come on out. We need to leave . . . *now*!"

I kissed her hand and forehead. She opened her eyes and smiled. Though my heart was pounding, I did not want to startle her.

There came another bang at the door.

"I'm comin'," I hollered, pulling my arm free. As I stood, she sat up, still covered with the sheet up to her chin, back against the wall and knees drawn to her chest.

I opened the door, enough for James to see my face. He was still clad as a Tejano, a straw hat dangled against his back by a string around his neck, a belt under his sash held a knife and two pistols. At his side was his long rifle. A shooting bag and powder horn hung around his neck.

"A patrol is on their way and they know we're here. We've gotta go, *now.*" He leaned into the doorway to see Francisca sitting on the bed.

"How do you know this?" I asked.

"One of Don Padilla's men rode in from the ranch no more

than a minute ago and said the bastards came back and that they were told by one of his neighbors that we were here." He paused to catch his breath. "An' they're coming for us."

Across the hallway, Dr. Bernard sat in the chair next to Padgett, who appeared to be asleep. Through the window, the sun shone just above the horizon.

I heard footsteps on the porch and into the front room. José appeared at James's side. *"La patrulla está aquí."*

I did not hesitate, for even I knew what he said. "Give me one minute." I shut the door and began gathering my clothes and weapons together. Francisca had not moved. I glanced at her once while I dressed myself. As I tried to tie the sash, she stood to help, quickly double binding the cloth so it would hold two pistols and my knife. I slung the bag with the letters to Austin and Obregon across my shoulders. The hunting rifle I was given still lay in the front room. My only thoughts now were how many caballeros rode our way.

"You cannot fight them, not here," Francisca said, as she pulled on her white skirt. In the morning light, I saw how dingy and stained it was, soaked with the blood of dead men, and the blood of men who would always remember the woman they owed their lives to. The evening before, we lay together, her fearlessness overwhelming, wringing every ounce of breath and sweat from me. Rather than blood, I gave tears, offering up my courage to be loved, and to love her. We held each other, for just one night, as if it was a lifetime.

At that moment, as she stood before me half-naked, I saw her truly afraid.

"I'll fight 'em on the porch if I have to."

"No, you must escape! If General Urrea or the Colonel Portilla find that his caballeros were killed on Don Padilla's land, they will send their army to kill every last Tejano that lives here. All of them."

She was silent for a few seconds. Then, "I was witness to such a thing, southwest of here. Just before we came to Goliad. There was a fight and only three soldados lost their lives. The cost to the owner of the ranchero, Don Rodríguez and his men . . . who had lived there for many, many years." She lowered her head. "Long before the Americans."

If they were intent on killing James and I, they would certainly kill Padgett where he lay, the doctor in his chair, all of Don Padilla's men, and Francisca as she attempted one last time to save us all.

Those murderin' bastards . . . I whispered. *Killin' their own damn folks.*

"And you brought Padgett and Bernard here?"

She looked up with tears in her eyes. "We had nowhere else to go, no other friends to turn to."

Another bang came on the door. "Zeb, the horses are in back and ready."

She pulled on her blouse and I held her one last time. We kissed. She pushed me away. *"You must leave."*

I opened the door and heard the galloping of horses. "What about my friends?"

Bernard still sat with Padgett. "He's taken a bad turn in the night, I'm afraid we cannot move him now, else he will die."

". . . and you, Doctor?"

"They will not kill me, as long as they know who I am." He smiled. "I've saved Mexicans' lives before, I can do it again."

With no more time for words, I faced Francisca.

She grasped my hand. "I will return to my husband, of course." She raised the inside of my palm to her lips, my fingers brushing her wet cheek. With a kiss, she let go and turned away.

I went to fetch the rifle and shooting bag that still lay in the front room. From the Tejano's camp came loud talk, then arguing. I peeked out the window. No farther than four strides away, facing the lodge, sat three caballeros on horseback. As one of them dismounted and walked toward the porch, I stepped into the hallway. Francisca followed me through the kitchen to the back door. Both *vaqueros* offered their horses to James and me.

She stood in the doorway. "I will always remember you, my Zebadiah Creed, *mi amor.*"

James and I mounted the horses. As I glanced to her with a smile, Francisca turned into the kitchen and disappeared.

"Seguir el río de Guadalupe norte," José said, pointing to a narrow road just past the woodpile that vanished into the trees.

Without hesitation, we both kicked our heels, hard, leaving our friends behind.

I could not think that I may never see them again.

We rode through thin forest, headed north to find the Guadalupe River. At a split in the road, we stopped to catch our bearings. The patrol damn near caught up with us. Seemed they knew where we were going, as if someone pointed to them our way, else there was only one true path through those woods to the river and off Don Padilla's land.

We took a blind turn. Across the width of the entire road lay a fallen pine tree. James pulled his horse up to jump, clearing its branches. My horse stumbled, pitching me forward, beyond the tree and onto the road. I kept my knife and bag, but my pistols were thrown several feet and disappeared into tall grass. Three caballeros slowed to a stop and raised their long rifles, pointing them at me. James charged back with a pistol in one hand, and fired. I heard a body hit the ground. The two riders still on their horses shot at James and missed. I stood now, wheezing, with my breath nearly knocked out of me. Black gun smoke roiled over the broken tree limbs, sending me to coughing. I hobbled up the road to find my thrown weapons. The first pistol I picked up had lost its prime. I could not find the other one. I stepped back toward the tree with my knife pulled. A caballero barreled his horse over its branches straight at me, his lance raised. I stepped aside, grabbed the shaft of the weapon, and yanked, pulling the rider from his horse. He landed on his feet running, wrenched the lance from my hands, and shoved me backward into a ditch at the side of the road. The caballero was upon me with his blade raised.

Shhh-boom! The man's left shoulder exploded from the front with a ball shot through, splattering me with his blood, and spinning him away. He cradled the lance in his right hand, and staggered toward James, now standing no more than two strides away. Dropping his long rifle to the road, James reached for a pistol tucked in his belt.

The caballero stopped. Blood seeped from the small hole in his back shoulder. *"Chico, no me has matado antes, y ahora tampoco podras . . ."*

James hesitated, looked at me, then to him, and said, "I ain't a little boy." He stepped back and aimed at the man's chest.

From behind the fallen tree, a click sounded. The third caballero stood with his rifle laid up on a branch aimed straight at James. With the second click, I pulled my knife. Fear and rage sent me to screaming, running at him. His rifle fired as he swiveled toward me. I leaped over the tree's branches, knife raised. I pierced the man's neck, cracking his collarbone, and sank the blade to its hilt. The caballero was dead before my knife slid from his body.

Shhh-boom!

James held out his smoking pistol, still aimed at the man who wavered before him. The lance tipped forward, then slipped through his fingers to the ground. He took one step toward James and fell.

I walked back from the tree, and with my friend, rolled over the dead caballero. It was then that I recognized him from the massacre, with a freshly healed scar on his face.

Son of a bitch, always comes back around . . .

"He would have killed you, Zeb."

"Yep, as he would have you."

"Should've killed him before," James said.

We gathered our weapons, mounted our horses, and rode some ways farther to find the rushing Guadalupe River, then headed north on the trail I had ridden down from Gonzales to Goliad, where no more than three weeks before, I had saved that woman's life.

And her mule.

Chapter 30

Groce Plantation, April 1836

The ferryman sat on the edge of his dock, staring out across the river, west toward the setting sun. The wood planks were scorched by fire. The flat-bottomed barge lay a few strides downriver, splayed out, half in water and half on the shore, burned, chopped to pieces, as if ten men came and hacked it apart with axes. The knotted rope that allowed the man for years to carry so many folks across the river had been cut, pulled from the far-side pulley, and left trailing in the water to disappear downstream.

"They burned my barge an' burned my home."

James and I sat on our horses, on shore.

He turned and nodded. "I 'member you. Both of ya. Yer dress don't mean nothin', I 'member your faces, and eyes, and words, and whatcha did. An' you . . ." He glanced up at James. ". . . puked on my boat." He looked at me. "And you asked what day it was, with the bells ringin', it's Sunday, lookin' for the big fella. Hell, I 'member ever body I take 'cross this river, ever body."

"How long ago?" I asked.

"Least a week." The ferryman's appearance, his thin and haggard look, was as if for all this time he sat on the dock in desolation, not moving but to fish water from the river to drink.

I looked back up the slope toward where the town once stood. "Who burned it?"

"General Houston."

"Hmm . . ."

"Wasn't two days later, the whole damn Mexican army come through, built their own barges an' boats an' crossed. I stood right over there an' watched 'em. They didn't care whether I lived or died. Their general rode the boat over as if he was George Washington. He come ashore, looked at me, an' saluted, an' rode right on through the burned-up town like it was nothin', an' was gone."

"How long you been sittin' on this dock?" James asked.

He shook his head. "Since that day, I suppose."

After refusing what little food we could offer, we left him there alone, watching the twilight disappear into the night.

"Houston burned Gonzales down to the ground?"

Deaf Smith rode beside me on his horse. "No, sir, *we* burned it down."

James and I had been overtaken by Deaf and his two men, on the road to Burnham's Crossing, not far from where Grainger had built his fire. Thinking we might be spies for Santa Anna, they lay in hiding, then stepped from the pines with their rifles pointed straight at us. When he saw beyond our disguises, I had never seen a smile so broad as his.

Five days and nights we rode north along the Guadalupe River, hiding from small, Mexican patrols and entire armies it seemed, on the march east. Some folks we saw on the run, mostly women and children, in wagons carrying their meager belongings, in a panic to get to the border and over into Louisiana and the United States. We saw no Tejanos, only white patrioteers unsettled from their new way of living on this Mexican frontier of Texas.

Now, we rode east with my friend Deaf, to join Houston.

"Did ya burn all the farms and ranches we passed on our

way here?" I asked.

Deaf shook his head. "I'm supposin' the Mexican army done that, after they stole everything they could to eat an' drink. Listen, if we hadn't burned the town, that damn Santa Anna would have been better off. The general an' I couldn't sit well with that happenin'."

"The general . . . how is he?" I did not ask whether he had raised his army for fear of becoming more sorely disappointed and morose than I already was.

Smith took his time answering. "He is under the gun. Some men call him a coward for his constant retreat. A few others, very few like myself, understand why he moves the way he does. We will not be caught again in a corner."

"So, he has raised an army . . ."

"Yes, sir, last count more than twelve hundred men. More showin' up every day. Most good men, some rascals that cause him trouble, rarin' to fight but ain't ready."

I sat back in my saddle, somewhat relieved, yet still anxious as hell. "Ya know Santa Anna's got three or more armies headed this a way with more than twelve hundred soldados each. That ain't countin' the caballeros."

Deaf nodded and smiled. "Yes, sir, I know, an' I know where they all are, most of 'em anyway. Seems they're all split up an' goin' ever which a way. Santa Anna, he's headed south an' whether he knows or not, straight into the swamps." He wore a big grin. "An' that's where we'll take him."

We rode slow, taking our time up the road. The more talk, the more anxious I grew. "How are we able to ride in the open, with armies all around?"

"Hell, they're all scattered out ahead of us, not around. You forget, Zebadiah Creed, my spies are everywhere."

"Does one happen by the name of Obregon?"

"How in hell do you know him?" he asked.

"Your memory is short, my friend. We first met at the, as you say, damnedest poker game you ever played in, with Bowie losin' an' Grainger winnin' his land?"

"Yes, sir, I remember . . . him and Grainger rode together back from Goliad to tell the tale of nearly bein' captured and runnin' out before. Later, we found out from one of Horton's riders all about losin' the battle at Coleto Creek . . ." He stopped his horse. "I expect you fellas can tell a tale a might closer to the truth than Grainger or Obregon?"

James began to speak, then lowered his head. "They killed 'em all and burned 'em."

"Who killed who, son?"

"The Mexican soldiers. Lined us up one morning and . . ."

The dark skin of Deaf's face turned pale. "How many?"

"Shot all of them but us, an' a handful of others."

"Son, I need to know how many men ya figure were killed."

"More than three hundred," I said, as matter-a'-fact as I could.

Deaf's face turned from pale to red, his eyes grew watery. "Son of a bitch . . ." Using the back of his filthy hand, he wiped the tears away. "How'd you fellas escape?"

"We ran to the bluff of the river an' jumped."

He stared at James, then me with a look of disbelief. His eyes hardened to anger, then softened, with some sense of commiseration.

"Ya know, it will be the two of you that tell the tale."

Deaf Smith turned his horse and with a swift kick, headed up the road. "Houston and the army's camped on Groce's plantation, we can be there by tomorrow. Fellas, we ride hard so keep up!"

Chapter 31

Most of the small villages and homesteads we rode through to Burnham's Crossing and on to Groce's plantation were deserted of both animals and people. Houses were abandoned with front doors left wide open. One such house we stopped at still had plates of food left on the supper table, gotten to by critters and the crows. Barns were either burned down along with the stores contained within, or stripped of their boards, most likely for firewood, leaving only a skeleton of a frame. Once, at the side of the road, we came upon a fat hog, its throat cut and left to bleed into the weeds and muck. By the rancid smell, it had been dead for several days. I thought, what a shame to waste all that good meat. Riding past, I felt the brush of buzzards' wings as they took flight. When we stopped to rest, the silence of the land was deafening. If Santa Anna and his armies were near, they were not making a sound. Deaf said all the people had scattered east toward the border. I spoke of the panicked folk trying to get across the rain-swollen Guadalupe and how I saved a woman from drowning. He gave a slight nod and rode on, hardly acknowledging my heroism. I followed in silence, embarrassed that I made such a deal of an act that most anyone else would naturally do, especially with Deaf, after all he had seen and done.

As we approached Burnham's Crossing, where I first met General Houston, I expected to find an army. We found the same open, empty field, this time trampled and muddy, with cold campfires scattered about, as if a thousand men had made camp and then abandoned the site for safer ground. Deaf guided us down to the shore to rest, near where barely a month before, the general and I had skipped rocks across the Colorado. This was the place where I shared my secrets with a man who seemed to understand my plight, as a warrior and son, fallen from grace and family shamed. I wanted to heed General Houston's kind words, that I had come far and would go farther still with many chances for redemption. Though on this day, standing between Deaf and James, all I felt was a deep, bitter hatred, toward Santa Anna and his armies, toward General Urrea for his betrayal, and toward myself for being taken in by my own willfulness and pride.

My heart burned.

James picked up a rock and skipped it out across the water. He laughed as it hopped eight times to plop into the river near the opposite shore. At that moment, staring at the young man, I wished to have his mettle, his liveliness to laugh about a simple thing as throwing a rock.

He must have noticed my look of envy.

"My daddy taught me," he said, and turned away.

With Deaf perhaps knowing the ferry was broken and no longer of use, we mounted our horses and forded at a narrow, shallow crook in the Colorado River and rode on. Evening came, we camped in the pines just off the road, without fire. Up at dawn the next morning, we were on our way at a full gallop.

The spring aroma of freshly turned soil filled my nose. Through the trees that lined the road, I glimpsed open fields, furrowed, black dirt, with negro women shouldering hang bags, bent over planting a new crop. Scattered about these fields sat a few men on horseback. I thought this strange as to how close our enemy was supposed to be. *Had we traveled all the way to Louisiana?* As I pulled up to ask Deaf about this, we rounded a bend and there before us, down a slope to a wide swath of bottomland next to the Brazos River, lay Houston's army.

Tents were scattered along a road that wound with the shore of the river, stretching north and around a bend. Some of the tents were bunched together, as if tribes had gathered to be a part of the army, yet needed to remain separate, individual from one another. Some flew flags of the different militias. Most camps flew a blue flag with one, yellow star in the middle. I was reminded of the few rendezvous I had attended as a trapper, along the Platte River, and earlier, when the bands of the Lakota Nation gathered on the north plains.

The smell of roasted beef mixed with smoke from the campfires made my stomach growl something fierce. I was hungry!

We entered the camps, the road muddy, puddles of stink water stood everywhere, as if it had rained for days with no letup. Deaf was greeted warmly with a few men giving cheers. While still in our disguises, James and I were looked upon with fear and suspicion, as if we might be captured spies. I pushed the wide hat off to hang at my back. As James did the same, he was the first to be recognized, by a man I knew well.

"I'll be damned if it isn't James Lee!" said Colonel J. C. Neill, sounding much more confident than the last I saw him the night before I left Gonzales for Goliad.

We pulled our horses to a stop. Colonel Neill and a crowd gathered around us. They were ragged-looking men wearing torn, filthy clothes. Some of their jackets resembled uniforms, most did not. James and I dismounted, our boots sinking into the mud, and stood together holding the reins of our horses; the crowd shambled in tighter. James inched closer to me. Deaf jumped to the ground and eased the men back to give us a bit of breathing room.

"I hear tell these fellas have been through quite a torment,"

Deaf said, glancing at the both of us, then back to the men. "You'll hear their tales in due time. Now where's the general, we must give him our reports."

One fellow spat on the ground and said, "The son-a-bitch . . . I mean, General Houston's in his tent over yonder by the river. For days we been a marchin' and a standin' tall in the goddamn rain, hardly no shootin'. Then he comes out late at night I hear, and . . . then he's fumblin' and a bumblin', if ya get my meaning."

I laid a hand on my knife and thought, *he's allowed to disrespect the general like this?*

Colonel Neill stepped forward to the man. "How dare you slander our general! The fact is, if anyone else says words like this about our commanding officer, well, sir . . ." He trailed off and pushed his way through the crowd to James and me. "I'll take you to him, gentlemen."

Deaf went up to the man and grabbed a handful of his right ear and twisted. The poor fellow yelped like a dog and took to his knees. "If ya ever . . ." Deaf said, and let go, leaving him kneeling in the mud, then leaned down to face him. "Turn you into a soldier yet."

We followed Neill, past camp after camp of frontiersmen, farmers, and townsmen. They had fared no better than the men I knew in Goliad, yet their eyes held a spark, a bit of fire to carry them on, something my friends had lost after the surrender at Coleto Creek. I saw no Tejanos or negros, the ones in this fight were all white men, their faces lined with grim resolve, willing to die for a piece of land, for a freedom and well-being they seemed not to find while living in America. As we walked past, I could see in their eyes the desperate need to fight for a cause they could easily lose, a cause I still did not understand.

Yet, their commander continued to retreat, to run away from the fight, away from their slim chance for freedom.

This they did not understand.

As we rode to greet Houston, Neill explained how some men were sick, bad water, he supposed. Most of the ill had been taken across the river to a camp near Groce's plantation. I decided then I would not be drinking any of the water.

The general's tent was set a few strides from the river, away from the rest of his army, guarded by two young men. Both looked familiar. Neill nodded to them and one entered the tent. The other stared at me, then said, "You don't remember me, do you?"

I looked hard at the soldier, one of the few in an actual uniform. I did know him. He looked older, though it had only been weeks since the last I saw him. "I'll be damned. Yes, you're Dick Scurry, the general's cook!"

"You survived."

I was taken aback by his statement. "You mean Goliad? Yes, I survived, James and I."

"And my brother, you helped my brother escape." His eyes welled with tears. "My brother is alive, as you promised."

The tent flap was jerked back, and Scurry's brother, Will, stepped forward, the boy Francisca pulled from the line of doomed men. Lost in our desperate attempt to save Padgett's life, I never knew what happened to him. I never thought to ask how she succeeded in keeping him alive. He seemed to recognize James and tried to smile, but only for a brief second, then gave a look of deep pain. James did not acknowledge him at all and turned away.

Both were about the same age, yet James had grown older in the last couple of months, wearing a weariness he perhaps would never lose.

Behind Will stood General Houston, in full uniform. From inside the tent came a woman's voice, though I could not understand her mumblings.

"There's Mama's horse," James said, pointing to a large, sky-grey mare staked to the ground behind the tent.

Houston gave us a sheepish smile and stepped into the sunlight of the afternoon. "Her name is Saracen. A fine horse she is." He lay a hand on the younger Scurry's shoulder to steady himself, and then let go.

James looked confused. "But Grainger . . ."

I shook my head, to let him know that this was not the time for an explanation.

The general stood, as if he wanted us to say or do something. He had changed, he now carried a sense of foreboding, a gauntness to his features, as if he knew all too well that he alone carried the weight of this war on his shoulders.

Dick Scurry leaned into me. "He expects a salute, sir."

I reluctantly did what he asked, as did James. Though with both of us not being true soldiers and unwilling to lower ourselves too far below another, our salutes were less than half-hearted. Especially with what we had been through.

"Sir, do you remember me?" I asked.

"Why, yes, yes, I do. You are the messenger that took my orders to Colonel Fannin." He paused, as if to recollect any conversations we may have had. "You're a friend of Grainger's."

"Yes, sir, I am. We have just come from Goliad . . . sir. Do you not know what has happened there?"

Deaf Smith must have been standing behind us and stepped up beside James and me. "General, we are here to give you our reports, sir."

Upon seeing Deaf, General Houston's eyes lit up and he offered a genuine smile. "My friend! How are things in the field? I need to know where the fiend is. Last we knew, he headed south to Harrisburg, is this still true?" He gazed beyond us, as if he were examining his whole army. His shoulders slumped back to where they were. "I have had a vision, that we shall meet Santa

Anna on the battlefield south of Harrisburg. In the swamps, there will be no escape for him and his armies. Yet, I know that . . . we are not yet ready for a victory."

Deaf nodded. "Yes, sir, you've shared this with me. And I have good news from my spies, he's split his armies and is indeed headin' to Harrisburg an' the gulf, chasin' after those bastards in the government. A small regiment he has. All we have to do is go an' get him."

General Houston turned his gaze to me. "And what of Fannin?"

I could not keep my eyes with his. "Colonel Fannin is . . . dead, sir."

"And his men?"

"Dead, sir. Except for only a handful."

He looked at Will Scurry, laid a hand back on his shoulder to again steady himself, and asked, "Did you know this?"

The boy began to tremble and did not answer.

"My brother doesn't talk anymore," said Dick Scurry.

Houston removed his hand and said, "Ah, yes, of course you did. I remember now." He seemed lost by his own answer, affected by the boy's condition.

Deaf nodded to James and me. "These two will tell the tale of Goliad."

A whistle blew. A steamboat whistle, an unmistakable sound that echoed through the camp. I had not heard this since myself and the Greys boarded a steamer that carried us from the schooner *Columbus,* up the Brazos to off-load at Brazoria and on to San Antonio. Though this was only seven months prior, it seemed a lifetime ago.

Houston wore a broad grin. "Yes, yes, transportation is here, finally. Sergeant Scurry, go and tell my colonels to make ready to cross this damn river, for we head east and south by the morrow!"

Houston turned and was about to enter his tent.

"Sir," I said. "I have a couple a' things left to discuss. I carry two letters from a certain Don Juan Antonio Padilla, one to a Stephen Austin and the other to Alexandros Robito Obregon."

He stared at me for a long second. "Both are gone, I'm afraid. Mr. Austin is in New Orleans and . . . Deaf, where is your man Obregon?"

Deaf Smith shrugged and did not answer.

I felt the cold shoulder from both of them.

"Ah, once a messenger, always a messenger, aye Mr. Creed?" Houston said.

I did not understand why our conversation had suddenly turned sour, as if he were subtly mocking me.

"One more question, sir. Where is Grainger?"

Houston stepped away from the tent and pointed across the river to a building, a large wood house with two imposing fireplaces set on a bluff overlooking the entire river basin we stood in.

"Jarod Groce's plantation house. He calls it the Bernardo Plantation. For God's sake, I don't know why. An old friend, as he and his son have been gracious enough to give up his land for our camp. Of course, it is he who we fight for, Mr. Creed. For him and the other cotton growers." He paused, then said, "Grainger is there, and has been for a week. Took the ferry over upon Groce's invitation."

I stared at the house and other buildings strewn along the bluffs of the river and remembered the negros in the field earlier in the morning.

"Tonight, I will dine with Texas aristocracy," the general said. "Though I am not looking forward to being brow-beaten by them. I would like for you and your young friend to join me. There, you may tell your tale of Goliad."

He turned to his tent, pulled back the flap, and disappeared.

I never saw the woman nor heard her speak again.

As the steamer took its berth, the soldiers of the camp began preparing to cross the river, east to find Santa Anna.

I crossed the Brazos to find Grainger and to ask him about those damn cows I was supposed to be helping him with.

CHAPTER 32

The two-wheeler was a wreck. It still floated, listing slightly to starboard, with holes blown through its walls by what appeared to be rifle shots and at least one cannon blast. Smaller than the liners cruising the Mississippi, this steamboat was made to navigate a twisting river like the Brazos, so narrow in some places that if folks on each side of the boat were to reach past the rails at the same time, they would touch overhanging trees. The steamer first berthed on the eastern shore, below the plantation house, to off-load two cannons. Dick Scurry said they were a gift from the city of Cincinnati. I had no idea why the folks there would invest in such expensive pieces and deliver them here to help us fight the Mexican army. Whatever the reason, I was grateful, as was everyone else who cheered their arrival.

Houston and I stood at the veranda rail gazing down to the crowded deck below, his mare tied to a post where he could keep constant watch on her care. With James standing by the horse, I believe the general now understood from where Grainger had gotten the animal. He did not say a word to the young man about their trade or why.

I still wore my Tejano clothes and he wore his uniform, along with a hat like Fannin's, without the feather.

"Mr. Creed, I owe you an apology," the general said.

I wondered, *what was he apologizing for, sending me to try and persuade a madman to change his course, to retreat, maybe saving the lives of all those men? For acknowledging me as only his messenger boy?* The very fact that we even stood side by side crossing the river together was not by my accord, but by his.

Earlier in the day, James and I had left his tent, leaving Deaf alone with him, and followed Neill to his camp. We were greeted warmly by four of his men lounging by a fire. Two I recognized from my brief stay in Gonzales. James knew them all. With skewered chunks of beef sizzling just beyond the flames and turnips buried in the coals, we shared quite the noonday feast. As we finished our meal, Dick Scurry appeared, requesting our presence to accompany General Houston on the excursion across the river and the general wanted James to personally escort his horse to ensure her safety. After leaving our earlier conversation in such dire limbo, I was shocked at the offer. However, I told Scurry to tell the general we would be honored.

Now standing next to Houston, overlooking what had become a floating exodus of anxious, desperate men, I sensed a confidence in him I had not witnessed earlier in the day, that by the steamboat arriving just in time, this was a sign to move toward the fight rather than run. Yet, there still seemed a deep lack of self-assurance in his broad decisions, that he was simply wandering the countryside dragging his army along with him, hoping for a break in his luck.

"Apology for what?" I asked.

"Why, for disrespecting you in front of Deaf and those two young brothers . . ."

I thought, *this is what he thinks he needs to apologize for?*

"And Colonel Neill?"

"Yes, yes, of course, him as well." Houston seemed annoyed by the mention of the man's name. He pulled a small bottle from his jacket and took a drink without offering any.

We watched as two reluctant oxen were led from shore, up the ramp and onto the steamboat. Placing them near Houston's horse was not an ideal location and James let the men who handled the animals know this. Houston hollered down, ordering them to move the damn oxen outboard and away from his horse. By doing so, the starboard list grew worse. I thought, *Why the hell don't they move 'em to the other side of the boat?* But then, with the several hundred men already crammed aboard, there was no way to herd the frightened animals through the crowd and passageways without causing a great commotion. James glanced up to me and the general and shook his head with exasperation.

Two blasts of the whistle from the pilothouse and the steamboat was underway. The dual paddlewheels strained as steam from the boiler pushed through heated pipes to move us away from the bank against the swift current of the river, stirring up silt, turning the water brown. The captain had tried to stop the flow of passengers after a certain number boarded, knowing the weight limit of his boat, but to no avail. Those anxious to cross the river would not be stopped. We were to travel upstream in an arc and use the river's downstream flow, allowing us to catch the landing on the far side. The pilot and captain had already accomplished this several times that day, twice with tremendous difficulty. Once, the landing was missed all together and the pilot had to swing back to the western shore and cross again. These boats were made to plow the waters up and downstream, not traverse from one side of the river to the other.

Houston continued to gaze down at James and the horse. "What is the boy's story?"

"He joined me and Grainger east of San Antonio, his mama sent him to find his papa. I left him in Gonzales to go and find you and met him again in Goliad."

"Did he find his father?"

For a few long seconds, I did not answer. As simple as the

answer was, I struggled to find the words. Jacob was not only James's father, he was my friend. "Yes, sir . . ."

"Why is he not here with us today?"

"He's dead, sir."

Houston lowered his head. "I see."

He continued to stare down at James. The lump in my throat grew larger.

"How did he die?"

"Shot by a Mexican soldier, savin' his son's life."

"How many more men were killed?"

"Oh, about four hundred, sir, lined up an' shot. Those who weren't dead were stabbed to death. All of 'em were piled up an' burned."

I seemed to have grown to feel too casual the more times I told the story, as if the words themselves carried me a little farther away from the horrors of that day. The fact was, I conversed with such ease and no emotion so as not to fall into tears.

"Fannin. The son of a bitch disobeyed my order to retreat," Houston said, as if to himself.

"Yes, sir, at first anyway. When we did leave the mission, it was too late, and the Mexican army caught us in a field. We . . ." I swallowed, "surrendered."

"Surrendered," he repeated, with a sneer. Then said, "Continue."

"They marched us back to the mission an' confined us for nearly a week. I had made a deal with the general to spare our lives, but he was called away. Somebody else was put in charge, and . . . one morning, they marched us out onto three different roads, tellin' us we were sailin' back to America, and . . ."

Houston interrupted me, his hands gripping the rail, making fists. "What deal?"

This should not have been a surprise, him asking about how

I might have come close to saving all those men. "I offered to give up my knife, Bowie's knife, to the general in charge, in exchange for our freedom. He was a collector of sorts, knowin' the value of the blade." The more I talked, the more I realized how foolish I must have sounded.

He glanced to the sash that held the weapon at my waist. "Your deal did not hold."

"No, sir, it did not."

There was a silence between us. His lips moved, as if he were swallowing the words I said, trying to answer questions that only he, as a general, a leader of men, might want to ask, but never would. Except for perhaps General Urrea himself, there was no one to provide him answers.

He took in a long breath, then, "And . . . how did you and the boy escape?"

"Slipped through a brush hedge, ran to the river, an' jumped. Hell, James couldn't even swim. I had to hold him under 'til they stopped shootin' at us, an' far enough away . . . to crawl out of the water." I closed my eyes. When I opened them, Houston was staring at me.

"You saved that boy's life."

I did not move, except to the rhythm of the steamboat.

"Look at me, son."

I caught his gaze.

"Sometimes, that's all we get to do."

I took a deep breath and glanced down at James, standing idly next to his mother's horse. Anything the general might say to comfort me was, in my mind, for naught. Though in my heart, I knew he was right.

There came a commotion below us, on the main deck. It appeared that one of the oxen had inched farther outboard, pushing against the main rail, causing the steamboat to tilt even more to starboard. With water splashed up on the deck and weighing over a thousand pounds, the second ox could not hold its place and slid into the other, shattering the rail and sending both into the river to vanish underwater. Only one popped up downriver. With a weak bellow, the ox sank.

No men were lost.

I shook my head and thought, *didn't see that comin'*.

"You goddamn louts!" General Houston shouted. "Did I not tell you to move those dumb animals and now we have no means of pulling our supply carts." He pointed to the man who let go of the harness, saving his own life. "You there, I will see you stand tall in front of me as soon as we disembark, you hear me?"

The poor soldier saluted and disappeared into the interior of the boat.

"Now, what were we discussing? Ah yes, Goliad and your escape . . . I want to know more; however, as we close in on the shore, I must be the first off the boat. We will continue this talk soon, aye?"

How quick Houston's temper had flared, from such a calm, intimate conversation we were having to an instant rage and back to calm, as if nothing happened. And with a casual shrug, he was gone, down to James and his horse.

Judith Ann Lee's horse.

As the steamboat landed, Houston attempted to mount the animal. She was not having it and reared up, nearly throwing the general backwards into the crowd of men behind him. James grabbed the reins, settled her, and began walking the general and the horse toward the shore. Houston would not have that. He jerked the reins back and tried again to leave the steamboat on his own. The horse bucked and finally, he dismounted. General Houston walked down the ramp in front of James and the mare. The clops of hooves echoed throughout the interior of the steamer muffled only by the press of men following from behind.

Watching this from the rail of the veranda, I was one of the last left on the boat. I lost them both in the crowd of horses and men, only to catch glimpses as they climbed up the steep road to the plantation proper.

In that moment, I felt alone, and not so sure I wanted to carry on, to continue this crusade toward the kind of freedom I was beginning to suspect most of these men wanted. A man laden with fears of losing something he had yet to gain, in my accord, would never be free. And . . . I was not so sure of their leader, one who constantly smelled of whiskey, driven to overwhelm his own self-doubt by leading others farther into the swamps, to kill a murderer who most likely had already defeated him. Yet, I was also under his spell as were all those other men, in a more unique way perhaps, with him able to talk to me as if I was his son, caring about my truth.

The truth was, my heart still burned for revenge, for lost friends and dead warriors.

I lifted my left hand off the rail. It did not shake.

Near the crest of the bluff, just as they were about to vanish over the top, James stopped and waved, motioning me to follow. I hesitated, then offered my response.

The crew of the steamboat bid me a farewell as I stepped off the deck onto the ramp and down to the shore.

Freedom ain't what ya think, it's what ya do.

CHAPTER 33

They were the blackest damn cannons I had ever seen, set side by side in front of the plantation house, pointed east, ready to be manned and fired. *Make sure they have plenty of water to cool those barrels,* I thought, as General Houston and his colonels gathered around them. Two gentlemen had traveled all the way from Cincinnati to make a formal presentation to the brave men of the revolution. I stood aside, watching the ceremony with Grainger. It was good to again be in his company.

"I hate cannons," I muttered under my breath.

Grainger responded with a chuckle. "These goobers don't know nothin' 'bout 'em. Can't see how they ever busted anything up shooting them, much less killed a man, or a hundred."

I looked at Grainger sideways and wondered how many men he had seen lying dead, blown apart by a cannonball. I shrugged and did not say anything in response.

Two women sat on the porch of the house, a mother and her daughter perhaps, in rocking chairs, not paying much attention to the escapades going on in front of them. Instead, they seemed to be sewing squares of fabric together into bags. I could not tell what they were for. Except for the quiet conversation between them, it was as if they were mere fixtures on the porch.

An older gentleman stepped in front of both barrels, faced the audience, his arms and hands held behind his back, and nodded to the men from Cincinnati. "I would like to thank these two fine gentlemen, who traveled all these arduous miles to provide us with another aspect of support we have throughout America, and beyond, for a cause held so deep in the hearts of men, to fight for a freedom from tyranny and injustice, so we may build a republic based on the equal rights of all God-fearing men," he paused and smiled, "and growing in this here fertile land, king cotton."

Most of his audience applauded. A few, myself and Houston's officers included, stood with their arms crossed showing no reaction.

"Who is he?" I asked Grainger.

"Why, partner, he's Jarod Groce, our guest and the original owner of this here land you're standin' on."

I spat, and again mumbled under my breath. "Ain't nobody owns the land."

I knew Grainger heard me for it was his turn to glance my way and say nothing.

Groce made way for General Houston. He stood tall against the backdrop of his two new weapons. "I would like to say thank you on behalf of my men, dead and still livin', to help us go and fight that son of a bitch Santa Anna and win this war."

All his officers cheered. It seemed that a trip across the river in a steamboat had changed their hearts and minds about the general and his leadership abilities. The other men who had accompanied the two upriver, whom I suspected by the look of their impeccable dress were politicians, stood in silence with frowns upon their faces. Their perfectly cut coats and the finest of beaver top hats reminded me of the men who populated Sophie le Roux's bordello in New Orleans. I took an instant disliking to them all.

Houston continued. "I have decided to offer one of my men the responsibilities of manning these fine cannons." And with a bit of a smirk, he asked Colonel Neill to join him. "Sir, I offer you a commission as the officer in charge of artillery." As soon as he said this, he gave Neill a quick handshake. Before Neill could offer a word of thanks, Houston pulled away and turned his back on him, the ceremony over.

"Whew there, partner. What the hell did the colonel do to Houston?" Grainger asked.

"I don't know. Whatever it was, it pissed him off good." I turned to ask him about his cows, our cows, when he walked over and shook hands with Groce, congratulating him for giving such a great speech. Grainger then followed Houston, Groce, and his entourage into the plantation house. I shrugged and went to find James.

The folks who fled their homesteads and villages for fear of the oncoming Mexican army, those who could not continue east, on to Nacogdoches and the Louisiana border, eased their journey at the open gates of Groce's plantation. One hundred or more, mostly women and children, filled chicken yards and nooks between the several barns, warehouses, and stables scattered throughout the property; some had fires, some did not. With what little belongings they had brought with them, they raised blankets and burlap bags for shelter. The plantation had become a place of refuge.

I passed a small camp next to the pig troughs. The smell of shit nearly bowled me over. Yet a mother and her three young daughters kneeled in silence beside a small fire. One of the girls stirred a pot hanging from a tripod of what looked like boiling gruel. The mother presented a wooden cup and dipped it into the thin porridge. She smiled as she gently held a hand against her youngest daughter's cheek and offered up sips, then wiped the corners of her mouth with the hem of a filthy dress. The child gave a smile back to her mother. As I continued to stare, they turned to me and the woman frowned. I lowered my head and moved on in search of James.

He stood overlooking a fence, staring down into a stand of maybe ten, one-room shacks. A communal area offered a large fireplace for cooking, with rough, hand-shorn tables scattered about. It being close to suppertime, a couple of old, negro women tended the fire. One of them opened an iron door on the side of the fireplace, and with a whoosh, let out a cloud that within seconds drifted up to James and me. I had never smelled anything so unique, so delicious, a sweet smoke I could taste. A couple of men carrying scatterguns wandered close to where we were, stood watching us, then walked down to the shacks and began unlocking padlocks, pulling chains from across the doors, and spooling them on the narrow porches. A chill went up my spine as I heard the clinks and rings echo up from the holler. I thought I had forgotten the sounds from being locked in the stockade. Out the doors, one by one, there stepped as many as thirty blinking, negro men and boys, onto porches, then to the common tables. Within seconds, a whiff of ancient soil and sweat mixed with the sweet smell of the beef, reminding me of another place, the plantation where I helped steal away three slaves and saved a man's life from burning to death. Broussard's plantation. That time and place was so far away from where I stood this day.

At the opposite end of the paddock, a gate opened and in streamed field women, their shoulders slumped and wearied, leaving their empty hang bags on a large table along the fence. They slowly joined the men. The older women dished out stew and tore chunks of beef from the smoker for everyone. After saying a prayer, they all began eating.

"Why were they locked up?" James asked.

"They're slaves."

"Yes, but why are they locked in their homes?"

I shook my head for I could not answer. The shacks had no windows, to let in fresh air and let out the stink. To have no freedom to feel the breeze, to see the green leaves of trees only once a day, bound up in chains, gave no hope of a life worth living. Yet, there they sat, with solemn dignity and grace, in prayer. I would not be so submissive and would most likely be dead.

We stood awhile, watching them eat. The overwhelming smell of the smoked meat reminded me that we had not eaten since noon. The men with guns leaned against the closed gate for a few minutes, then walked down through the tables and up to us.

"You goddamn Tejanos speak English?"

I looked at James and realized that we were still dressed in our disguises. "Yes, sir, we do," I said. "And we ain't Tejanos."

The man who spoke slammed the butt end of his gun against the wooden fence where James stood. "Move on. Ain't nothin' here for ya."

We both stepped back a foot. The fence being solid slats and painted black, we could only see their head and shoulders, as was the same for them looking at us.

"Once, I burned down some pieces of shit shacks like ya have here . . . an' freed a mama and her two sons." I stared straight at the son of a bitch.

The man growled and leveled his scattergun at my head. The other fellow did the same to James.

"Now, git, else you two'll feel the whip a' the overseer, or worse, same as these niggers you starin' at."

I slowly raised my hands above my head and took another short step backward, away from the fence and the two guns. James did the same, then pulled a pistol and aimed it at the head of the man standing in front of him. I lowered my hands, pulled both my pistols, and aimed them low at the two fellows. With the fence between us, they could not see them.

"I have gone against better men than you," James said, "I'm here standing, and they ain't."

"Son, I will blow your head clean off before you can even cock that pistol."

"Hold on, hold on!" I hollered. "We ain't here to hurt nobody. Fact is, we're here as guests of Master Groce, an' he would not take too kindly to you killin' him. Now this here young man has killed his fair share a' Mexicans, just in the last couple a' weeks. An' when he says he ain't afraid a' killin' you, nor dyin', well, sir, he's certainly telling the truth. Another fact is, with these two pistols I hold in my hand aimed at both your guts, at least one of ya's gonna die if we all go to shootin'. And you better believe my pistols are cocked."

There was a silence between us as the two clods decided what they wanted to do. Folks had gathered, standing on the far side of James and me, making sure not to be caught in a crossfire.

"Lower your pistols an' we'll lower these here scatterguns," said one of the men.

"You go first," I said. James and I held our pistols steady.

"Drop it, son. Nobody needs to die today, not for this," I whispered.

James slowly lowered his weapon, as did I and the other two. We turned on them and began walking past the crowd.

"I'm glad ya didn't cock that damn pistol," I said. "We'd be carryin' your body back to your mama's."

His face turned red and he did not say a word.

A young negro, the age of nine or ten, wearing black, shiny shoes, black pants and jacket with a clean, white smock, came running up to us. "Mista Creed, Mista James, Masta want both of ya's back to the big house. Miss Myra'll meetcha at the kitchen an' has new clothes for ya ta wear for supper. Yes, sir, ya must be quick, Missy don't cater much to dilly-dallying." And he made off without catching his breath, then looked back to see if we followed. "Say the masta, you's both heroes!" he hollered and ran back through the refugees.

The folks who stood before us parted way, their surprised looks turning into stares of apprehension. I shrugged and followed James through the crowd to the plantation house, wondering how much trouble it might have been if we had killed one or both of the master's slave keepers.

Both would've died from livin' a corrupt life they didn't know they were livin', I thought, *and we would've died heroes, for runnin' away.*

Chapter 34

Miss Myra was perhaps the largest woman I had ever seen, standing over six feet, at least. She wore a billowy, blue dress, covering her like a tent. She worked her way through the narrow hall, not coming close to touching the vase of flowers set on a wall table. She chattered her whole way from the kitchen side door where she had let us in, to opening the door to the small, storage room where we were to change our clothes.

"Now, I hate ta say it, you two is guests, but for the life a' me, I don't know why the masta insist on ya comin' through the kitchen. All I heard from him is how you's heroes a' somethin', that ya saved the lives a' so many men . . ." She paused to catch her breath. "If you's heroes, why you come through the kitchen?"

I shrugged as I had no answer for her.

"You know somethin' he don't then," she said.

She swung the door to the room open, hitting an object hidden in the dark. If there were windows, they were covered, keeping the waning, early evening light outside. Miss Myra shoved her way on in. The candle she carried lit up the space, showing us three broken chairs, a table, and woven baskets filled with dried corn. Laid out on the table were two sets of clothes. The pants and coats were almost identical, both black as coal with a slight sheen. Our shirts were the same, except in color, with James wearing blue and me wearing red, the opposite colors of the near ragged shirts Francisca had given us. Myra stepped out for us to change, then knocked and opened the door without waiting for James to finish pulling on his britches.

"Don't you worry, there ain't nothin' I ain't seen or felt a hundred time before," she said and laughed, her whole body jiggling like pudding. She glanced at both our pairs of boots, shook her head, and hollered, "Packy, get in here, now!" The young boy poked his head into the room. "Now, Packy, you take these here muddy boots an' clean 'em up. Master Groce don't cater to wearin' nothin' but shine on them toes." The boy picked up both pair and with a struggle to carry all four boots at once, took off in a run, stopping to retrieve one he dropped. Miss Myra leaned into the hallway. "An' don't you be messin' 'round, these two gentlemen need be presentable in ten minutes!"

James pulled a chair upright and tried sitting in it. One of the legs promptly broke and he tumbled to the floor in a heap. Missy and I started laughing as he refused either one of our help to pull him out of the broken pieces of wood. He stood, brushed off the dust, and laughed. "Should I try the other two?" he asked.

In a few minutes, Packy came back, dropping two boots to the floor. He checked for scuffs and set both newly shined pairs onto the table. I was amazed at how quick this young boy worked.

Miss Myra left and returned with a small hand mirror and comb. James held the mirror up to his face and stared for a few seconds, combed out his tangled hair, shook his head, then handed both the comb and mirror to me. I do not know who he thought he saw, the boy who left his mama's supper table weeks before, or the young man who survived his father's death and killed two men to protect his friend.

I glanced into the mirror. The grey eyes appeared to be the same the last time I looked, with Juliette, in Sophie le Roux's bedroom, as I dressed in preparation to face down Benjamin Brody in New Orleans's most famous opera house. I held a colder stare than before yet was unwilling to admit this to anyone. How some folks saw through to my soul might explain their hesitance to approach me. *So be it,* I thought, as I combed my hair and beard. Miss Myra gently took the mirror and comb back. I stared into her deep, black eyes. She smiled, unafraid. For an instant, I felt we shared an ancient sadness.

Packy appeared at the door. "Miss Myra, Masta wants these sirs in the big house now, he says!"

With one more look and a tug at our coats, she began to shuffle us out. I reached back to where my knife and pistols lay. Myra shook her head. "Masta don't allow his guests carryin' weapons."

I stood for a second, remembering the last time I went unarmed to a social event, in Sophie le Roux's parlor, where I finally met Baumgartner and fought him without a knife. I shook my head. *Hell, there ain't no need,* I thought, hesitated, then picked the knife up and slid it into my britches, covering it with my coat. *Just in case . . .* Myra shrugged, and we walked out the door.

A wide foot path attached the kitchen to the main house, covered by a canopy, latticed through with a blackberry thicket, its pink, spring flowers in full bloom. Three small torches lit the way. As we approached the house, I heard loud talk, mostly from Grainger and the man I recognized to be Jarod Groce.

We entered a long hall. A stone fireplace covered most of the far wall with a small fire burning in the middle. Though the weather outside had cooled, the air inside the house was heavy, warm, and smelled a bit smoky, as if the stones wept invisible smoke. A dining table stretched throughout half of the room with a full complement of plates, glasses, and silverware. A square, wood contraption, slats framing open spaces, a window in the air, hung from the ceiling a few feet over the middle of the table. A thin rope was attached to the top and run through pulleys across the ceiling to hang in the corner near the front window. I had no idea what this was meant for. Standing near the fireplace, deep in conversation, Jarod Groce and Grainger stopped talking as we approached and turned to face James and me.

"Masta, I introduce Mista Zeb an' Mista James."

Grainger did not move as Jared Groce faced us and bowed, again with his arms behind him. He did not reach out to shake our hands.

"It is indeed an honor to welcome such fine, young men into our humble household."

James returned his bow as I followed suit. Bowing to another was not my strongest show of respect. However, I was standing in the man's home, and I felt compelled to do so.

"Come, come, gentlemen, and have a drink with us, before our other supper guests arrive." He nodded toward Grainger. "I take it you two know each other?"

Grainger and I gave a glance and a nod. I wondered how much of our exploits he had mentioned to our host.

"I take it he's been a houseguest for a while now, missin' all the mud an' sickness of the camp?" I asked.

Groce gave Grainger the slightest of a raised eyebrow, smiled, and said, "Shall we have those drinks, gentlemen? I will share with you the absolute best Scotch whisky a man can ask for."

I shuddered hearing this, for the last time I had drunk scotch, I killed my brother's murderer.

Groce led us to a small table along one of the inner walls. Grainger stepped up and poured us all drinks from a crystal carafe. He hesitated, handing a glass to James. "How old are you?"

I took the glass and gave it to James. "He's old enough to

fight and kill a man or two, he's damn sure old enough to drink."

Again, I wondered why Grainger was so hard with James. There was no time between them nor situation or event to have caused such resentment.

Grainger offered the old gentleman a glass. Groce slowly reached out, his left hand bent at the wrist with fingers gnarled, twisted, and grasped the drink.

"Well then," Groce said, "to the great cause for independence and to victory!"

We raised our glasses. James and Grainger drained theirs as Groce and I sipped ours. The smoky taste took me back to the bloody knife I could still feel in my hand after running it through Baumgartner's neck. I shook off the memory and swallowed the rest of the scotch in one gulp.

Grainger would not catch my glance, then said, it seemed, to no one in particular, "Ya drink like you finally mean it . . ."

The four of us stood quiet, I felt rather uncomfortable, only assuming to whom he spoke of.

I looked at James and said, "Been through a lot lately, I suppose."

There came heavy bootsteps on the porch and in through the front door strode General Houston with two men following behind.

"Gentlemen, I am so damn tired. I have drilled these men, some goosecaps, some real rounders, most good, fearless men. They just need more training, and I intend to keep giving it to them!"

The man closest to Houston said, "Yes, sir, but you have squandered your strength by languishing in that bottomland, in the rain, for near a third of your army is still sick, sir. I can attest to this because I have cared for the poor souls, across the river and now here on drier land . . . and by the good grace of Mr. Groce, your men are gaining their health back.

"And when they are all well, then, sir, we will go and fight the enemy, and not before. In the meantime, I will continue to train those who can stand and fire a gun."

The three men had stopped just inside the door, their loud talk resonating through the hall, then silence. The third one, quiet through the conversation, said, "Gentlemen, I'm in need of a drink." He nodded toward the four of us still standing near the table with the scotch. "I'm afraid that my father and his guests have begun the night, and we must catch up."

Jarod Groce acknowledged the man and said, "Gentlemen, may I introduce to you the true owner of Bernardo Plantation, my son, Lamar Groce."

The resemblance was remarkable, but for the years, both could have been twin brothers. Lamar was not crippled in his arms and hands as the elder Groce appeared to be.

"Ah, my heroes!" Houston said, "No more do you look like damn Tejanos." He gave an approving nod and began walking around the table to greet us, motioning the other two to follow. "Gentlemen, come and meet my young friends."

The seven of us gathered around the small drink table with Grainger pouring scotch for everyone. His only hesitation was offering more to James. I glanced at him and frowned. He winked at me and filled the glass to the top.

Lamar raised his glass and turned to General Houston. The rest of us followed suit. "I toast to the one who shall take us to victory . . ." He then looked squarely at me with the slightest of smirks. "And to those who have survived thus far."

I slowly raised my glass, keeping my gaze locked with his, and downed the scotch. My head began to spin, for I had not partaken in spirits for a long while. He broke my stare to look down at my shiny boots, then turned to James, who was also becoming a bit unsteady on his feet, and looked at his. James followed Lamar's gaze, shrugged, and gulped down his drink.

The elder Groce must have noticed James's sway. "Son, you might want to hold out for a while; supper will be served, I am sure, very soon." He turned to his son. "Lamar, will your wife and my lovely granddaughter be joining us?"

"Yes, sir, they should be along shortly." As soon as he said this, the mother and her daughter who, earlier in the day were sewing on the porch, stepped into the room from a door near the fireplace. Their dresses were made of the finest silk and cotton, both wore the same shimmering, gold-colored fabrics, though with the daughter wearing less a low cut than her mother. The girl glanced at us, in particular, James. Then she saw Jarod Groce.

"Poppy!" she said and ran to her grandfather. He laughed and gave her a hug the best he could. She did not pay any mind to his crippled condition.

"Hello, my young sunshine. Did you and your mother finish those sandbags you were working so hard on?"

"Yes, sir, we sewed thirty or more, then gave them to Joseph to fill."

"Good, good, he should have them done by now." He turned to Houston. "General, could you use my granddaughter in any more ways for the war effort?" He hugged her again, reaching for her mother's hand. "Both would prove to be the turning point for our cause, I am sure of it."

Lamar stood between Grainger and the other man whom we had not yet been introduced to, quiet, sipping his scotch, observing his wife and daughter fawn over his father. He took a step back and hollered, "Myra!"

As if she was standing right outside, Miss Myra immediately pushed the door to the kitchen open. "Yes, Masta?"

"In five minutes, we will be ready for dinner."

"Yes, Masta," she answered and disappeared. Within seconds, in came four or five servants. They laid out on the table a roasted turkey, slabs of broiled beef with potatoes and greens. And what looked like those damn oysters Scurry had me try a month or so before. Within seconds came flies to invade the food.

"Myra, get Packy in here, now!" said Lamar.

She stepped out the door, ushered in the young boy, and pointed him toward the corner where the thin rope hung down. He grasped it and tugged. The window frame hanging over the table slowly swung up. The boy let go of his grip and the frame fell, swinging to the other side. He pulled again, allowing the wood contraption to fan across the food. As if as one, the flies lifted into the air and seemed to disappear for a second, then tried to land back on the food. There came the whoosh of the window fan, back and forth until the flies finally gave up and flew away. Packy continued to reach up and pull down, let go of the rope, reach up as far as his little arms would go, and pull down, as if he were ringing a silent bell. Myra stood next to him, smiling with approval. Lamar Groce said nothing, ignoring them both.

Mrs. Groce stepped forward. "Shall we finish our introductions and sit for supper then?"

"Yes, yes, of course," said the elder Groce. "Gentlemen and ladies . . ." he nodded to his granddaughter and smiled. "We have in our midst, two genuine heroes, survivors of what I have heard to be a most brutal act of savagery. What these young men went through, no one here can imagine. Perhaps it is more fitting that our leader of the cause introduce them?" He bowed to General Houston.

I stared at the general, hoping he might tell the truth. That our deeds were not heroic at all.

The general cleared his throat. "These gentlemen are two of only a few who were not killed by the rifles and swords of the Mexican devils. I present to you Zebadiah Creed and James . . ." He leaned toward the young man and whispered, "What is your last name?"

"Lee, sir, James Lee."

"Well, there you are, Mr. Lee. Ladies and gentlemen, I give you the heroes who survived Goliad."

Everyone clapped, except for Miss Myra and Packy.

I glanced to James and hoped that he might understand the difference between the two words *survive* and *hero.*

The gentleman we had not yet been introduced to offered his hand. "Dr. Anson Jones," he said, and stepped away.

With a rather weak grip, Lamar Groce shook both our hands and opened his arms to his wife and daughter. "Gentlemen, these two allow me to be who I am, my lovely wife, Jessica, and daughter, Caroline."

They both curtsied at the same time. His wife said, "Well, then, gentlemen, supper is served."

We took our seats with Lamar at one end of the table along with his wife on his left and daughter on the right. His father sat at the other end. I took a chair next to Grainger and across from the doctor. Lamar offered his wife her chair. James was shown to sit next to young Caroline. He clumsily pulled her chair back and as she slid down, she pulled a napkin into her lap, all the while her father staring at them both. Across from her daughter, Jessica gave them both a subtle smile.

Lamar said a prayer, asking the Good Lord to bless the food, and the revolution, for it was truly in God's hands now. I sat quiet, barely giving an amen as James nearly hollered it out, startling us all. Again, Jessica smiled and was the last to utter the word.

After passing around and helping ourselves to the wonderful cooked food, we ate in silence. All I could think of was the thing that would better this meal. "Might there be biscuits?"

"Myra, will you go and fetch the man some biscuits?" asked Jessica.

The servant left and for a few seconds, but for the swoosh of the shoofly, there was silence at the table. From the open windows came a gentle, evening shower.

"Damn," said the doctor, glancing toward Groce's wife. "Please excuse my language, ma'am, but except for the rain, we would perhaps be farther down the road to finding Santa Anna."

Houston did not take the bait and, instead, sat quiet and ate his supper.

"You do know, since your army has crossed that river," he nodded to the Brazos less than a quarter mile from the house, "you are obliged to chase after . . . we have investors waiting, you know."

Houston finished chewing and swallowed, took a drink of the wine that had been served, and said, "Good doctor, I am well aware of the opportunities of those who have paid for this fight, their business dealings and otherwise. You do not need to remind me." He glanced at the elder Groce, then to the son, he said, "I will take the fight to Santa Anna within two weeks and be done with this."

Lamar Groce gently laid down his fork, wiped his mouth with his napkin, and said, "Sir, the longer this goes on, the longer I am in peril of missing a full planting. As it is now, I can send only the women to the fields for I am afraid the men will run away as they may find out that they are in fact free men by Mexican law. I do not have the time nor inclination to go hunt after my property that we have paid for in sum. What I need is a complete crop planted, tended, harvested, baled, and shipped to my exporters in New Orleans, as do all my fellow cotton growers along the Brazos. If we were to miss because you cannot put down this . . ." He waved a hand, as if he were shooing away a fly. ". . . invasion. Then I ask sir, do we have the right man?"

James leaned over and whispered, "So that's why those poor fellas were locked up."

I simply nodded, for that was all I could do in light of whose table we sat at. The burn inside my gut grew.

The general slammed his fist to the table. "If you do not trust my instinct, prowess, and experience as this army's general, then, sir, you are welcome to have Rusk take the reins; he's here now with the troops. Or perhaps, send a message to Burnett, who has run away to Galveston with the rest of the counsel, in fear of their lives, and he may take my place. Hell, send a message to New Orleans and call your good friend Stephen Austin, who has sat out this war completely, and ask him, would he kindly come back to Texas and finish up this small problem of Santa Anna and his five- or six-thousand-man army invasion, so you can call in your crops on time."

As Houston spoke, the shoofly swung slower to hang still above the middle of the table. Flies, invisible seconds before, appeared above us, landing on what was left of supper. Lamar Groce turned toward Packy and Myra. "If you don't wake that boy up, I will."

Myra laid down the pan of biscuits she had just brought in and shook the child. He instantly pulled the rope down and flies again were gone.

"Mr. Creed, you have been to the front lines and back, what do you think of our dilemma?" asked Dr. Jones.

I glanced to the boy pulling the rope with Myra standing beside him. She snapped her fingers as if she had forgotten something and picked up the pan, walked to me, and with a wide serving knife, offered me a biscuit. "I's so sorry sir, they's not nearly as hot now. Butter?" She held out a small dish and set it on the table and placed the biscuit on my plate. Again, we shared a look, of a mutual bitterness soothed by years of resigned, enforced compromise. The only difference between her and me? I was free, and she was not.

"Thank you, Myra. Mr. Creed, we await your answer," said Jessica.

"I think you might be mis-reckonin' what this man Santa Anna, with his army, plans to do. If you pick up a gun to fight against him, or go blastin' those damn cannons, his aim is to kill ya, outright, no capture, no quarter, ain't no capitulatin' as Fannin tried to do, no terms of surrender." I lowered my head and gently rubbed the handle of Bowie's knife hidden behind the fabric of my coat. "To keep the flag of Mexico flyin' over this here land is his only goal."

From the other end of the table, Jarod Groce said, "For years we have tried reasoning with these unyielding Mexicans. They see no value in our ways, our means of a life we have come to make here."

"You mean ownin' slaves," I said.

"If not them, then who would pick our cotton?" asked Jessica.

Food had dulled the scotch and the knot in my gut grew tighter. I buttered the biscuit and was about to take a bite. I then realized, simple, crystal clear . . . everything about these white folk was about owning black folk. This was their cause.

I laid the biscuit down without tasting it and gave General Houston a glance. He caught my gaze and then looked away, as if he might be embarrassed. *Was this also his cause?* I asked myself.

I pulled the long knife from under my coat and set it on the table beside my plate. But for the *ahs* from a couple of the men and the slow creak of pulleys above our heads, the room was silent. The rain had stopped, yet, in the distance, thunder sounded, as if from somewhere beyond, Bowie was there, watching us.

"This here knife once belonged to Jim Bowie. I'm sure you all know who he is. He died a couple a days after he gave it to me, probably killed four or five soldados before they finally got him. Travis too. Funny, I hear the only one who survived the Alamo was Travis's slave name a' Joe, who the Mexicans set free. And what I hear about ole Joe? Hell, he's thrown back into chains cause he's a goddamn negro, an' he ain't ever gonna be free in Texas."

"Mr. Creed watch your . . ." said Jarod.

"I ain't finished. This here knife, well, I've had to kill a couple a Mexican soldados, both tryin' to save this boy's life. I promised his mama I would see him back home. I also tried with this here knife to capitulate a surrender with a general name of Urrea to save, oh, 'bout four hundred men fightin' for your cause. Let's just say, Urrea loved well-made weapons. After a week sittin' in a shithole prison, he left, and another man took charge. There came an order to kill us all, which they did. Lined us up an' shot down nearly everybody, except for a few who ran away." I felt James staring at me. "This young man's papa saved him, stood an' took a ball through the neck. And as I say, we ain't dead," I pounded my fist on the table making the knife and all the dishes rattle, "because we ran away."

I was out of breath, spent, and slumped in my chair. I was not sure just what I had said. I wanted desperately to cry, scream out, clutch the knife, and break all the fine dishes on the long table. But I did not. I sat there and slowly slid the blade back under my coat. Again, there was thunder, closer. The storm was not quite upon us.

"Whew there, partner, you been through quite the turmoil, you an' the boy." Grainger leaned forward and nodded to James. "I say we toast, to your courage and survival." He raised his glass, and everyone followed suit, except me. "To the great cause of stayin' alive . . ." He drained his wine, as the rest drank their own.

There came a loud snore, then a snort from the corner, and

the shoofly slowed to a stop. Lamar turned toward the boy, scraping his chair on the wood floor as he stood. Everyone watched in silence as he strode to the fireplace and picked something up off the mantel. Myra had left the room.

"Daddy, he's just fallen asleep, let me wake him?" Caroline weakly asked.

Lamar raised a finger to his lips and whispered, "Shhh . . ." He walked back across the room to where the young boy stood with his head resting on his hands clutching the rope. He let out another snort and opened his eyes. His master stood before him. Packy panicked and pulled the rope hard, making the shoofly once again wave back and forth across the table. Lamar reached over and with his left hand held the rope from moving. The boy continued to jerk down but the shoofly had fallen still. Finally, he stopped and let go. Lamar released the rope and the end spooled down around Packy's shiny, little shoes. In his master's right hand was a leather riding crop.

"What's he going to do?" whispered James.

I suspected he knew what was about to happen, as did the rest of us at the table.

"Son," Jarod Groce called, "let Myra take care of him, she knows best."

Ignoring his father, Lamar gently guided the boy to the middle of the room and stood above him slapping the short whip against his own thigh. "Now, Packy, I warned you once. You're old enough to know what twice means, don't you?"

The boy gave the slightest of nods, his whole body shaking.

"Take your coat off, then your shirt."

Crack came the thunder, closer now, almost over the plantation.

I sat and watched. Not the spectacle that was about to happen, but the folks gathered around the table. Lamar's wife sat stone-faced, as did his daughter. This was not the first of these beatings by her father. Her grandfather was uncomfortable, but not enough to again call out his son. By his ever so slight grin, the doctor was clearly being entertained, and Grainger, he sat beside me and drank more wine. General Houston? I saw no emotion. James, however, was halfway out of his seat. I grabbed his arm and pulled him back down, leaned in, and whispered, "You can do nothing."

Packy shed the coat and began unbuttoning his shirt.

Lamar bent down and examined the boy's shoes. "There's a scuff . . ." He shook his head. "And a bit of mud. Damn, you can't do nothing right?"

The shirt hung open on Packy. Lamar placed the riding crop in his teeth, turned him around, and as if he were his own son, removed the shirt. Bright scars shined across the young boy's back.

I cringed, held my breath, and reached for my knife. James laid a hand on mine. I could feel Grainger staring at me. I glanced at him as he gave me a shake of the head.

The door to the kitchen swung open.

"Masta . . ." Myra's voice shook. "Masta, he ain't but a boy, a goodun at that. He don't mean nothin' by fallin' asleep. He's a hard-workin' boy," she pleaded.

In walked another servant. Myra pushed her back and blocked the door.

The riding crop hung loose in Lamar's right hand. He laid his left hand on top of Packy's head, rubbing his nappy hair. He turned and stared at me over his shoulder. "Something you better understand, he's my nigger, and I can do with him whatever I want."

The legs of my chair scraped across the floor. I stood still with the palm of my hand resting on the handle of the concealed knife. Glancing around the table, I saw no support for the child, only a resignation for the act that was about to begin. I pushed my chair a little farther back and walked toward Myra. I heard another chair and James was behind me.

"I know what happened today, between you and my keepers," Lamar Groce said, "and if you interfere with my operations again, as the rightful owner of this plantation, I will hang you myself."

Myra stepped out of the way.

The last sounds I heard from the dining hall were the whistle of the whip, slap of leather to flesh, and the whimpers of a child.

Chapter 35

I did not want to wear the clothes I had on. The pants and shirt of Lamar Groce felt like poison on my skin. Yet, I had no choice. In the storage room lay the dirty, bloodstained shirt and britches Don Padilla had so graciously given me. I could not bring myself to wearing them. I wanted buckskins and moccasins. So far was I from my mountains.

I gathered my pistols and bag. James did the same. Myra was in the kitchen. I did not approach her, I would not want her in trouble with her master, nor did I have any words to say. James and I stopped outside under the blackberry-bramble lattice. I wondered what to do.

"I ain't never heard a child beat like that before," James said, in a timid voice.

I nodded. Memories of my beatings as a slave to the Lakota rose up and caught in my throat. I swallowed, pushing them back down into my gut. Only steps away, from behind the closed door to the hall, I heard the whoosh of the shoofly and murmur of conversation, then laughter. Nothing had changed but for the fresh welts on the young boy's back.

"I'm leavin'," I said, and stepped through the lattice to the front of the house. The rain had let up to a sprinkle. I rounded the corner and headed toward the outbuildings of the plantation. *Someone surely has a shirt and britches I can borrow,* I thought. From behind me, there came a short whistle.

"Whew there, partner, you ain't runnin' off yet, are ya?"

I turned back toward the porch. Grainger stood in shadows of the lamplight leaning against a column, smoking. James stumbled into me.

"You two ain't leavin', are ya?" he asked again, tapping the pipe on the heel of his boot. Ashes and sparks flew with the breeze and he stepped down to the ground. "All you went through, fer nothin' . . . like, like, them flickers of burned up tobacco?" He cradled the bowl of the pipe until it cooled and placed it in his coat pocket.

Laughter burst through the open windows of the hall from both the men and the women. The earlier incident was forgotten.

I walked up and faced Grainger, in close. He was a head taller, maybe stronger, but that did not matter. The smell of wine and scotch left his breath and drifted away, like the ashes of his pipe.

"Grainger, I don't know what scheme you're pullin', I don't care. You been through this whole fight rubbin' with the generals, makin' yourself bigger than you are."

He sighed, broadened his shoulders, and smiled, "Zeb, you don't know how large I am."

I moved an inch closer. I was not to be intimidated.

He looked past me to James. "What about your papa? You gonna let him die in that field for nothin'?"

James offered no response to his taunting.

"Well, then, I for one believe the general when his says he can find ole Santa Anna and kill him. I'll wager you the land I own an' won fair an' square, this here war's over in two weeks, as the general well claims. I aim to be a part of all that's comin' after. Now I know that you don't take too kindly to slavin', but ya gotta take the good with the bad."

We continued to face each other.

"The good for me is cattle on the open range. One day, I'll

be sendin' tons of beef back east and they'll be sending me their money to eat it. Now, if I gotta hang around these yahoos to make damn sure that happens, well, sir, that's just what I'll do." He smiled and laid a hand on my shoulder. "Now, partner, you're in on it, whether you know it or not. I can't tell ya the hows or what abouts just yet, when this thing's all over . . ." He looked down his nose at me. "So, if you an' the boy decide to leave, then so be it. You'll more'n likely be shot as deserters, or Santa Anna's been itchin' to kill ya for this long, he might just do it."

Before I could consider his threat, the front door opened and out stepped General Houston. "Ah, my young warrior and his protégé." He lit his cigar, taking time to fire the end completely, and walked off the porch to stand next to Granger.

I took a couple of steps back to face them both. I did not welcome another lecture from this man.

From behind me, James asked, "Why'd you give my mama's horse away?"

Both Houston and Grainger turned to the other and grinned.

"I was truthful when I told your friend here, that I needed a more statesman-like look, and your mama has provided that," said the general.

"Well, sir, I don't think my mama would've approved. I can tell you, she don't care much about statesmanship. Fact is, she don't care too much about anything the law has to offer, except when it has to do with gettin' back our land and keepin' it."

Grainger lowered his head, then looked at James. "Fact is, son, when this here war's over, she's gonna be so much better off than she ever did dream."

"How do you know that, Grainger?" I asked.

"You'll just have to trust me now, won'tcha."

"Of course I don't trust ya."

Grainger showed a look of surprise. "Zeb, I'm shocked that

you would say such a thing. I'm the nicest fella you know."

"Have you ever heard of the Order of the Lone Star?" Houston asked.

Though Don Padilla had mentioned this, I shook my head.

"A circle of highly influential, important men has come together, under one flag, to give us large sums of money, men to fight, and artillery." He motioned to the cannons still sitting behind us in the dark. "They are making damn sure we do not lose this fight. Yes, keeping the cotton plantations alive is a small part of it, but only here in the east. Out west is why we revolt, for the land that stretches from here to Santa Fe and the Rocky Mountains. Millions of leagues to call Texas."

Another pompous lecture.

"And what of the Comanche?" I asked.

His answer came after a long draw off his cigar. "We will have plenty of time attending to them. A newly formed militia is riding south of here. They call themselves the Rangers, Texas Rangers. Good men, the best. They will see to the Comanche's needs."

My thoughts spun. I swore I did not trust either of them. James stepped up beside me. *And what of the boy?* I asked myself. *And his mother . . .*

Houston blew smoke into the air and asked, "Zeb, do you have the two letters Padilla tasked you to deliver?"

I touched the breast pocket of my coat and felt the crinkle of paper. I had placed the letters there as I donned on the fresh clothes. I nodded.

"May I see them?"

I hesitated, then I shook my head. "They were not to be delivered to you, sir, but to Stephen Austin and Señor Obregon."

"I know, but I am their commanding officer as I am yours. So please, hand over the letters."

I pulled the first one out and unfolded it. Written in Spanish, I could not read the words, except Obregon's name along with Padilla's signature. The Austin letter, I could read, as it began with "Dear Friend." In what little light there was, I could not make out the rest, and moved closer to the porch lamp. After reading, I handed Houston both letters. His expression as he read told me Padilla's words did not spell good news for him and his republic. He then read Obregon's letter, shrugged, and handed them back, perhaps changing his mind as to their importance.

He stood square with James and me. "If you insist on leaving, as volunteers, I cannot stop you. However, you will both be considered mere messenger boys, cowards who ran away from the fight, no matter your opinion . . . of what *the cause* might be."

Behind Houston, the door opened and out onto the porch stepped Caroline, then her mother. Her father, grandfather, and the doctor remained inside. Through the windows, I could see them smoking, the shoofly swaying back and forth, swirling their cigar smoke throughout the hall.

"Why, Mr. Lee, I was a hoping you were still here. Mother, if it's proper, may James join us on the porch for a spell?" asked the young woman.

James hesitated, glanced to me, then Houston. Grainger caught his eye and gave the slightest of nods. The four of us stood frozen, as if our conversation never happened. As if the evening was starting anew, which in the light of what happened earlier with Packy, seemed to have never happened at all.

"Zeb, I'll catch up with you," he said, and climbed the steps onto the porch.

I folded and placed the two letters back into my breast pocket and walked away.

The rain fell, harder. Without a hat, my hair and beard matted to my head and face. I shivered, then sneezed. *I'll be damned if I fall ill.*

I did not know who or what I was looking for. A sign perhaps of the way forward, a path that might lead me to a true understanding and meaning of why I wandered a slave plantation in the middle of the night surrounded by folks, unsettled, devastated by recent events that they had no control over. Yet, in my mind I heard General Urrea's words as he questioned Jacob as to why he thought Mexico was his home if he was not a citizen. This led me to think of Judith Lee and her problems keeping the land Jacob spoke about, as theirs, free and clear. And then, for some reason, I thought of Grainger and his plans to raise cattle. *Where is his land?* I asked myself. *Must be close to the Lees homestead, somewhere east of San Antonio?* Hell, I was ready to believe this fight was finished and Grainger's plans were in place.

What were Grainger's plans? I had yet to receive a straight answer from him and my place within his grand vision. I did not care, *I'm headed a long way from here an' away from these damn Texas folk, all of 'em.*

The silhouette of a person just inside a barn, framed by the light of a dim lantern, offered a soft whistle. I stood alone in the near downpour, the door and dryness inviting, and stepped toward the light. A young man turned for me to see his face. He seemed familiar, as someone I had once noticed from afar.

"I know you," he said. "You were at the flooding river . . ."

I had crossed so many rivers, seen so many people. His accent reminded me of the German, Ehrenberg.

"When?" I asked.

The light showed that we were in a warehouse surrounded by cotton bales, some stacked three high. We were not alone. Two families shared the dry space with baling equipment and other sundry items hanging down from the rafters. Though not too crowded, there was little privacy, especially for the women and children. Good that there were no animals, the smell of these folks along with the cotton dust was overwhelming enough. As I entered, everyone became quiet.

"A month or so ago, the Guadalupe," said the young man.

He brought me back from my distraction. Memories of a morning, saving that woman's life, came flooding back to mind, the crack of the tree slamming into her wagon, the choking brays of the mules. Throwing myself into the water, climbing through the floating tree she clung to and spinning her to the surface. The tip of the hat her husband gave me from afar and the blank stare she gave before they drove off with their son east onto the savannah, fleeing the onslaught of Santa Anna and his armies. *Of all places to be reminded of this,* I mused.

"There was a flood, I pulled a woman from the water," I said.

"She is my sister."

I recognized him as the boy driving the smaller wagon. He was not a boy but a man of nineteen or twenty, only short in stature.

"I thought she was your mother. How is she?"

"She is here."

He nodded for me to follow, around and behind the bales to a narrow space against the wall. A faint glow from a lamp lit the white cotton, turning it to the color of gold. On a canvas cot lay the woman, asleep.

"Is she sick?" I asked, my voice low so as not to wake her.

He shook his head, then shrugged. "A little."

"Where's the man who tried rescuing her?"

"Dead," he said, without hesitation. "Not too long after the flood, our wagon's axle was sheared by a hidden tree stump as we rode back to Cat Spring. With no tools to repair the break and no one to help, we abandoned that wagon, as we did our larger wagon to the river, and rode our horse or walked on toward the town carrying only a rifle and pistol. The mule carried what little supplies we had not lost." He spoke as a matter of fact, with a regular tone of voice. "Marta was sick, like she drank most of the water she was swept up in."

She was smaller than I remembered, as if she had dried out and shrunk to less than half her size.

"How did you know I was here?" I asked.

"I was in the crowd watching you face down those men today."

"What do you want?"

He hesitated, then said, "Bring her back. Save her, like you saved her from the river."

"I don't know how you mean. If she's sick, she needs a doctor."

"She isn't sick like that . . . it's, it's more in her head."

He seemed to be looking for something I was unable to give. I could save someone from drowning, but to save a person from dying of their own free will? I was no healer, no medicine man.

The woman stirred, then opened her eyes. I remembered them being crystal blue, yet now they were dull, out of focus. She stared at me and shrank even more, as if afraid I might harm her. The young man kneeled and brushed back her hair. "Marta, this is the man who saved you from drowning, remember?" Her eyes softened, and she relaxed.

He looked up at me and asked, "What is your name?"

"Zebadiah Creed. You can call me Zeb."

"Ah yes, I have heard of you, there is talk. This makes sense now that it be you."

Talk, I wondered. Who the hell was talking about me?

"What's your name," I asked.

"Peter, sir, Peter von Haus."

Marta tried sitting up. With her brother's help, she leaned

against the wall, her legs dangling from the cot. He offered water from a skin bag, she refused.

"She has not drunk in a day. She has not eaten in a week." He stood and motioned me into him close and whispered, "I believe she is dying."

I had seen her demise in other women, during my time with the Lakota. Women who had lost their warrior husbands, through sickness or accident, but especially in battle. They felt they had no place left in the world, no one to share a life. Some women moved through grief to find another mate. Some survived off the generosity of the tribe and grew old, wise, to become leaders among her people. Others lost their will to live and eventually wondered off alone, into the wilderness to die.

"The river caused her condition?" I asked.

Peter shook his head and began to speak. Marta placed both hands over her ears and rocked back and forth, humming a simple tune, as if she could not bear to hear their story.

"She does this when I tell folks our tale."

I was tired and wanted to sit. And with such contentious conversation at the supper table, I had not eaten so well. *The biscuit I left on the plate would taste mighty good now,* I thought, then asked, "Would you like to speak about this where she can't hear you?"

"No, sir, she cannot be left alone as she begins to wail. I shall continue . . .

"Because of our loss of the second wagon, we were forced to walk with Marta riding the horse. Eventually all who traveled east that day left us in their dust."

I struggled to stay with his story, as worn out as I was. "Would she mind if I shared her cot? I'm dead on my feet."

Peter looked at me warily, then waved a hand for Marta to move. She stopped rocking, glanced my way, and scooted over, then commenced to rocking again. I sat down. With the sag of the canvas, she leaned toward me, then wiggled her way to the edge of the cot and stayed still.

Peter cleared his throat. "We are German."

I shrugged as I did not know how this made a difference. I wondered where Ehrenberg was, if he was even still alive.

"A Mexican patrol suddenly came upon us, on horses. Dusk it was, we were just about to enter a grove of trees to settle for the evening. Stefan, always ready with a pistol, surprised us by shooting and killing one of the riders. Our horse and mule ran off, never to be found. With their lances, the other two corralled us together. One of the men spoke loudly in Spanish, and without warning, ran Stefan through, cracking his ribs and into the heart." As Peter spoke, I did not hear any anger or grief in his voice, only, perhaps, a lingering sense of shock.

Marta rocked back and forth again, more vigorous, anxious, shaking her head and saying no, no, under her breath.

"The rider shoved Stefan's body off the lance with a boot and to the ground. Another rider dismounted, drew his sword, and struck me in the head with the handle. I woke later to the blackness of night, my skull split, blood caked in my hair. I found Marta lying a ways away in the brush, moaning. I attempted to comfort her, she would not let me. She tried to crawl away, to where I do not know. I grabbed her by the feet. She screamed and kicked me in the face. I sat as close as possible, with her moaning and crying. Not once through the night did she stop. Morning came, I could see how brutalized she was, her dress tore up. I almost left her to find my own way but did not. For days we walked from there to here, most by ourselves."

With all that I had seen and felt, the blood, murder, and treachery, this mischance encounter brought me to coughing, my belly tied into knots.

Had I saved her from drowning only to go through this torture?

Marta stopped rocking, laid her hands gently in her lap, and sat staring at a bale not three feet in front her, it's gold-lit cotton spilling from the burlap cloth. She hummed a simple tune, one that I had heard before, sung by the murderer Rudy Dupree, then John Murrell's band of cutthroats. What was the song? *Ah, Rock of Ages . . .*

The rain had stopped, all was quiet but for the humming of a hymn and Peter's breathing.

"I don't know what I can do."

"Comfort her, with your story."

I was not sure what he meant. My tale of escape? My story of revenge? Which might help her understand that life is worth living no matter what happens. You survive, through the day, the week, the year, until the anger, grief, and guilt are burned up.

I commenced to telling them about my brother, what kind of man he was, the fact that he could out-hunt, out-ride, and out-trap me. A gentle man that would scalp you in a second if you wronged him. He was the one killed, murdered because of a seeming random set of circumstances. I thought we had done the right thing bringing our furs downriver on our own. I was left for dead and my brother lost his life for it.

"What happened to the murderers?" Peter asked.

"One lost his head to a guillotine, and the other? I drove a knife through his neck."

"I want to find the bastards who did this to us and kill them."

I listened to his words for revenge and thought, *how will you find, out of thousands of Mexican troops, the two that murdered your friend and raped your sister?*

"If you leave, who will take care of her?" I asked.

"The Groces, of course. They opened their home and plantation. They must have some sense of compassion?"

I thought of the riding crop dangling from Lamar Groce's hand as he held Packy by the head. "I have found them not to be compassionate at all."

"If I have to stay and look after her, then you must go and kill them."

I was confused. "How can I do that? I'm on my way back to Missouri. I'm finished with this fight."

He gave me a look of surprise. "Why?"

I thought, *how can I explain, to this man who was going through so much hatred and grief, the reason why we fought was to keep slavery alive in Texas?*

"You go and kill them, because . . . because you saved my sister's life, so she can be left for dead on the cold ground, by murdering Mexicans."

"This don't make sense. She floated by. I jumped in and pulled her out of the water. I saved her life because I had to. Whatever happens after, ain't my concern."

"Where we come from, in Germany, when you pull someone from death's door, you are in some part responsible for their life, from then on."

At that moment, a tiny piece of me thought, *maybe I should've let her drown.*

"In our world, sir, we are all connected . . . for the good and for the bad."

I thought of Jacob, his blood pumping out his neck onto his son, the smoke of a hundred Mexican rifles fired at once, and the four hundred men shot dead in an hour. My heart again clutched my throat.

I was tired, of talking, of running, of fighting. Farther back of the narrow space, there were two bales, side by side, with a blanket to cover them. *I could sleep here for a while, let Houston and his army go and find Santa Anna. I would walk to the mountains, find my brother's wife and son and let them know about his death, and then make my way to Missouri and Anna. That's my plan.*

For how long my eyes were closed, I did not know. I sat on the cot with my back against the wall. Marta's head lay upon my shoulder. Peter was nowhere near. The rain seemed to weep, the wind moaning through the cotton warehouse. Blood rain we called it, my brother and me.

Marta stirred and spoke something in German. I leaned forward, laying her back down on the cot, and covered her with my coat. I stretched out on the two bales of cotton. *Comfortable,* I thought, *just like a bed.*

The fruit of the tree shimmers crimson in the brilliant sun. I walk between two wagon ruts. Looking to my left, then right, across the burning, hot prairie, a thousand wagon ruts run straight to the tree. Spokes of a wheel stretch for miles beyond the horizon. I am not alone, for the more I look out through the haze, folks appear, apparitions on horseback, in buckboards, covered wagons. Some walking, like myself. I carry nothing but a knife, they carry all their life's possessions. I do not know why I am drawn to the tree, dragging my feet through the grass. I glance down. Chains surround my ankles, chains wrap my waist, hang from my wrists. Yet, I move forward, unencumbered, free.

There is a woman's voice whose words I cannot understand, calling across the land. Beckoning us to join her. Closer, crowded, choking, noisy, dangerous, pistols drawn. Wagons are abandoned, and folks scramble up the trunk of the tree, into the branches and disappear. I stand stomping my feet, angry, furious that I cannot climb, weighted down by the chains that bind me.

A presence appears out of the prairie dust.

"Good to see you, brother," said Jonathan.

I attempt to give him a hug. He steps out of reach. "We mustn't touch."

From anger comes sadness and I miss him deeply. I cry out "You have abandoned me!"

He shakes his head. "No, you've needed to go alone. All the folks in this tree, you have helped, in some way. Look up, brother."

The red bulbs of fruit spread plentifully throughout the tree are torn away and eaten by those folks hanging from branches. Blood juice drips from their mouths and they spit the seeds to the ground. Sprouts appear near me, tiny trees.

My chains fall to the ground in a heap. Jonathan hands me an axe.

"You may chop down the tree." He points up. "All those people will die." He points down at the chains I have yet to step from, lying loose around my boots, and then toward the distant horizon. The growing trees are at my waist. I hear the rattle of bridles and reins, the rumble of wood wheels, the thunder of ten thousand rifles shot, mumbling voices, laughter, and death screams. I feel the breath of millions.

My brother is no longer beside me. The foreign voice calls out. I stand holding the axe, looking up.

I am shaken, gentle-like. James peered down at me.

"Zeb, I thought you truly left! Quick now, we must go."

I wiped my eyes. Daylight showed through the cracks in the wall I lay next to. The cot was empty except for my coat, neatly folded. "Where is Peter and Marta?"

"Don't know them. I found you by chance poking my head into this building. An old woman said you were back here alone and had been most of the night. Come on, Zeb," James said. "We've got to go, else the army will leave us behind. I've been made a sergeant by General Houston to help Colonel Neill with the twin sisters, the cannons. He promises me a uniform when the fighting's done. Caroline says I'll look mighty fine!" He stopped and then looked down at me with mournful eyes. "We go for Daddy."

I stared at him for a few long seconds, the dream disappeared. Perhaps I had also dreamt of Peter and Marta, their plight to reach safe arms, my part in their grievances and redemption. I shook off the last evening's darkness, picked up my coat, and followed James past the cotton bales. Near the open door stood Grainger.

"Whew there, partner, we thought we lost you for good this time."

I blinked at the morning sun. Grainger gave me a grin, as he had when we first met six months before, him showing me how to walk the sea-swept decks aboard the schooner *Columbus,* bringing us from New Orleans to Texas. To kill a few Mexicans, as Billy Frieze would say. I adjusted my knife, nodded to them both, and we went to find Houston, his army, and Santa Anna.

I needed to finish this.

Chapter 36

San Jacinto, Late April 1836

I stood with Burleson and his men as part of the formations that lined up near perfect along the rise, just past the woods where we were camped. Some said that by the time we reached Buffalo Bayou three days before, our numbers were well above eight hundred. Some I knew from before the fall of the Alamo. Others I did not want to know for I had enough of their patriotic dreams of what kind of country they would build.

After this battle, I will be far gone.

General Houston rode Judith Lee's grey mare, proudly parading back and forth along the front line. The man and the horse made a stunning show of grace and leadership with his words of encouragement and laying a path to glory.

"We shall take the field today, in honor of those true Texans who have died . . ." He paused and glanced to me. "Not in vain, but to further our great cause in creating a free state, separate from anyone's rule but our own!"

The entire army cheered him on. By his words and by our overlooking the enemy not more than a mile away across a sweeping prairie, did General Houston finally seem to gain the respect of every man he led into this fight.

James manned one of the "two sisters," the cannons rolled all the way from Groce's plantation. Throughout our march to this place, he maintained his assurance that he would stand with Colonel Neill and rain down fire upon the enemy. However, the day before the battle, Neill had been wounded by a cannon blast from the Mexican artillery and was not able to stand with us. In a rage, James wrote on one of the cannonballs, "For Col. Neill" and was determined to blast the ball square onto Santa Anna's tent.

Grainger rode with Colonel Lamar's cavalry on his black stallion. He was again friendly toward me despite his ill behavior at the plantation. I had not figured us to be as close as we were during our earlier travels to San Antonio and on to Judith Lee's. At this time, though, if he were to die, I would certainly grieve his loss, but no more so than James Lee, as I held the young man in such high regard. And not once did Grainger mention his cows to me. I glanced to my right and caught his eye. We gave each other a nod.

I smelled Mexican beef broiling over campfires. The aroma did not distract me like it did at the Alamo. Rather than hard, corn tortillas, I had a belly full of fresh-butchered beef and biscuits from our own noon meal. In that moment, though, I remembered lying in a field near Goliad next to Jacob Lee, blood spurting from a ball shot through his neck, a bayonet thrust into his chest. James and me running to the river. That was all this battle meant to me. Like many of us, I was ready to get on with the fight and be done with my avengement.

No more than four hundred yards ahead of us, down a gentle slope of prairie, sat Santa Anna and his army enjoying their late afternoon lunch and siesta. As if completely unafraid of whatever military offensive we might muster.

The trees behind us concealed our silhouettes. We kept our weapons low, so the sun glints would not betray us. All were quiet along the front, waiting for word, our final command to charge.

General Houston turned from us, trotted toward our enemy, and casually ordered, "Trail arms, forward!"

The late afternoon sun waned behind us, the tall grass our only concealment as we crept down the slope. Everyone held their rifle slings and shooting bags from making noise. Other than the swoosh of the brush of grass, we advanced in silence. Only General Houston could be seen by the few soldados guarding their barricade. Ahead and to our left, amongst a grove of oaks, came the first shots, cries, loud yelling in English and Spanish.

Here we go!

I stood up and charged, our rallying words, screamed out, *"Remember the Alamo! Remember Goliad!"*

In front of me, Houston rode hard straight at the enemy camp. A volley of shots from behind the barricades echoed up to us. In an instant, he and his horse fell to the ground. As I ran past, through the gun smoke, the general was helped to his feet with a pistol in hand. The horse lay still.

A vow broken with Judith Lee.

Within fifty feet of their meager defenses, I kneeled, primed my rifle, and fired. The soldado I aimed at had turned to run away. He fell forward through a tent with a ball shot into his back. I reloaded and fired at another soldado, missing as he ducked behind an upturned wagon. I ran, breaking through the barricade, then I was on him, bashing his face and head with the butt end of my rifle, pummeling his shattered nose and skull against the wooden bed of the wagon. I dropped the rifle, pulled my knife, and grabbed a handful of blood-soaked hair. He stared at me through eyes nearly swollen shut, unfocused until he saw my blade, and began to scream. Jerking him to the ground and with my knee at his throat I screamed back, *"For Jacob Lee, you bastard!"* He fell silent and gave an upward glance, as if asking, *Why me?* I wiped off the dust and sweat from my face and leaned into his neck, choking off any more cries. I cut a circle at the crown of his head, perfect, and with a yank, peeled his scalp away. Blood squeezed from the hair dripped down my sleeve as I held it up to the sky. I slowly stood, my heart pounding, and began to sing a death song, then stopped and stared down at the poor man, his eyes still upon me. As the blood wept from the scalp, my anger and hatred, all the anguish buried so deep I thought I might not be human anymore, began to seep away. I offered a silent prayer to the great spirit, *Wakatanka.* Wringing out every drop of blood, I slid the scalp into my belt, picked up my rifle, and ran, letting the man die on his own.

To my left and right, we had over run their defenses. The cries of the soldados were not cries as they died, but of shocking surprise before death. In minutes, we were through the camp, chasing those still alive into the waters of the bayou that lay beyond. We scattered along the shore and some of the Texans began shooting. The surface of the dark water swirled in red, the screams for forgiveness choked off as the soldados sank, their last words heard on Earth. An officer emerged from the water in front of me, near the shore, and stood up with his arms raised. He cried, *"Yo no estaba en Goliad!"* I raised my rifle, pulled the hammer back two clicks, and aimed. He slowly closed his eyes and turned his head away from me. I lay my finger against the trigger. He stood silent, at attention, proud. I stared at him down the barrel of my rifle. I tried squeezing the trigger and . . . *boom!* The officer fell backward and sank into the bloody muck. I lowered my rifle. At the same time, a fellow name of Sparks lowered his smoking pistol. He began to reload. The look he gave me was one of disgust. He primed his pistol and followed some of the others to the farther shore by stepping on the saddles of drowned horses sticking out of the water.

I walked back up through their camp, carrying my rifle loose in hand. Those soldados only wounded had been skewered to death. I felt nothing as I stepped away from the slaughter, no remorse, no compassion, and certainly no forgiveness for any of these dead men.

Yet, I harbored no hatred. I just felt empty and tired.

My only thought was, where might James be and how I was sure he had survived this fight. I had to go find him.

Twilight settled. With no fires lit, it became harder to see. I passed a body, facedown in the grass with long, black hair and wearing a white skirt awash in blood. My heart rose up and for the first time since crossing the Brazos, my hands began to tremble.

It would not be impossible? my mind screamed.

For a while, I knelt beside her. I thought of the time in the chapel she smiled, the way she cared for Padgett. The song she sang in grief for a former life she shared about with no one, but me. The two of us lying in moonlight, the smell of mescal on her fingers, her passionate cries in Spanish. The last glance she gave before staving off the patrol that set out to kill James and me.

The thought of seeing Francisca like this . . . I could not bear.

I closed my eyes and rolled her over. The woman I looked down upon was not her. Tears welled up and I wept in silence, in the dark, on the last battlefield of the day.

Chapter 37

Santa Anna has escaped!

Throughout camp were murmured those words. Yet for a while, in the dark of night around the fires, no one seemed to care. Most everyone rejoiced in our victory with drink and boisterous talk of their kills, except for me and a few others. No smiles creased our faces blackened with powder. No glad words were spoken. For a few moments, before I went looking for James, I sat with Grainger, resting at the campfire of those who were left of the old New Orleans Greys. Even with my dour disposition, he and I seemed to be friends once again. I was certainly glad to see him still alive.

"I swear, partner, you are lookin' a mess," he chided, and offered me the bottle he held.

I nodded and took a drink, a long slug, and handed the bottle back to him. I had to admit, he appeared much healthier than I was as he had ridden his horse for most of the fight, though fortune must have favored him. General Houston rode three horses, all were shot out from under him and he lay near his tent beneath a tree with an ankle shattered by a rifle ball. Not one of us who were on foot was wounded, though most were covered in blood. In the morning, before heading west, I would go and wash myself off in the bayou beyond our camp.

This time spent together reminded me of standing at the well of the Alamo, not two months earlier, drinking from the bottle he stole from Travis, discussing our plans for escape.

"We've come a long way from there to here," I said to myself.

"From where?" Grainger asked.

"The Alamo."

"Hmmm," was all he said.

We sat for a moment in silence, my mind on the dead woman I found lying on the prairie. My hands still shook. I spat into the fire. "Who would kill a woman out here? Wasn't there enough killin' for one day?" I took the bottle away from him and had another strong drink. My head began to swirl a little.

"I heard about that. Fact is, the man who did the killin' . . . well, a rumor says he didn't fight, hid in the grass 'til we was cleanin' up, goin' around makin' sure the dead stayed dead, if ya know what I mean . . ." He stopped and lowered his head. "Heard he ran her through with his saber, then laughed as she fell to the ground."

I handed the bottle back and calmly asked, "Who is he?"

"Well now, Zeb, if I tell ya, you're gonna run off an' find him an' no telling what you might do."

"Only a goddamn coward would do this," I said, seething with anger. I gritted my teeth and once again asked, "Who is he, Grainger?"

He hesitated, then, "A colonel name a' Forbes, so the rumors say."

I pulled both pistols from my belt, laid them on the ground, and stood, adjusting the Bowie knife and scalp.

Grainger also stood. "Now, Zeb, don't you go off doin' something . . ."

Before he could finish his sentence, I walked away.

I found James with his fellow cannoneers, at a fire built between the "two sisters," pulled back from the rise they were fired from, still pointed toward the battlefield, the last of the cannonballs and grapeshot piled neatly on display. I did not see the one James wrote on for Col. Neill, nor did I see the colonel.

"Zeb!" he hollered. "I was just going to find you." He gave a hug and stepped back, his face showing shock, then concern. He looked me up and down. "Zeb, you, you got blood all over you. Are you wounded?"

Shaking my head, I said, "Nope, I came through the battle unscathed. Just lookin' a mess, I suppose."

"Zeb, ya don't look too happy."

I tried to smile. "I am damn glad you are alive, my friend, an' this goddamn war's over."

"We're going home, Zeb."

I nodded. "Yes, you're goin' home, to your mama." Saying those simple words made me sad. Then I thought, *Hell, I should be glad he's got a home to go back to.*

From across the camp came a call, mocking words yelled out, then came a response that I did not understand. James and I continued talking, with him explaining how those cannons turned the tide of the battle. I did not remember ever hearing a shot fired. Then someone reminded us that to the east was the rest of the Mexican army, much larger than the small battalion of men we just defeated. I heard it again. *Who killed the woman?* And the response throughout camp . . . *Colonel Forbes done it!*

"I've gotta go," I said.

"Ah, Zeb, stay with us, won't you?" James pleaded.

"Gotta go do somethin', I'll be back soon enough."

The young man shrugged and smiled. He seemed truly happy. He turned back to his friends and they continued to celebrate their victory.

I found Forbes among the first caches, war bounty dragged from the battlefield, not far from where Houston lay. He was surrounded by a junior officer and three enlisted types and all seemed to ignore the inflammatory remarks hollered across the camp. I waited for him to set the Mexican sword down that he held to the firelight. A short man he was, clean-shaven, nervous.

The weapon seemed too large for him to handle. The few seconds I stood staring at him, he caught my eye twice, and looked away both times as if embarrassed. He laid the sword on top of a barrel, opened a small chest and smiled, glanced back, picked up the sword, and walked straight at me.

"I ask, man, do you take issue?"

I looked him up and down. There was no dust nor gun smoke grime on his face, no blood on his clothing. With my left hand resting gently on the handle of my knife, I said, "Lookin' mighty clean for just comin' from a fight."

In seconds, we were surrounded by Texans, volunteers, officers, and the like, some carrying torches. There was no call and response, only silence.

Forbes stopped a couple of strides in front of me, still pointing the sword. "Again, I ask, do you take issue with me, sir? If so, stake your claim," he said, with a quiver in his voice.

I stared at him and took a step forward. The sword he held dipped ever so slightly. He switched hands, his weaker one, then held the sword with both hands, sagging at the wrists. A couple of the men snickered.

Another step. "I'm hearin' you hid out 'til all the real killin' was done, is that true? Hid in the grass like a goddamn rat?"

Forbes glanced around at the crowd closing in. "Sir, I fought as well as any man here."

More snickers. Some men shook their heads and scoffed out loud.

Another step forward, and the tip of the blade touched my chest. "You gonna run me through like ya did that woman? Hell, ya musta used a tiny pecker sword to kill her, ya can't keep that one straight."

Instead of responding, he looked at my hand on the knife, then his eyes grew wide. I felt the sharp tip push at my shirt, as if he was poking me with his finger.

"You . . . you're the one," he said.

The men surrounding us gathered closer, gazing at my belt. No matter that Forbes still had a sword against my chest.

"It is him," someone exclaimed.

Another said, "It's one thing to kill 'em, but to take a man's scalp? Why, that's pure savagery."

The fighters of the day all began talking amongst themselves, now staring at me and the bloody scalp that hung from my belt. I did not know what was happening. In a second, the course had turned, and I was the one being scorned.

Sparks stepped from the crowd. "Hell, he couldn't shoot one of 'em just standin' in the water waiting to be killed." He proudly smiled. "Had to do it myself."

From the back, someone said, "He's one of 'em to survive Goliad . . . by running away."

I stood still, letting them chirp like birds, my resentment toward most of those yahoos swelling up to my face, then burned away. I could not fight them all, nor would it help to call each one out, starting with Clark, to defend myself. Nor would I give the pleasure of looking them in the eye.

At that moment, I knew my time with these men had ended.

I squared with Forbes. The weight of the heavy sword had weakened both his shoulders. With my right arm, I knocked the blade away, peeled the handle from his hands, and thrust the sword into the soft earth behind me. I looked him in the eye, grabbed a handful of hair, and raised my knife to his forehead.

"Admit to murderin' that woman, I won't take your scalp."

Silence gripped the camp. I felt a presence behind me, annoying, like a bee buzzing around my head.

Grainger whispered in my ear. "If ya scalp him . . . now, I'm not sayin' that he don't deserve to be scalped, seein' what he did to that woman. But, Zeb, if he dies, they'll be hangin' you for murder."

Forbes' eyes were squeezed tight, I held my blade on his skin just below his hairline, and sliced, gentle-like, across his forehead, then stopped. He did not cry out but remained quiet, in shock.

"Open your eyes, you coward."

He cracked his eyes open to slits. Tears streamed down his face mixed with the blood seeping from the cut. I would not let him wipe it away and jerked his hair, hard, as if I were pulling every strand from the top of his head. I let go, then snatched the scalp from my belt and held it up to his face for all to see. He screamed so loud my ears hurt, the bastards around us gave out a collective gasp. I grabbed the back of his head and drew him in close.

"Here's somethin' to remind ya that you didn't die tonight."

With the point of my Bowie knife, I nicked his left cheek by an inch, and shoved him to the ground. Forbes rubbed the top of his head. Realizing his hair and scalp were intact, he promptly pissed his britches and passed out.

There was not one utterance among the crowd, other than Grainger saying, "Zeb, Houston wants us."

I wiped my blade and slid it into my belt. The scalp, I clinched in my fist. My former comrades in arms parted way with no words for me or Forbes.

Chapter 38

Houston lay under an old, snarled oak tree, on a pallet of blankets, his left ankle wrapped tight but still seeping blood. On a camp stool next to him sat Will Scurry tending a small fire to see by. Scurry looked up and smiled as Grainger and I approached. Houston did not and motioned both of us to squat opposite the fire. It felt as if we were to be either praised or admonished, maybe both.

The general moved his leg slightly, wincing in pain, and lay on his side with a hand propping his head up, quiet for a long minute staring at the fire. He took a drink from a small bottle and licked his lips, as Padgett had done with the absinthe. Finally, ". . . Shot right out from under me, all three of them. Hers was the best horse I've had, your friend Judith Lee. And I thank you Grainger, for showing me the importance of presentation."

Grainger nodded, pulled a flask from his jacket, and offered it to Houston. Scurry fetched the drink and gave it to him. "Ah . . . now I could always count on you, my friend." After a long slug, he passed the flask back to Grainger. "Yes, sir, I count you as one of only a very few to call a friend." He looked at me. "Are you my friend, Mr. Creed?" He paused, then without my answer, said, "Of course not, you have no friends, Zebadiah. A great warrior most often walks alone, as well I know."

I was not sure what General Houston was talking about. He seemed to be rambling on, out of it.

"Sir, what can we do for ya?" Grainger asked.

"Scurry, would you ask my fellow warrior if I may handle the prize he holds at his belt?"

The young man hesitated, not knowing what the general was asking. I stood, pulled the scalp, and offered it to him. Scurry reached over, and with his thumb and forefinger, snatched away the hair and gave it to Houston.

He seemed to fondle it. I knew this was not the first time he had held another man's scalp in his hand.

"Taken in battle, a just reward."

He gave it to Scurry to give back to me, and without hesitation, said, "I want you two to go and find that murdering son of a bitch. And if you can't bring him to me alive, well, then, Mr. Creed, you will bring back his scalp for my belt."

He took another drink from the small bottle, closed his eyes, and rolled over to face the darkness.

My shoulders sank, and I hung my head staring at the ground. If this meant going after anyone other than Santa Anna, I would have refused. For Houston to personally ask me to bring back his scalp, from one warrior to another, I could not say no.

I squared up, glanced to Grainger, and nodded. *One more I suppose and that's it . . . then I'm headin' west.*

He slapped me on the back and said, "Let's go."

We walked to the Greys' camp, the evening quiet, except for: *"Who killed the woman?"*; a pause, then, *"Colonel Forbes done it!"* Twice the call, twice the response, each time with laughter. And then: *"Who scalped the Mexican?"* Silence. A solitary voice hollered out, *"The damn savage, Zebadiah Creed!"*

No one laughed.

Grainger and I rode with Deaf Smith.

The morning sun shone down hot on the Mexican camp, the

battlefield. We made our way past the bodies of soldados littering the prairie alongside dead horses, broken carts, and wagons, the smell no better or worse than the death stink at our battle at Coleto Creek. After a while, I imagined all battlefields smelled the same and that if I were to grow accustomed to it, then I would become the monster I sometimes felt I was.

The Mexican army had burned our dead, but we would not be so kind as we left theirs scattered across the prairie.

A small group of Texans were gathering valuables, bounty, possibly from Santa Anna's tent, even more chests than were taken the night before, filled with clothes, fine dishes, a candelabra. One of the men was Forbes, wearing a straw hat that did not quite cover the bandage wrapped across his forehead. He turned to face us as we rode by, glanced to the ground, and quickly resumed his direction to the others loading the loot into a wagon. Smith left us, sauntered over to Forbes, and spit on him. He rejoined Grainger and me and we rode on.

After a mile or so, we reached Vince's Bridge, or what was left of it.

"The damn thing wouldn't burn so we chopped it in two," Deaf said. "Ain't no way we was lettin' them bastards get away."

We sat on our horses looking out across the stretch of bayou the bridge had crossed. Maybe a hundred bodies still floated in the shallow water. The slaughter of the soldados was repulsive. Some would say, not near as repulsive as taking a scalp and leaving the man for dead. I had no answer.

A half a mile north of the broken bridge, we passed a couple men from Burleson's camp. It seemed we were not the only ones searching for Santa Anna. They spoke of a large field with a single tree where a couple of prisoners had been found the night before. The rest are more than likely long gone, one of the men said, and they headed back south to cross the water to the other side, closer to the bay.

After they were out of hearing distance, Deaf said, "Hell, he ain't over there, he's afraid of the water, the coward son of a bitch."

The bayou edged along a huge swath of prairie, more a savannah, with grass as tall as a man. In the middle stood a lone tree. Through the grass ran trails, hardly visible, though allowing enough access to find a man or two hiding out among the rough blades.

Grainger suggested, "We split up, I betcha we can flush out a handful of the bastards if we each go our own way zigzaggin', an' meet at the tree."

"Do you really think they're still hidin' here from last night?" I asked.

"Hell, a whole herd a' cattle can hide and not be seen but for the bent grass," Grainger said.

Deaf and I looked at each other and shrugged. "Holler if yer needin' help. We catch any of 'em," Deaf said, nodding toward my knife. "I wager we can get 'em to talk."

I did not know how particularly effective this plan might be; however, if I did find ole Santa Anna hiding there, I believed I would need no help in dragging him up off the ground.

We split the grassland into thirds, took our places at the outer ring of trees, and began riding our way to the center. Within half an hour, Deaf hollered out, "I got one!" Grainger had been riding to my right. I glanced his way and could not see him. I went to help Deaf. He was still on his horse holding his rifle on a young soldado, maybe as old as James, covered with grass and stickers. He appeared to be unarmed, holding up his hands to the sky. He spoke Spanish, fast, in a panic, as if we would kill him right then. I did not blame the boy for being frightened, for I am sure he witnessed most of his comrades shot dead the afternoon before.

"Dónde está Santa Anna?" Deaf asked.

The young man shook his head vigorously. *"No sé, no sé!"*

Smith pulled the hammer back two clicks and aimed the rifle at the boy's head. *"Una última vez, pregunto, dónde está Santa Anna?"*

He shrunk back, his eyes squeezed shut, held his hands over his face, and with one finger, pointed toward the tree. *"Nos íbamos a reunir en el árbol al mediodía,"* he cried.

"Now that's more like it," Smith said and lowered the barrel to the soldado's chest.

Shhh-boom! The boy was dead before he fell to the ground.

My horse reeled in shock, as I did. I had seen Deaf Smith kill but had not known him to be this cold-blooded.

He looked me in the eye and shrugged, "Far as I'm concerned, we're still at war." He calmly reloaded his rifle, glanced up at the sun, and trotted off toward the tree.

I was deciding on whether to follow, when I heard Grainger call out from the opposite side of the prairie. He called again, my name, "Zeb, where are ya? I need ya. I think I got him!"

Deaf did not seem to hear Grainger's cries for help and kept riding. *If it ain't him, then Deaf maybe can catch him,* I thought, leaving the dead boy lay. I did not think of him again, as in my mind, we were about to catch Santa Anna. I kicked my horse into a gallop through the tall grass.

Grainger was nowhere to be seen.

I rode along the trees and brush that separated the prairie from the waters of the bayou and hollered out for him. I heard a horse whinny, entered the thick trees and brushwood, and headed toward the sound, as if Grainger himself had just made the faint trail I followed. I burst through a thicket into a small clearing, empty but for his black stallion tied to a bush. At the edge of the shore stood Grainger, with his hands behind his back. Two other men stood on either side of him with scatterguns cradled in their arms. Behind them, in the water, lay a boat, a scow, with a fourth fellow manning the oars. Just beyond, the bayou opened to the Galveston Bay where I could see the masts of a small coastal schooner anchored, much like the *Columbus.* I swiveled in my saddle and glanced around me to see if I was followed, that they were there to meet others and not me, then I looked for a Mexican soldado that might be Santa Anna. There was no one.

"Zeb, you come on down off that horse," Grainger said. "We're done with this here fight."

I recognized the man on Grainger's right, the scoundrel he sent back to Broussard, the bounty hunter with the bleeding gut, the night of the bushwhacking. The other fellow was Cobbs, the one who left us at the battle of Coleto Creek, riding Still Wind, along with Obregon, and my friend who now stood before me.

"Grainger, what the hell is goin' on?"

I reined my horse backward, closer to the trees.

Grainger slowly moved his hands from behind his back and pointed two pistols at me. His two men leveled their scatter-guns.

"Like I said, don't want no trouble, partner, this is all part of the deal. Now, come on down an' we'll talk."

If I got off the horse, I was done for, so I sat, not moving. I could not think, of why, or how, I just knew I had to get away, make it through to the field.

"I know what you're thinkin'. If ya try to run, Zeb, Cobbs here will shoot your ride right out from under ya. Now throw down your pistols and get off the goddamn horse."

By the look in his eye, I knew he meant it. I had seen that cold stare before.

How could I be so stupid.

"You son of a bitch . . ." I said.

"You are right about that, my friend. Cobbs, shoot the horse."

Cobbs cradled his gun, pulled a pistol, and stepped forward.

I held up my hands, "No! No!" Then reached for my pistols and one at a time dropped them to the ground.

"That's better, partner. Now come on down an' I'll explain everything."

"I ain't your goddamn partner."

"Well, you might think twice after I tell 'bout all my plans, our plans."

I eased myself off the horse and stepped toward the three of them, the pistols and scatterguns still aimed at me. Cobbs again pulled his pistol, walked up to the horse, and shot a ball straight into its head. The poor animal fell over, shaking the ground, retching in pain, dying, then still.

"Why the hell did you do that!" I hollered, glaring at him.

He laughed, moved back to stand beside Grainger, and shrugged. "Don't need it where you're goin'."

I stood only a stride in front of them.

"Now the knife," Grainger said.

I laid my palm upon its handle, hesitating. If I gave it to him, I would more than likely never hold it in my hand again.

"Don't throw it, toss it in the dirt."

From behind me, through the trees, came a young voice. "Zeb, you there? I come to tell you, early this morning, they found Santa Anna!"

I pulled the Bowie knife, stepped up to Broussard's man, and slid the blade into his gut, twice. His eyes grew wide and he dropped the scattergun, then fell to his knees and forward to the ground.

Shhh-boom!

Smoke swirled from one of Grainger's pistols.

Beyond the dead horse, a few steps into the clearing, stood James holding his belly, blood seeping from between his fingers. He looked down at the wound and gasped, back up to Grainger, then to me.

"Zeb?"

Grainger and I squared, a loaded pistol pointed at my chest, my bloody knife in hand. A swift thrust to his groin. He sidestepped, flipped the spent pistol, and with the handle, cracked me in the skull.

My last glimpse, his eyes cold, confused. His voice, "Damn kid."

And the world went black.

Chapter 39

In the dark, somewhere above my head, the sea lapped against the hull of the ship, gentle, not nearly as rough a sea as what we sailed through to get to Texas. I lay on a straw mattress on three barrels, above the seeping seawater and rats, in chains; maybe two days since I witnessed James murdered. Though with no sun and my head still split, I could not swear how the time had passed.

I asked Cobbs to send down the son of a bitch Grainger. He shook his head, laid the gruel on the steps, and slammed the hatch shut. What light entered the hold, came from square breathing holes built into it. Once, I saw a shadow cross, as if someone stood still for a few moments. I hollered out *Grainger*! Twice. The shadow disappeared.

I lay in silence. When I closed my eyes and tried to sleep, all I saw was James holding his belly, blood pouring through his fingers. His shocked voice calling my name. Above the noise of the ship and water, I thought I heard Grainger laughing.

The seas picked up, sometimes crashing against the hull of the ship. If I held out my arms, toward the bulkhead where the chains were attached, I could sit on the steps. With the ship heaving to and fro, I could not sit for long, but if Grainger did come down, then I could wrap the chains around his neck and . . .

Someone opened the hatch, letting it slam backward to the deck. One of the crew came down the ladder with Cobbs following, two pistols pulled. The sailor unlocked the chains at my wrists. Without a word, Cobbs motioned up and followed me out of the hold. The light of the oil lamps hurt my eyes. Up another deck, and we were alone in the crew's mess. He offered a seat and the cook set a plate of boiled beef and potatoes, and a cup of beer in front of me.

I could not remember the last time I had eaten this good.

"Ya might have a biscuit?" I asked. The cook frowned but nodded. He left and came back with a half a piece of bread and dropped it onto the plate of food. I picked it up, sniffed at the mold, and laid the bread back down. After eating half the meal, I pushed it away and asked, "Where's the bastard?"

From the shadows came, "Right here, Zeb."

I stood, and Cobbs pointed both pistols at me.

"Whew there, partner, you look a mess." Grainger stepped into the light. "No matter, we'll be comin' to the end of our journey soon enough. Now sit back down an' we'll talk awhile."

He sat opposite me for a long second, both of us staring at the other, my belly so tight I might've thrown up the food I had just eaten. Grainger sat stone faced. I had never seen him weigh so heavy in his demeaner. He opened his mouth to speak, hesitated, and pulled Bowie's knife from his belt, my knife, and laid it on the table.

"I always meant to ask. Did you really try to make a deal with that damn Mexican general, tradin' this here piece for the lives a' those poor fellas at Goliad?"

With my hands folded, not two feet from the knife, I did not answer.

"Ah, no matter. They all died an' now I have the damn thing." He held the blade up to the light, blood still tainting the steel. "Hell, I remember when Bowie gave this to you." He looked wistful, then almost envious.

I could not let my eyes stray from his. Except when I coughed.

"You don't sound good, partner."

I did not respond and went back to staring at him.

He squared his shoulders, then leaned in toward me. "Let me tell ya a story, Zeb."

"Tell me why you shot James?"

He lowered his head and would not look at me as he spoke. "That was not supposed to happen, I promise ya." He fiddled with the knife. Finally, "The land that Judith and Jacob Lee owned? Well, sir, it's my land." He looked up. "Won it fair an' square, in that goddamn poker game. It was Bowie's, and after his wife an' daughter died, Judith an' Jacob seemed to win their dispute. The one she mentioned at her supper table. Remember Zeb, she said Travis had helped them keep the land? Seems Bowie just about gave up on everything but winnin' this here war, then he got sick and . . . well, you know."

"Grainger, what in hell does that have to do with me? You kidnappin' me an' all?"

He glanced away, then back. "There's money on yer head, Zeb. Lots of it."

I touched where he knocked me in the skull. The wound had been hurriedly sown shut. I felt skin crusting up and wondered if it was festering.

"Now here's the deal. We take you back to stand trial for Brody's murder. You'll be found not guilty, 'cause you didn't kill him, right? I get the bounty money an' you go free. It's as simple as that, my friend."

"How much?"

"Five hundred dollars, Zeb."

"Buys you a lot of cows, don't it, Grainger."

"*Yes, yes,* you got it!" He sounded genuinely excited.

"Got one question, where's the return on my investment, and James's?"

He lowered his head again, stroked the blade of the knife,

and said, "When you're free . . ." He looked up and smiled. ". . . you come an' live with Judith an' me, on our land . . . as a true partner. We'll build the biggest cattle ranch in Texas!"

I sat with my hands still folded on the table and glanced to Cobbs. He had lowered the pistols and did not seem to be paying much attention to our conversation. *I could slit his throat before I was shot dead.*

Grainger picked up the knife and placed it back into his belt. "I know what you're a thinkin', Zeb. An' ain't nothin' gonna bring back your boy James, ya hear? Now you got some time to think. We're gonna be rich, my friend!" He stood, as did Cobbs, again pointing his pistols at me.

"Judith Lee," I said.

"What about her?"

"Judith Lee's boy, not mine. James was Judith Lee's boy."

"Hmmm . . ." he said and nodded to Cobbs.

He locked me back up in the dark hold, this time without the chains binding my wrists. I never knew whether it was day or night. My cough grew worse, keeping me awake with my thoughts.

I had survived the massacre of nearly four hundred men to be betrayed by my best friend, *how could I let this happen?* I had not figured on returning to New Orleans, ever. And here I was being brought back a prisoner, accused of murdering a man I did not kill, yet should have, as Madame Sophie le Roux had expected me to do. I tried to make sense of it, but could not, and was left with little hope.

I knew though that if I did survive this injustice, I would hunt down Grainger and kill him.

From the hold, I heard the sounds of the Mississippi, the blaring horns of the steamers, the bargemen hollering to one another as they maneuvered their way up and down the wide river, past the small schooner headed for port. The musty smell of the swamps we passed brought memories of my time not seven months before, of Pawpaw's shack and constant rain, Olgens Pierre helping me from the fish nets I found myself entangled in. The gator's fat tail being boiled away. Billy Frieze's funeral pyre in flames.

But for the lines being thrown to shore, I could not tell that we had moored. Footsteps sounded on the deck above. The hatch was unchained and opened with a slam. Cobbs stood again with two pistols, beckoning me to join him. A sailor bound my hands and feet in irons and I shuffled up to the main deck. The sun shone bright, blinding me for a minute. I closed my eyes and then opened them. At the quarterdeck, Grainger was given a bag of coin by a man immaculately dressed in a French coat and beaver top hat.

He approached me. "*Monsieur* Creed, I am Marcus Broussard. Let me be the first to welcome you back to New Orleans, sir. I do believe you owe me for freeing three of my best slaves." He paused to look me up and down. The scalp I still held tucked in my belt must have caught his eye. "I hear good news from Texas. You come direct from battle, I presume?" He started to turn away toward the brow, then, "Oh . . . and you're charged for the murder of Benjamin Brody."

Past Broussard, among the crowd on the wharf, I caught a glimpse of Sophie le Roux wearing her finest yellow dress. She curtsied, gave me a wink, and disappeared.

As I left the schooner, shuffling past Grainger, he cradled the bag of money, his head down. I heard him mumble, "Sorry there, Zeb."

"You know I'll be comin' for you," I said, and felt Cobb's pistol at my back. "You know I'll be comin' for you . . . Partner."

Read on for an excerpt from *Blue Rivers of Heaven*,
the third novel in The Tales of Zebadiah Creed series
coming soon!

Chapter 1

Orleans Parish Prison, Early Summer 1836

Day and night had disappeared. I did not know when the sun rose or the moon shone. All was dark with the occasional flicker of a torch as the guard brought food, slop I would not feed to a dog. I ate every bit. There came a constant moan from somewhere deep within the prison, behind walls as thick as the expanse of my hand. An insane agony I could not fathom. I wondered, this person must only sleep when I sleep, and I slept in fits and dreams. Sometimes, I woke thinking it might be me with the moan, and insanity.

For the murder of Benjamin Brody, I sat in this place. I admitted taking his scalp while fighting an honorable duel months before, over stolen furs and my brother's death. Though I could have easily slit his throat, I left him alive.

The clothes I wore still stank of Texas. Battlefield blood soaked into the cloth and dried, a stain map of my recent plight, could hardly be seen for the rot, the holes and tears uncovering scars. Yet, no matter how threadbare these clothes became, I smelled of Texas.

How I yearned for buckskin, clean air, and cool water.

A rustle in the next cell and I knew his questioning, then his stories, would begin anew.

"Hey Scalper, you awake?"

I did not answer. I never answered.

"I can hear ya breathing different. You ain't much of a snorer.

Good for you. I heard some men die in their sleep from snorin', just stopped breathin'." He laughed, sounds from the back of his throat caught between his teeth. "Hell, I killed a bastard once, for snorin' too loud. We was on a hunt. Slept like a tiny baby after." He laughed again. "Not him, I tell ya, *me, me.* I slept like the tot, not him. He could no longer sleep; the bastard had a knife in his throat!" He howled, as if his words were the funniest ever said.

Of the many men I had met who were true killers, this one bragged the most. He reminded me of Grainger. Less convincing perhaps, and less conniving, for it was because of Grainger and a $500 bounty that I sat in this black, shit hole. *I will kill him.* The thought spun constant through my mind; my gut filled with rocks. *I will find my way out of here and kill Grainger.*

"Hey, Scalper . . ."

He had leaned closer toward my cell, within the distance of a few feet. But for the wall between us, I could reach out and shut him up for good.

"I know why you're here." His voice changed, becoming deeper, serious, hard.

"Oh, not what they told ya as to why you're here, but the truth."

"Why should I believe you?" I asked, the first words I spoke to the man in the cell next to me.

"You have nothing left to lose, my friend. For they will hang you, with no ceremony, no spectacle to show the fine men and women of New Orleans that your travesties will be accounted for, as well be theirs. You will die and no one will know." His words carried a different tone, a cadence to his speech he had not shown until I asked my question, as if a new man had taken his place.

"You call me 'Scalper,' why?"

He laughed with a much more gentle, refined sound than

before. "Ah Mr. Creed, your reputation most certainly precedes you."

He knew my name.

There came a silence between us, for how many minutes I did not know. Time meant nothing to me. My own breath and heartbeat were all I heard. I stood and reached for the wall. Though this prison had been built only a few years before, the rough cut stone felt ancient, with a thin layer of slime coating the rock. As I followed the wall from corner to corner, then finally to the iron bars of the door, the scurries of the rats told me that I was not alone in my cell. In the darkness, I faced the passageway.

"Who are you?" I asked. "And how do you know who I am?"

He laughed again, then sighed. "Why, I thought you knew. Everyone knows who the Scalper is." He must have stood at the same place in his cell as I stood in mine, side by side, not three feet from each other. "Your tales have become famous, my friend. Here in New Orleans and beyond."

"Who are you?" I asked again.

"In some circles, this question might get you killed."

"I ain't afraid, with or without this rock between us."

Another sigh, and he said, "Ah, Mr. Creed, you are afraid, else you would not have engaged with me. Besides, this rock will not stand between us for very much longer, my friend."

I cringed at him calling me this. The last friends I had either betrayed me or were killed.

"I ain't your friend."

"Hmm, no, not yet. Though, we will have history together."

I felt obliged not to acknowledge him any further, my mind shaken as to how this man imprisoned next to me knew so much. I stepped to the back of the cell and squatted against the wall. *I will not speak to him again,* I thought.

How soon after our conversation the light appeared, I could

not tell. A guard stood at my cell door holding a torch. Behind him, a shadow moved, then a man in a top hat appeared, short, rotund, breathing heavily. Sweat glistened on his forehead and chubby cheeks. He removed the hat and brushed a hand across his bald head.

"Mr. Creed, I am here to serve as your attorney, appointed by the court. Though the judge is obligated to provide you with defense in trial . . ." He cleared his throat. "It is customary to pay as you can for my services. Have you any coin, sir?"

I laughed. The last of my coins had been lost in a poker game six months before near San Antonio.

"Sir, I take that as a no." He placed his hat back on his head and tapped it down. "I will do what I can then, sir."

"When is the trial?" I asked.

Impatience sounded in his voice, high, whining. "Tomorrow. Mr. Creed, your trial is tomorrow morning. So, now I must ask you, did you murder Benjamin Brody?"

"No, I did not."

"This is how I thought you might reply . . . that is all." He began to turn away, then took out a handkerchief and wiped the sweat off his brow. "If you were to plead guilty, sir, I can promise the hanging a man would be proud of."

He paused, as if waiting for an immediate answer, then turned to the guard. "I will be bringing him fresh clothes. Ensure that he is properly washed. We don't want him stinking up the courtroom . . . courthouse." With another wipe of the brow, the lawyer and the guard left, leaving me again in darkness.

From the next cell came a sigh, then, "Ah, I wish you luck, Mr. Creed."

"Ain't no luck," I said.

"Then, Scalper, I wish you the best."

I leaned back against the wall, and waited, listening for the moan. But for the scurry of the rats and the snores of my fellow prisoner, all was quiet.

ABOUT THE AUTHOR

Originally from Oklahoma, **Mark C. Jackson** currently resides in Chula Vista, California, along with his lovely wife, Judy; their cat, Brooke; and dog, Hazel Nut. He is a standing member of the Western Writers of America and winner of an American Fiction Award, Best Adventure/Historical for his first book, *An Eye for an Eye (The Tales of Zebadiah Creed),* also published by Five Star. This is his second novel of the series. www.markcjacksonwriter.com

The employees of Five Star Publishing hope you have enjoyed this book.

Our Five Star novels explore little-known chapters from America's history, stories told from unique perspectives that will entertain a broad range of readers.

Other Five Star books are available at your local library, bookstore, all major book distributors, and directly from Five Star/Gale.

Connect with Five Star Publishing

Visit us on Facebook:
https://www.facebook.com/FiveStarCengage

Email:
FiveStar@cengage.com

For information about titles and placing orders:
(800) 223-1244
gale.orders@cengage.com

To share your comments, write to us:
Five Star Publishing
Attn: Publisher
10 Water St., Suite 310
Waterville, ME 04901